THE GENEVA DECISION

SEELEY JAMES

Published by

Machined Media

12402 N 68th St

Scottsdale, AZ 85254

THE GENEVA DECISION, Sabel Origins #1

Copyright © 2012, 2013, 2015, 2018, 2019 Seeley James

Original publication v1.0-6.1 on 30-Nov-2012

This version is v1.0-7.32, 12-April, 2019

Cover design: Pete Garceau

Cover photograph: Andrew Montooth

Digital ISBN: 978-0-9886996-0-1

Print ISBN: 978-0-9886996-1-8

Distribution Print ISBN: 978-0-9886996-0-1

ACKNOWLEDGMENTS

My heartfelt thanks to the beta readers and supporters who made this book the best book possible. Alphabetically: Melissa "Iceterrors" Capo-Murray, Alun Humphreys, Ken Newland, Jeannine Chatterton-Papineau, LoriAnn Shisk, Gloria Smith, Gail Weiss, and Sue Whitney.

- Amazing Editor: Mary Maddox, horror and dark fantasy novelist, and author of the Daemon World Series http://marymaddox.com
- Extraordinary Editor and Idea man: Lance Charnes, author of the highly acclaimed *Doha 12, SOUTH,* and *THE COLLLECTION.* http://wombatgroup.com
- Medical Advisor: Louis Kirby, famed neurologist and author of *Shadow of Eden.* http://louiskirby.com
- Romantic Ideas Editor: Pam Safinuk

A special thanks to my wife whose support, despite being reluctant to say the least, has been above and beyond the call of duty. Last but not least, my children, Nicole, Amelia, and Christopher, ranging from age sixteen to forty-three, who have kept my imagination fresh and full of ideas.

Once you read this book, you're going to want more!

Join the VIP List:
SeeleyJames.com/VIP

For Serena

CHAPTER 1

Geneva, Switzerland
20-May, 8PM

AN ASSASSIN TWISTED BETWEEN MEN in tuxedos and women in ball gowns on a beautiful evening in May backlit by the golden sunlight glancing off Geneva's Lake Léman. It was such a surprise that Pia Sabel rechecked all the visual signs: sweat on his brow, bulging eyes, pulsing neck veins, purposeful stride. He disappeared in the shadows before emerging into the light again.

From the age of ten, off-duty Secret Service agents had permanently etched those signs in her mind but, until that moment, it had all been theory.

The assassin weaved through the forest of people in the small park, just a silhouette in the lingering rays. Then he disappeared again and the string quartet played Vivaldi.

She wondered if she'd imagined him just to get back at her father. He insisted she attend the party. She was to meet Clément Marot at the Banque Marot reception in the roped off park on the lake. She studied the crowd again. The man was gone, either evaporated or nonexistent. Which could be a problem. It wouldn't have been the first time she imagined an assassin.

Pia sighed and resumed her search for Marot. Any man there could be the banker. It was Geneva after all. She pulled out her phone and took another glance at Marot's picture.

When she looked up, she saw the assassin again.

He was crossing the park at some distance. His stride was picking up pace as if he were nearing his target. Then he disappeared behind waiters bearing silver trays of champagne flutes. She looked around at the reception guests who politely laughed at each other's cocktail wit.

Her stomach squeezed.

She reached into her purse and clicked her panic button. Agent Marty waited on the far side of the boulevard, Quai du Mont Blanc. Could he reach her in time to help? She looked around for security people then remembered there were none. The safest city in Europe had few of them. The very reason Marot wanted to hire Sabel Security.

Shouldering her way between guests, she put herself on an intercept path. With a little luck, she could cut him off and maybe delay him until help arrived. But she reached the balustrade and a magnificent view of Jet d'Eau, Geneva's famous fountain, with no sign of the assassin. She stepped onto a park bench and searched again. His predatory pace would make him easy to find.

Instead, she found Clément Marot chatting with people in the far corner. The assassin stepped out from between two guests on Marot's left, pulled his hand out of his pocket, and pointed something at Marot's temple.

Marot's head came apart.

The bang echoed off the hotel façade and across the water.

Marot collapsed on the ground like a dropped cloth. Sharp shouts and cries erupted as a small crowd moved around the victim. Some tried to move back, others to move in, but they cancelled each other out.

Pia Sabel watched the assassin. He held a gun in his hand and aimed at bystanders' faces. Everyone in his path stepped back a good ten yards, crushing together until there was little room to move. Once they moved, the gunman strode toward the street. After five paces, some men swirled in behind him. He turned around and threatened them with the gun, then resumed his march.

Pia slid her hand around the Glock in her purse's hidden holster but left it there. Too provocative. Too many innocent bystanders.

She sized him up. Average height for a European, he was an inch shorter than Pia. She'd sparred with enough men at the gym to know a fight with him could go badly. Very badly. But there was another move that might work. Dangerous, but someone had to do something.

Threading her way between guests, Pia took up a position in the killer's path. Standing on tiptoe to see over a tall man's shoulder, she watched him. His wary eyes scanned the crowd, daring anyone to stop him. His cold gaze locked with hers for a second before moving on. Then he hesitated, something had caught his eye. He looked in her direction again.

To keep the element of surprise, she turned her back, bent her knees, and lowered herself below the shoulder in front of her. She tried to use all her senses. She watched people's eyes to track his movement. She tried to feel the static charge in the air through her skin. She listened for his footsteps.

Her human shield stepped back, clearing the killer's path.

She coiled the powerful springs in her legs and listened to the killer's footsteps approaching.

Pia exploded into his path, pivoting on her right foot and hooking her left ankle around his. Momentum carried his bodyweight forward, but before he could recover, her left forearm slammed hard into his shoulder blade. The assassin crashed face first onto the concrete pathway. She jumped into the air above him, her gown billowing around her like an unfurling parachute and came down hard. Her knees drove into his back on either side of his spine, halfway between the ribs and the hipbone. The impact forced the air from his lungs and pounded his kidneys.

Emboldened by her initiative, a heavy man stomped on the killer's wrist until the gun fell free. Another man picked it up. Someone hurled epithets in French while other voices called for police and doctors.

Multiple vehicles converged on the scene, their sirens shrieking. Their blue and white lights splashed off nearby windows before spilling into the park. Pia, panting from the adrenaline rush, patted down the killer. In one pocket, a book of matches with a handwritten phone number and a bus ticket from Douala, Cameroon. In another pocket, a wad of cash comprised of several euros and other bills that read Banque des États l'Afrique Centrale. Nothing else—no other weapons, no ID, no wallet, no phone. He writhed and struggled against the men holding him.

Agent Marty pushed through the crowd, looked at Pia and the man under her knees. He said, "Hey boss, you OK?"

CHAPTER 2

20-May, 8:30PM

PIA NODDED, TOOK A DEEP breath, and pointed.

"Killed Marot. He was heading to the street, probably had an accomplice. Cuffs?"

Marty whipped out the plasticuffs and took over.

Grabbing a fistful of her gown, Pia kicked off her heels and pushed through the astonished crowd. She ran toward the quai fifty yards away, jumped the velvet rope, and surveyed the broad sidewalk. Thirty meters to her right, a lone gray Peugeot idled at the curb in the no-parking zone. It was empty, the driver's door open, no license plate. A tall man, pale with blond spiky hair and a thin goatee, stood not far from the car, just outside the rope. He strained on his toes to peer into the crowd.

His face snapped her way. Their eyes locked.

He turned to run. Should she pull her pistol or try to tackle him? She was not a confident marksman on the range but was a world-class sprinter. She gave chase.

He bolted for the idling car. She angled to cut him off. He had the advantage in distance while she had the advantage in speed. His large black boots clumped across the sidewalk. She closed the gap, but it wasn't enough.

In a last ditch effort, she threw herself into a slide tackle. Her feet nearly clipped his ankles but caught only a bit of his heel. He stumbled and jumped into the car. By the time she grabbed her Glock, he had the door closed and, half a second later, tore away.

Her darts would never penetrate the car's sheet metal.

Should have brought bullets.

He was gone.

★ ★ ★

SHE CLUTCHED HER GOWN AT the shredded hip and limped back toward Agent Marty. As police cars and emergency vehicles swarmed the street, officers and emergency responders pushed through the crowd. Pia followed in their wake.

Agent Jonelle, hair slicked into a tight bun at the nape of her neck, came alongside Pia.

Pia glanced over. "Thought I gave you the night off."

"Awfully kind of you, Ms. Sabel. But you know I don't work for you, right?"

"You work for Dad, then?"

"Mr. Sabel told me to keep your past in the past and unplug any pranks you might think funny." She paused as they walked. "And I'm here to help you run Sabel Security before you run it into the ground."

Without breaking stride Pia turned to stare at the woman. She turned forward again, looking ahead twenty yards. Several police officers had arrived and formed a circle to the right of Marty and the killer. Two, a man and a woman, wore blue windbreakers with POLICE CANTONALE stenciled in white from shoulder to shoulder. The rest were uniformed officers.

"Those were Dad's words?" she asked.

"Pretty much—but cleaned up some."

"Great."

The woman in the windbreaker stepped forward to meet them. She carried a purse slung over her shoulder bandolier-style, the way Pia liked to carry hers. She extended a hand, smiled, and gushed something in rapid-fire French. The only words Pia understood were the two that matched the woman's nameplate, *Capitaine Villeneuve*. Villeneuve didn't wait for a response but hurried on toward three uniformed officers, shouting orders as she went.

Must have been her official thank you.

Pia approached a pudgy officer next to Marty. His name badge read *Duchamps*.

"His accomplice is getting away in a small gray Peugeot, no plates," she said. "You can catch him if you hurry."

Duchamps stared at her, then turned to Marty. Marty translated and Duchamps stared some more. After an awkward second, he pulled a handheld radio out and repeated the description.

Jonelle tapped her shoulder. "What makes you think they're working together?"

"They were both soldiers."

Marty extended his free hand, holding her Vivier heels. She smiled thank you.

Pia examined her captive while Jonelle waited for an explanation. Since he wasn't facedown with her knees in his kidneys, she could get a look at him. He had a swarthy complexion, black beard, dark eyes, and a high and tight haircut. A broken nose and bloody shirt. No longer struggling, he seemed oddly calm. Not subdued. Not worried.

"This guy was aiming at people's heads," Pia said. "Marty told me that's how soldiers aim in case the enemy is wearing body armor. And the other guy wore Army boots."

Marty dragged the killer to his feet and pushed him toward the officers. Duchamps took one arm, Capitaine Villeneuve took the other, and they walked toward a squad car on the street.

"Pardon me," the tall man in the windbreaker said. "I must have your statement." When their eyes met, he smiled and pointed his pen at her. "You are Pia Sabel, the Olympic footballer, oui?"

Pia nodded. Fans of women's soccer had dwindled since the games ended.

He was handsome and lean, like a distance runner, his skin drawn tight over sinewy muscles. Coin-sized curls and strong features. His words rumbled in a rich baritone.

"I thought this. Your tackle of Louisa Nécib in the Olympics was, ehm…" He snapped his fingers as he searched for the right word. "Notorious."

She shrugged. "In France."

He smiled. "Oh, pardon me. I am from Chamonix, just across the border. And also Capitaine Villeneuve. We are on special assignment to the Canton. But no matter. So then, I need your statement." He patted his pockets before finding the pen and pad already in his hand. "Just the few questions, if you please. You tackled him, he fell face first causing the broken nose. I have this from the others. You took items from the pockets. What were these?"

"I was looking for weapons. Patted him down. I put them all back." Pia described the contents of the killer's pockets.

"Oui." He jotted. "Anything that distinguishes the items?"

"The matchbook had *Objet Trouvé, Valois Maritime* embossed on the outside and a phone number on the inside."

Jonelle said, "Excuse me?"

At the same time, Alphonse said, "Do you remember the number?"

"Just +41-22, something something."

Alphonse nodded. "Country and city codes of Geneva."

"Yes."

"Perhaps the clue, oui?" he said.

He whistled to Capitaine Villeneuve, who knelt by the patrol car's open back door. Absorbed at that moment with securing the prisoner in the back seat, Villeneuve didn't respond. Duchamps waited in the front, his mind and eyes elsewhere. Alphonse stretched to wave and whistled once more before giving up.

Pia said, "Probably the number of whoever hired him."

"Hired? Assassin? How do you think this?"

"An Arab working with a Nordic-looking guy, both soldiers, they picked a public space with no video cameras, they weren't afraid of any resistance from the crowd. That's a lot of planning. These guys are pros."

Alphonse's mouth hung open. "Many conclusions for such, ehm, petite evidence." His smile took the sting out of his words.

"Still."

"Excuse me," Agent Jonelle said. "Valois Maritime is a shipping company. The *Objet Trouvé* is one of their ships. It's listed on the meeting agenda."

Alphonse looked at Pia.

Pia looked at Jonelle. "Agenda?"

"Yes. On your phone, under calendar. The meeting with Clément Marot."

Pia scrambled to retrieve her phone, pulled up the calendar and the meeting notes.

```
Sécurité - Banque Marot
1. Questions Internal
2. Questions International
3. Priorities Premier:
   • Objet Trouvé - Valois Maritime, Marseille
   • Étoile de Lyon - Total SA, Paris
   • Zorka Moscoq - Lukoil, Moscow
   • Altid Trigg - Statoil, Stavanger
```

Alphonse read over her shoulder. He said, "You will send this to me?"

"Sure," Pia said.

Just beyond him, Pia saw an officer escorting a college boy in a tuxedo with an older woman on his arm. Their faces turned down, their posture weak and bent—the son and widow. She wanted to say something to them, do something that would make them feel better.

The officer escorting them broke off and walked over to her. He said something in French. She raised her brows and slowly shook her head. He said, "Madame Marot has requested you keep the meeting tomorrow."

"I can do that."

As he walked away, a frantic woman in an off-white sequined dress intercepted him. She gestured and pointed with outstretched arms, her body bent at the knees and waist, her neck strained. The officer shrugged and pointed to another officer. The frantic woman ran in that direction. He rejoined the bereaved and led them forward.

A loud shout caught Pia's attention. Capitaine Villeneuve ran toward a knot of uniformed officers, yelling at them as she ran. Alphonse looked up from jotting on his pad, leaned an ear toward his Capitaine and stiffened. His eyes opened wide, and he shouted back to Villeneuve. He turned back to Pia. "My apologies. I must go. We finish your statement soon, oui?"

"Sure."

He sprinted toward the quai, where Capitaine Villeneuve had assembled three uniformed officers. She gestured in every direction. The group split up, running.

Jonelle turned to Marty. "You speak French—what was that about?"

"They said al-Jabal escaped."

Pia said, "You mean the killer? How the hell did that happen?"

CHAPTER 3

20-May, 9:30PM

AGENT MARTY FORKED HIS FISH, unwilling to look at either woman. Jonelle uncrossed her arms, leaned forward, and finished her last two bites. Pia trimmed the last slice of steak and ate it. She tried to think of the best way to get Jonelle in line, but nothing clever came to her.

Pia said, "It's the right thing to do."

Jonelle looked at Marty, who shrugged, then back at Pia.

"You're on her turf, sticking your nose into her investigation. If I were Capitaine Villeneuve, I'd lock you up first time you touched something."

The hotel's restaurant sparkled in white with gold trim. Pia set her knife and fork on the china and pushed it away. She said, "You were an MP for, what, ten years?"

"Twelve."

"And how many murders did you investigate?"

No one spoke as the bus boy cleared the plates. The waiter stepped in, scraping the crumbs from the linen with a silver scraper. Pia caught his eye and signaled for the check.

"Too many," Jonelle said. "You put ten thousand eighteen-year-old boys in the desert for months on end, something bad's going to happen. No worse crime rate than anywhere else per capita."

"And they had at least twenty lethal weapons each," Marty said. "Identical weapons. Worst conditions for finding evidence."

Jonelle shot a glance his way. "You're not helping."

"I looked up Chamonix while I was changing," Pia said. "It's a ski village in the mountains an hour from here. Guess how many murders they've had in the last ten years."

Jonelle sighed. "OK, so she pulls drunks out of gutters and cars out of snowbanks. She's still a trained peace officer—you're a rich kid who was lucky enough to tackle a killer without getting hurt. You gave them the bad guy, and they blew it. Big problem, but not our problem. Our client—*potential* client—is dead. We have no legal standing here. No ethical reason to get involved."

"Moral reason."

Agent Marty said, "She's right."

Jonelle glared at him. He put his hands up and leaned back.

"Your father made significant financial promises to me if you remain in the job and are successful over the next five years." Jonelle stabbed a finger toward Pia. "I don't have stacks of money stashed in my Gulfstream's cargo hold. That means I want to do what's right for Sabel Security, what's right for the business. At the moment, we're looking at good press: *Pia Sabel Captures Killer*. That's a win. Leave it alone."

"He murdered my client."

"Your client is a banker. A Swiss banker. Who caters to the ultra-rich. Not a sympathetic person."

"I should have stopped him."

"Not true," Marty said. "You might have prevented it, or you might have been killed trying. You might have scared him into a rampage killing and ended up with a lot more dead bodies. You could have made it worse, not better."

"Look," Jonelle said, "we meet with Madame Marot in the morning, give her our condolences, and head home. Either she hires us or she doesn't hire—"

"We're here, and the locals aren't equipped," Pia said. "They're nice enough, but they lack the experience you and Marty bring."

"They didn't ask for our help. We can't help them."

"That's not how we make decisions at Sabel anymore. We don't help people based on whether we can or can't, should or shouldn't, or if it's convenient. We help people who need help."

Pia's gaze wandered outside the restaurant windows where spotlights clicked off in the park. Police were clearing out. A reporter lingered with a cameraman, trying to dig one last word out of an officer who kept his head down and his mouth shut. Just as her gaze was moving on, Pia spotted the woman in the off-white dress running across the park. The woman approached the officer. Her hands outstretched, her knees and waist bent, she was still frantic an hour later.

Pia glanced at Marty. He followed her gaze outside and shrugged.

She said, "The boy in the lobby?"

"Want me to get the mom?" he said.

Pia nodded and stood.

Jonelle looked up at her. "What's going on? Where are you going?"

"There's someone who needs help," Pia said with a nod out the window. She ran to the lobby while Marty ran outside.

Two chairs faced each other over a small table in a secluded corner. In one chair sat a boy of six or seven playing with two toy cars. If his mother had come through looking for him, she could have easily missed him. Pia and Marty had seen him because they looked in secluded corners out of habit and training. Pia dropped to her knees six feet away and observed him. He glanced at her and sank his head to his chest. His eyes were red and a trail of snot trailed sideways off his face. The crying was over and he was living in abject fear. He glanced around the room before he returned to Pia.

She patted her knees and opened her arms. "Hi. Do you speak English?"

He shook his head and pulled his knees up. He folded his arms across them and sank his face into the box they formed.

She said, "Mére?"

He kept his head locked down. She realized that 'mother' and 'sea' probably sounded the same in her terrible accent. She tried desperately to remember something in French. Behind her, heels clicked rapidly across marble. The woman in off-white swished by her and swept the boy up in her arms. Neither boy nor mother spoke; they clenched their arms around each other.

Pia stood, watching for a second before joining Marty a few steps away.

★   ★   ★

BACK IN THE RESTAURANT, SHE signed the check and led her team outside. She zipped up her USA track suit. She said, "Where do we start?"

Jonelle started to say something.

Pia cut her off. "Because I'm in charge now, and things are going to be different. Discussion is over."

"I'm sure it was tough to witness another murder—"

"Just…" Pia chopped the air with her hand. "Get started."

Jonelle shook her head. Pia's agents huddled over Jonelle's phone-map for a moment, pointing things out to each other, then looked up without saying a word. They started walking up the narrow lane beside the hotel. Marty shoved his hands in his pockets and took the left side. He scanned the buildings top to bottom. Jonelle took the right.

Pia tagged along, three paces back. "What're we looking for?"

Marty looked over his shoulder from ten yards up the narrow Rue des Pâquis and held a finger to his lips. He went back to scanning the storefronts from the street to the roofline.

Pia said, "Just trying to learn."

"Learn quietly," Jonelle said. "Imagine you're this al-Jabal guy. Your ride left without you. The city's locked down, nobody goes in or out without a lot of scrutiny. Did you have a backup plan? If not, what're you going to do?"

"Lay low until the heat's off?" Pia said.

"You make it sound like a cheap thriller, but yes. He hides somewhere. Finds an empty apartment, a construction site, a flat roof. Maybe he has a friend."

"Why aren't they doing that?" Pia pointed down the lane as a patrol car passed by on the well-lit four-lane cross street, Rue des Alpes.

"Lazy police work," Jonelle said. "It feels like you're doing something when you seal off the checkpoints, bridges, trains, major streets. Lights and sirens and policemen everywhere you look gives people the impression you're putting it all out there. Le Capitaine's hoping the killer makes a break for it. He won't." Jonelle kept walking, looking at everything. "Sooner or later you have to do the work. You have to get out and walk the beat."

"We do the same in soccer. We call it 'doing the work'. Finding open space when your teammate has the ball or marking your player when she loses it." She paused and took a long breath. "At least… used to, when I played."

In the sickly orange light of the sodium lamp suspended five stories above the street, Jonelle stopped and stared at her.

"OK, I'll be quiet," Pia said. "Do your thing."

Jonelle's expression softened. "Sorry, I forgot to mention something. You've only been on the job for a day, and you got a lot done, considering. Not just taking down al-Jabal—spotting the accomplice, figuring them for soldiers, catching the make and model of the car. You put all those things together yourself?"

Pia smiled. "Bodyguards talk about security everywhere I go. Been hearing it all my life."

"The assassin part—you really think that too?"

"Only thing that makes sense," Pia said. "Don't you think?"

"You don't want to prejudice your intake of the evidence. Compartmentalize your theories until you have something solid to back them up."

"That wasn't solid?"

"No," Jonelle said. "But as theories go, not bad."

"What's your theory, then?"

"I don't have one. But I do have statistics, and those show that the vast majority of murders involve a family member. On top of that, women are involved in most noncontact murders like poisoning and assassination. I'd take a close look at the wife."

Jonelle turned in a slow circle, looked up at the buildings, roof lines, the doors of restaurants and shops that opened into the lane.

Pia looked at the same buildings, unsure what a hiding place might look like. Still close to the hotel, they were surrounded by offices closed for the night. Few places to hide. They walked up Rue Sismondi, working a grid uphill from the lake.

After looking at buildings the others already checked, Pia pulled out her phone and turned to the Internet. Jonelle and Marty kept pacing the grid, their eyes working every door and window. In the space of a city block, the neighborhood changed from tourist shops and cafés to sex shops and bars. A scattering of people strolled on the main streets. They turned down another narrow lane and worked it up to Rue Docteur Alfred-Vincent, then turned uphill again and made their way toward the next cross street, Rue de Berne.

"We're trying to keep a low profile here," Jonelle said. "It's bad enough that you're wearing your USA track suit, but put the phone away. You're lighting up the street and making yourself a target."

Pia clicked it off. "I was looking up the *Objet Trouvé*."

"And?"

"It was hijacked by pirates in Cameroon."

Jonelle raised a brow. "Cameroon? Like the bus ticket?"

Up the hill, Agent Marty gave a low whistle and waved them over. They trotted to his position. From the edge of a building, he pointed down Rue de Berne at a group of narrow storefronts: Cartes Telephoniques, Barillon Hotel, Marrakech, Parfums de Paris, Funny Horse Saloon, Berne Shop.

Jonelle followed Marty's gaze, checking the street, turned back to him and nodded. She said, "Worth a look. You take the back."

Marty looked right down a long block, then left. And looked back at Jonelle. He shook his head. "No alley. Probably a closed courtyard inside the block. Access could be difficult. Let's do a walk-by first."

Jonelle and Marty turned into the larger street and took the sidewalk opposite the shops.

Pia tagged along, quiet for a few steps. Then she said, "Wait. What did you see?"

CHAPTER 4

20-May, 10PM

"WE'RE LOOKING FOR AN ARAB." Jonelle pointed across the street. "In twelve blocks that's the only place we've seen with Arabic in the window."

Pia glanced at the storefront and recognized two words: *Marrakech* and a huge *OUVRET* on a sign hung in a darkened window. Was the store open or closed? She crossed the street to have a look. Jonelle hissed her name, calling her back. She kept going—just a closer look from a public sidewalk, no big deal. She cupped her hands on the glass and looked inside. A modest store of fashionable dresses with Arabic motifs. Everything was dark except for a sliver of light coming from the back room.

She tried the door. It swung open and a bell tinkled. Pia stepped inside.

Jonelle crossed the street, pushed in behind her and hissed in her ear. "Jesus, what are you doing?"

Marty crossed to their side, looking left and right as he came.

Jonelle tiptoed through the small showroom, circling wide around a doorway at the back of the shop and disappeared from Pia's sight. Light from the street did nothing but create silhouettes and cast shadows. The scent of Arabian jasmine filled the air. Pia found herself standing in the middle of the room, unsure of her next move. Her confidence drained away and left her cold.

A man's voice called out in Arabic.

Her heart rate exploded into high gear. From his tone Pia assumed he expected someone, hence the open door, and was agitated by the silent approach. Jonelle gestured from behind a rack of clothing. Pia had no idea what the hand signal meant. Sounds of movement and another Arabic greeting floated from the back room, the voice sounding closer.

Pia pulled two hijabs off a shelf. She wound the cloth around her knuckles.

Lights erupted overhead.

A big man appeared through the small doorway. He shouted and pointed a gun in Pia's face.

Jonelle pulled her gun and crouched, but she was two display racks away at the back of the showroom.

Half frightened and half angry, the man approached Pia, gun held steady.

Pia put her hands up, not quite raising them above shoulder level. The man took another step toward her. He glanced at the merchandise in her hand and demanded something of her in Arabic, then in French.

She shook her head. "I don't understand. Do you speak English?"

He peered at her, his fear gone, his anger rising, and shouted again in Arabic. She took a step closer putting her left foot forward, tilting her ear toward him as if straining to understand him. She moved her shoulder just inside his gun, her hands still slightly above her shoulders but closing in, her face scrunched as if she were trying to translate his words.

He shouted again.

A face popped in from the back room: swarthy complexion, trim beard, haircut high and tight.

Al-Jabal.

He turned and fled into the back room.

The big man craned behind him, following Pia's gaze. As he turned back, she burst off her back foot, snapping two lightning fast jabs to the big man's right eye. Her surprise attack went as expected: he dropped his gun, brought up his hands, and leaned away. Twisting her body and springing from her legs, she landed an uppercut under his jaw that snapped his head backward. He staggered. She finished him off with a right cross, smacking his temple with the heel of her hand. He collapsed at her feet.

Jonelle walked up and shot him, leaving the small dart in his neck.

Marty burst in through the door and aimed at the back room. Jonelle ran to the open doorway and crouched near the jamb, covering the left side of the room. Marty stepped close enough to peer inside and lowered his gun.

"Gone," he said. "There's a courtyard out back."

Jonelle shot a nasty look at Pia. "What the hell did you think you were doing—"

"He's getting away!" Pia started for the back door.

Marty grabbed her collar and yanked her back.

Jonelle said, "If I were him I'd be standing outside, waiting to shoot anyone who pops out that door. Wouldn't you?"

Pia winced.

Jonelle held her palm in Pia's face: Stay.

Pia gritted her teeth.

Marty grabbed the door handle, waited for Jonelle's nod, then burst outside, rolling across the small courtyard's brick. A shot pinged off the wall behind him. Marty popped into a crouching position and took aim. Jonelle leaned out the door, aiming downrange but holding her fire. The sound of running feet echoed off the surrounding walls. Marty gave chase, ran a few feet, looked back and shook his head.

Sabel Security dart's were powered by miniature rocket motors that limited range and accuracy. But Pia felt the tradeoff was worth it: less noise and less collateral damage. Not to mention fewer lawsuits and they were relatively legal in most countries.

"He's gone," Marty said. "The construction site must go through to the street."

They came back inside. Jonelle shook a finger in Pia's face.

"Let's get a couple things straight. When you're on an operation with a former Army major like me and a former Marine lieutenant like Marty, you stay behind us, not in front of us. We had an unspoken plan based on years of experience, and we had the element of surprise—"

"He looked pretty surprised after my first jab."

Marty burst out laughing. After a glance from Jonelle, he choked his laugh, turned away, and pulled out his phone.

"You were aggressive and lucky," Jonelle said. "What if al-Jabal had been the first through that door? He'd have recognized you and shot you in the head. In my book, the only thing that ranks lower than working for a spoiled rich kid is working for a dead rich kid. Bad for my street cred."

"Police are on their way," Marty said.

Jonelle knelt next to the shopkeeper, pulled out an injector and stabbed it into his leg. Pia knelt next to her and checked the man's pulse.

"Why did you shoot him?" Pia asked.

"Wanted to make sure he didn't shake it off and come at us from the back."

"When I put them down, they stay down."

"Better safe than sorry," Jonelle said. "But yeah, that was one hard hit."

Pia grinned. "Been working on it for ten years."

"Don't get carried away by the danger-rush. It can kill you and your team if you're not careful." Jonelle stood. "OK. Let's look for evidence. Something to explain ourselves to *Le Capitaine*."

Stacks of clothes labeled in Arabic, a pair of men's sneakers, a small desk, two chairs near the door. Nothing incriminating and no sign of al-Jabal. They returned to the front room and checked the storeowner's gun, a Sig Sauer P225.

"Same gun al-Jabal used to kill Marot," Pia said.

"Standard issue for the Swiss militia," Marty said. "That's every Swiss male between nineteen and thirty-four. Must be a million of these in Switzerland."

Within minutes, the small shop filled with paramedics and police. Lieutenant Alphonse Lamartine arrived and took statements from them. Shortly after he finished, the officers in the room stood a little straighter, concentrated a little harder on their tasks. Capitaine Villeneuve's commanding air preceded her into the shop.

Pia was impressed. In the store's light, she could see Le Capitaine a bit better. She had auburn hair, maybe mid-thirties, and wore a yellow shirt with a red logo under her bright blue windbreaker. As bad a color combination as Pia could imagine.

Villeneuve listened to Alphonse's report on the situation, then spoke to him in French.

"She wants to know more about the tranquilizer dart," Alphonse said.

"Will the shopkeeper suffer injury?"

"No," Jonelle said. "The dart is filled—"

Villeneuve stopped Jonelle with a wave of her hand and pointed at Pia.

"Pardon," Alphonse said, "but she wants to hear it from your company president."

Jonelle turned to Pia. "You ordered us to use them, probably best if you explain it anyway."

Pia looked Villeneuve in the eye. "The dart carries two doses. The first is a concentrate of Inland Taipan snake venom, a neurotoxin that affects the central nervous system with flaccid paralysis within one second of injection and lasts up to twenty minutes. The target is alert but immobile during this phase. The second dose is zolpidem, a sleep medication. It puts the target under for about four hours but takes five to ten minutes to take effect. For a few minutes, the target can hear and see but can't move. He can't pull the trigger on his gun."

Alphonse said, "Nonlethal weapon. You compete with Taser?"

"Not yet. We still need some… testing."

He tilted his head.

Pia said, "Some people have allergic reactions to the venom. We carry an antidote just in case."

"How many people have allergic reactions?"

Pia shrugged and sighed.

Alphonse translated and Villeneuve nodded. She inspected the place with her hands folded behind her back. She looked in the back room, in the cabinets, out in the courtyard. She called out questions, and Alphonse translated.

"No sign of al-Jabal when you fired at him in back?" he asked.

"We didn't fire at him," Pia said. "He took a shot at Agent Marty."

"Did you find any proof of al-Jabal's presence here?"

"No. We saw him. He ran for it. We looked around." Her hands came up, then fell back to her sides. "Nothing."

Alphonse nodded. Villeneuve came back and stood next to him. She crossed her arms, faced Pia, and spoke.

"Le Capitaine recognizes your contributions to the safety of the canton this evening," Alphonse said, "You subdued the murderer at the party and then the Swiss citizen in his shop. It is unfortunate that there is no proof of the killer's presence here. It is her wish that you refrain from assisting the police any further. Your intentions are honorable, no doubt, but the results," he motioned toward the shopkeeper, "are uncertain."

"I understand." Pia said. "I'm sorry. I'm sure you have a big operation going on."

Pia could feel Jonelle watching her.

"Le Capitaine wishes me to escort you back to the hotel," Alphonse said. "I will be with you in one moment."

Alphonse and Villeneuve spoke in the corner of the store.

Pia looked at Jonelle, glanced over at Villeneuve and back. She said, "Good thing she didn't arrest me. So, we're done here. I blew it. I should've let you and Marty do your thing. Now she thinks I'm a wacko with a hero complex."

"You're not a wacko with hero complex," Jonelle said. "You're a spoiled rich kid with a hero complex. She should know the difference."

They zipped their jackets and stepped outside. Alphonse finished up and joined them. The sidewalk was only wide enough for two, so Jonelle and Marty hung back several steps.

Pia said, "Escorting me back—is she punishing you?"

He shrugged and clasped his hands behind his back as he walked.

"Oui, more or less. She is in the foul mood. Much pressure now. The police chief told her, *You lost him—you must find him.* She thinks I encourage you with the... admiration. But, no matter—escorting you is not the punishment. And it is the nice night for the walk, oui?"

CHAPTER 5

20-May, 11PM

SHE TUGGED HER JACKET CLOSE against the falling temperature as they strolled along Rue des Alpes. Their route took them out of the neighborhood of shops and cafés toward the glass and steel office buildings closer to the hotel. Their conversation was casual, ranging from women's soccer to the Olympics and the next women's World Cup. Alphonse had become a fan as a teenager when his diplomat father lived in Washington, DC. He'd dated a woman who lost to Pia's high school team and recalled being stunned by Pia's domination of the field.

"You play like Cristiano Ronaldo," he said. "And you would leave football to run Sabel Security?"

"No choice."

"But you are too young. Twenty-five?"

"So were Mark Zuckerberg and Sergey Brin."

"No, I mean too young to give up the promising career. I don't understand this."

Pia inhaled the crisp air through her nose in a long deep breath, pinched her lips, and let her breath out. They crossed beneath a stoplight where Pia saw a strip of plastic in the gutter and pointed to it.

"Hey. These are the plasticuffs we put on al-Jabal." she said.

"Perhaps." Alphonse looked around. "This is where Duchamps stopped for traffic and was clubbed on the head."

"They were cut with something curved. You can see where the plastic fits together." She pointed to the ends, where a slice was evident.

He picked them up, looked curiously at them, nodded. "Thank you. We will have someone look at these for tool marks. Maybe another clue, oui?"

Pia smiled. He smiled.

Jonelle and Marty closed in on them.

From three paces away, Jonelle said, "Fingerprints?"

Alphonse looked at her.

Jonelle said, "Gloves, evidence bag? You guys lost the prisoner before you had a chance to take his fingerprints. That strip of plastic might be a chance to discover his real identity."

Alphonse winced in the sodium light. He gripped the plasticuff by the edges between his thumb and forefinger, then dropped it into his windbreaker's inside pocket. He looked up at Jonelle and gave a stiff nod.

They resumed their walk.

Alphonse said, "You must forgive our awkward approach to handling murders, Ms. Sabel. Geneva has the lowest homicide rate in Europe. Few officers have any real experience transporting criminals. All we know is what the manuals tell us."

"I thought you were on loan from France."

"The truth is, we have even less homicide in Chamonix."

They strolled on. When they reached the cross street, Quai du Mont-Blanc, he stopped and pointed in the opposite direction.

"I highly recommend seeing the view from Pont de la Machine, the city's first hydroelectric plant. Today it holds the gallery and café. Closed now, I'm sure. But the city view is worth the walk."

Without waiting for an answer, he strode onto the footbridge across the Rhone River.

Pia glanced at her agents, shrugged, then followed him.

In the middle of the dark river, a darker building waited. Three hundred yards to her left, upstream, Lake Léman poured into the Rhone, passed beneath the bridge, and headed toward the Mediterranean Sea.

"You know," she said as she caught up, "Sabel Security was asked by Clément Marot to meet with him about the *Objet Trouvé*."

Alphonse smiled. "Pardon. Could you do me the favor?"

"Sure. What?"

"Don't pronounce French without the effort." He smiled. "It is pronounced *objet trouvé*—it means 'the object as it is found.' Like natural art. Example, driftwood is the *objet trouvé*." He sighed and muttered, "Américains."

She smiled weakly and continued walking. Behind her back she flashed Marty her hand signal for privacy. Marty tugged Jonelle's arm, and they stayed close to the street end of the bridge. It was quiet on the lake. A rare car travelled the streets on either side of the river.

They stopped in front of the old power plant and faced Lake Léman. Five-story buildings, shouldered together, lined both sides of the river. They were lit up like Christmas in reds and greens and blues, their lights reflected in mesmerizing patterns on the water's dark surface. Pia made a picture frame with her fingers and clicked, mimicking the noise of a camera. She giggled and shoved her hands in her pockets.

"Anyway," she said, leaning her back against the railing, "I looked it up. Pirates commandeered the ship off the coast of Cameroon three months ago. Remember, al-Jabal had a Cameroon bus ticket in his pockets, and—"

"Oh. No. No." He stepped back, glaring at her. "Tonight, three officers left their posts at the train station to answer your call at the dress shop. Al-Jabal could have walked three blocks and taken the train to Paris because of you. You mean well, you did well, but you upset Le Capitaine's plans. It is most difficult to work distracted."

"What? I thought you—"

"No, I am not discussing this investigation with you. Last summer you played soccer in the Olympics. Last week you played soccer for Potomac Women's Club. You are good. Maybe as good as Sandrine Soubeyrand. Maybe. But tonight, you play detective—in a country where you do not speak any languages. Why? Because your father gives you the company like the toy. Do you really think the job is so easy? Yes, you tackle the killer. Thank you. The rest you leave to professionals."

He turned to the river, leaned his elbows on the railing and huffed.

His glanced at her and shrugged. "Even if we are not so professional, we do what we can."

Pia studied his profile. "Um. I'm sorry, Alphonse. I didn't mean to wreck your…"

Her voice trailed off, and she looked for a new conversation.

Alphonse wore a pin in his jacket with the same logo she'd seen on Capitaine Villeneuve's shirt. Pia pointed to it. She said, "Is that a police fraternity of some kind?"

He glanced at it, confused for a moment. Then came that great smile.

"Oh, no. It is the Association Nationale des Professionels de la Sécurité des Pistes, ANPSP. How do you say in America? Ski Patrol, oui?"

She nodded. "Your capitaine had the same logo on her shirt."

"For many years, she heads the school for the training. In Chamonix, it is common for the gendarme to take the second job doing the ski rescues. I am instructor there also."

They inhaled the chilled night air as the conversation died. Pia thought of several things to say and pushed them back. She glanced at a diagram affixed to the railing. It showed the hydroelectric system as it was built in 1887: the lake, intake, penstock, turbines, and generators. Annotated in four languages.

While she stared at the sign, she considered her attraction to him. Was it his looks? No, he was handsome but not exceptionally so. His demeanor? Maybe. Most of her boyfriends had been fine until they grasped the extent of her wealth. Then they turned into self-prostrating suck-ups. Alphonse's directness was refreshing, even admirable. At least, so far.

His phone chirped three times before he took the call, quickly turning around and taking a few steps. She listened to his voice. Maybe it was his baritone. While she listened, she recognized the words *Pont de la Machine* and wondered if she might learn French someday. She was impressed that he spoke English so well.

Alphonse spun around. "I must leave at once. Terrible news. There has been another shooting. Another murdered banker."

He turned and ran down the footbridge, past Jonelle and Marty and into the darkness.

Jonelle put her palms out, asking if everything was OK. Pia considered yelling to her and decided to text instead. A car pulled up at the opposite end of the footbridge as she thumbed out the news to Jonelle. Some other couple would arrive to take in the romantic sights.

Until then, she would savor the mood.

A second murdered banker in the world's banking capital. What was going on? Should she try to figure it out or take Jonelle's advice and leave it alone? Marot had never hired them to do anything. Her inexperience had made matters worse at the dress shop. If she stuck around trying to solve Geneva's problems, she was bound to make more mistakes. Jonelle was right. Murdered bankers were not her—

Pia's ears picked up a noise. Someone was running. She knew the sound of running footsteps, athletes on grass, people on treadmills, college girls in boy's dorms. This was different—not an athlete's precision-planted steps but aggressive steps, angry steps.

She looked over her shoulder toward the far shore. A man charged straight toward her. His posture was aggressive. Too aggressive. Her muscles froze. Halfway up the bridge, forty yards out, he stopped and raised an arm. He pointed at her—a blond guy, spiky hair, black boots. Al-Jabal's accomplice. Beyond him was a small gray car, the driver's door open.

She dropped into a squat, then burst up and sideways as a shot banged through the air. She'd faked out defenders around the world, but bullets were faster. Her tricks would probably not work for long against the soldier. She leaned left and snuck a peek over the railing. The plant's intake platform floated on the water below her, a few yards out. She spun around and ran right as another bang shattered the quiet night.

Behind her, Agents Marty and Jonelle were closing in as fast as they could but were still not close enough for Sabel darts. She ran for the building, looking for refuge—a column, a bay to hide behind, anything. She needed a few seconds of cover to dig out her gun and return fire. Nothing. The building was a flat brick front.

She glanced at the shooter, planted her feet and flew backward two yards in a single bound, forcing another miss. His third shot shattered the glass inches from where she'd been. She landed on her butt and rolled in a backward somersault.

Her memory reeled in lessons from the firing range. A Sig Sauer held eight bullets. He had five left. If she jumped, she might make it to the intake platform. It was lower, unlit, and would force him to turn his back to Jonelle and Marty if he wanted to shoot her. A risk he might not take. They'd arrive before he could kill her. Maybe. It was her best chance.

She ran for the railing.

From the car on the street, an Arabic voice shouted, "*Eyreh be afass seder emmak!*"

She'd heard that phrase during games in the Middle East. The ugliest insult an Arab could muster.

Al-Jabal.

Pia vaulted the railing.

In midair she realized her mistake: the platform was too far.

She plunged into shocking cold water. Something tugged at her torso, pulling her down. The current of the Rhone flowed out of Lake Léman and into a narrow penstock, or inlet tube, that once fed the power plant's turbines. She was in that current, slipping into that penstock. She had to swim out immediately or get sucked into a kilometer-long tube. Clawing at the water, she struggled upward, sinking as much as she rose. She shrugged off her jacket and kicked off her shoes. Graceful efficiency, a swim coach had once told her when describing underwater swimming form. She'd have to be less panicked to reach graceful.

Her lungs burned. A land-athlete, she lived and breathed air without a second thought. The more she fought, the more air she wanted, which meant she needed to make better progress against the current. Otherwise, fatigue would force her lungs to do what they craved, to expand and fill regardless of the consequences. Already she had to exert even more energy to keep her mouth closed.

She wondered why she'd even made the jump. She was no gymnast, no vaulter. She was tall and strong and fast, not light and lithe and fluid. The platform had been a mistake, possibly a deadly one.

She clawed harder and kicked. She felt eddies of water behind the trailing edge of her skin, the sign of ineffective paddling. The exertion of swimming against infinite tons of water used up the remaining oxygen in her blood. She was exhausted. She had nothing left. She struggled to commit her arms to one more stroke.

Dying in that freezing river because of al-Jabal was not an option. The bad guys were not going to win this game. Pia Sabel always won.

It was time to fight. She willed herself to make it out alive. Recalling her instructor's guidance to treat the water as a solid object, she pressed her fingers together, imagining them pushing against a rock wall, and pressed hard against it. Progress. Her knees locked, and her kicks gained traction. She fought back another overwhelming urge to gasp for air. Her arms moved upward with better form and downward with more power. Stroke by stroke, she made a little progress and got away from the strongest part of the current.

The water lightened above her. City lights—the surface had to be close. Her body burned with an uncontrollable desire to breathe in anything. Just a little farther. Another stroke or two. Her muscles ached; her lungs were on fire. She pushed herself harder than she imagined possible.

Kicking her way to the surface, she broke through and sucked in lungs full of air. For a minute that was all she could do—breathe.

She looked around for a way out. Nothing but darkness. A wall separated her from the open river, while the current tried to tug her back into the deep. Exhausted, she swam along the wall until she reached her intended destination, the platform, and hauled herself onto it.

Marty's voice reached her ears. He and Jonelle found an access walkway and made their way toward her.

Brushing the water off her tracksuit, she thought about the escalation. The assassin was trying to kill her. She stood up and met her agents halfway across the platform. Marty handed her his leather jacket.

She slipped it on, shivering. "Did you get them?"

"The darts don't have much range," Jonelle said. "They ran for it."

"Still think this is none of our business?"

Jonelle's face tightened.

"Trouble is, he's on the other side of the Capitaine's roadblocks," Marty said, "and we don't have a car."

"That's OK. I know where he's going." Pia shivered again as she began the soggy walk to the hotel. "What kind of person says, '*Eyreh be afass seder emmak,*'—*A thousand dicks in your mother's ribcage*—anyway?"

CHAPTER 6

PIA SABEL SAT UP IN bed, looked at the clock, and threw her pillow across the room. She put on a robe, dropped into a chair in the suite's living room, and pulled out her phone. After a mental check on the time difference, she dialed. He picked up on the third ring.

"She's a bitch, Dad."

"I know, princess. You should try the new pills."

"Drugs are never the answer. I'd rather have a shrieking ghost-mom visit me every night."

They were quiet for a moment, listening to each other breathe over the phone. She liked that he always made time for her.

He sighed. "I take it your mom was blaming you for letting Marot die?"

"Yes."

"You know it wasn't your fau—"

"I know." It sounded sharper than she intended. "Sorry, I'm—"

"Agent Jonelle's report says you're planning to go after them. Is that true?"

"Of course."

"I'm not going to allow that. Your job is a desk job. Stick to the four S's: Sell Sabel Security services. That means wining and dining clients, not fieldwork. I never wanted—"

"You forced me out of soccer. You told me to take some responsibility. I am."

"But not in the field. You're a natural-born leader, princess. The company needs you in the office, running the operation, making the customers happy. This is nonnegotiable, Pia. Come back to Washington and take the helm."

"They tried to kill me, Dad. Bad for business if that goes unanswered."

"Send the professionals after them. It's too dangerous."

Pia waited a beat. "Danger doesn't matter. What's the worst that could happen?"

"I'm not having that discussion again. Your attitude toward staying alive is…" His voice quaked before trailing off.

"I believe what I believe," she said. "You just don't get what it's like for women, Dad. When a man walks down the street, only one out of a thousand people is even capable of hurting him. When the average woman walks down the street, more than half could kill her. I have two advantages: I'm not afraid to die; and I hit first. You know that rule from *The Art of War*: walk away from a fight if you can? *The Art of War* was written about men fighting other men of equal strengths. Women don't have that kind of equality. Remember when my college roommate, Rachel, was attacked? That rapist could have beaten me, but I put him down before he had a chance to think. I can't worry about the danger—I just wade in."

"It's your afterlife theory I don't like," he said.

"That I'll be with my parents?"

"Yes."

"Sorry, Dad." Pia took a moment to think. "You moved the world for me. You took me in and gave me everything I needed to succeed. But I'm taking the helm my way. That's nonnegotiable."

"Pia, you come home this inst—"

"Not happening."

She paused and listened to him breathe. Or was he steaming?

"You know what I learned from you? When you take over a company, you take total control. You've been taking me to board meetings since I was nine, and I listened. You always tell the executives that you make all the decisions, so you can tell whose decisions are working and whose aren't. That's what I'm doing."

"And I always take the brightest executive and make him my mentor," he said. "I keep my ears open to the voice of experience. I don't have mass resignations."

That stung.

"You're right. I'll come home in a day or so," Pia said. "I need to pick up more agents, do something about the employee confidence problem, and pick a mentor."

"Wait—"

"Gotta go. Love you. Bye."

She clicked off while he was drawing a breath. What followed that breath would have been a rant about who controlled what, and who built which company, and how gratitude should manifest itself.

Pia called her pilot and asked him to look up all possible routes, by rail, car, or air, out of Geneva that would get a fugitive to Brussels. No matter which option the assassins chose, she intended to intercept them. She told her pilot to file flight plans for any routes the police might have left unguarded. All she needed to know was: when would they make their break?

CHAPTER 7

21-May, 3:30AM

THE MORNING 10K WAS SACRED to Pia, a necessity for a clear mind. She chose the city streets over the hotel's treadmill, reasoning that unless al-Jabal and his spiky-haired pal knew of her lifelong battle with insomnia, they wouldn't expect her on the streets at three-thirty. Besides, she hated treadmills. She told Agent Marty only that she was going for a run when she walked through the suite's outer room.

Running along the empty Quai des Bergues on the Rhone's northern shore, she drank in the cool alpine air. She crossed over on the Rue des Deux-Ponts, her path taking her into an industrial neighborhood. Fresh bread, newspapers, and dairy were being loaded from warehouses to trucks. Then diesel fumes stung her nose as each truck pulled out of a bay and trundled by.

She changed her route to escape the smoke and made a turn back toward the lake, which brought her to the University of Geneva's impressive campus. She circled it and found Rue Henri-Fazy, which led her into Old Town. The district dated back to the first millennium and was made of narrow passages paved with uneven cobblestone. Not the best footing for a runner.

As she looked for the quickest route back to a smooth surface, the flash of police lights caught her eye. Farther down the Grand Rue, harsh blue and white light shot out from a narrow side street. She slowed to a walk and approached the corner, where an ambulance backed into a tight lane. An officer moved scooters to one side, widening the path. As she resumed her run, the officer saw her, stopped what he was doing, and ran toward her.

He called out, "Arrêtez!"

She stopped twenty yards away and waited for him.

He issued rapid-fire commands in French and made frantic hand gestures that looked like he wanted her on the ground, something she wasn't willing to do without good cause.

She shrugged. "American. I don't understand."

He stopped two yards away, holding his hand up, and talked into a microphone dangling from his shoulder. He held a short conversation over the radio. The policeman stared at her. They waited in a tense standoff until a tall silhouette squeezed past the ambulance and approached them, his windbreaker pulled tight against the chill.

Lieutenant Alphonse Lamartine.

He called her name. She jogged to him. Alphonse stood just outside the glow of the ambulance headlights, rumpled and ruffled. He trotted out to meet her halfway.

"What are you doing here?" he asked.

She stopped, still three yards away. His tone.

He continued toward her, stopped an arm's length from her, stiff and formal.

"You are out late tonight, oui?"

"No, I'm an early riser." She nodded toward the ambulance. "Did something happen?"

He stared.

Overcome by his unexpected scrutiny, words spilled out of her. She explained her insomnia, her run, where she'd been, the empty streets. Still he said nothing. She pulled up her running app on her phone, handed it to him, and showed him how it mapped and timed her.

He nodded, looked at the phone, and stayed quiet for a full minute. His face scrunched up as if to say something, then relaxed.

Finally, he said, "Sixteen minutes, over five kilometers, this is quite rapid."

She shrugged.

"No wonder you gave al-Jabal the slip on the bridge." He waited. "Were you seen at the hotel before you left?"

"Agent Marty is on night duty. He can confirm it. If the hotel has cameras—"

"On your run, did you see anyone?"

"Bread trucks."

"Not al-Jabal?"

Pia's breath hung for a second. Her fingers slid across her runner's pack, checked the Glock holstered there. "He's still loose?"

"Oui. Two more murdered bankers."

They looked at each other in the dim light without speaking.

She said, "Wait, you left me on the bridge because of a murder—now there's another one?"

"Two more. First Marot at the park. Then, Madame Bachmann of Genève Banque International at her home. Now we discover the president of Genève Banque and his partner, both murdered within the few hours."

"And I'm out running through the neighborhood."

"Oui." He sighed. "You make yourself the target for interrogation. So often, the criminal returns to the scene to examine the police progress. You are here, at the scene. No doubt the alibi will prove true, you have no motive, you subdued the killer, yet procedure says you must be questioned."

Pia pursed her lips. "Guess so."

Alphonse pulled out his phone, still holding Pia's in his hand. He dialed the hotel and checked her story. The desk clerk had noticed her leave, and video cameras recorded all the exits. A technician would make them available for inspection during business hours. Alphonse hung up and stared at her phone.

He asked, "These calls you make, the few minutes ago. Who are they?"

"Alphonse, I'm not connected to this."

"My question requires the answer."

"My pilot and my father."

Alphonse hit redial. He spoke for a few moments in French, then handed the phone to Pia. She reassured her father that everything was fine and hung up.

"Your father speaks languages," Alphonse said. "And you?"

She glanced away and blew a breath. "I studied soccer. Every day. All day. Learned a little German."

He ran through a series of quick, short questions about her running habits, her route, her departure from the main boulevard toward Old Town, her reason for running past the ambulance. She answered with quick, short replies.

"Look, Alphonse," she said. "You know I'm not involved, and I don't know how to explain it any better than that. Jesus, they tried to kill me. If you like, I'll give you one of our security phones. It'll tell you where I am at all times. You can follow me or call me or text me, everywhere I go."

Alphonse drew a deep breath and kept his eyes on the phone.

"Le Capitaine will require the thorough investigation. She may not assign this task to me. Come to think, I am certain she will not. She thinks I do not have the dispassionate observations where you are concerned."

"I have nothing to hide." She pulled her spare phone out of her pack and handed it to him. "Keep this. I want you to know where I am."

At the last statement, he stepped back and took a long look at her. He forced a nervous smile. He said, "No boyfriends will call this number?"

She smiled. "No boyfriends. I break phones all the time. My people give me a spare. Consider this your personal satellite phone, works anywhere above ground. You can text me, call me, video chat, locate, anything you want. I don't want you to have any doubts."

He smiled and pocketed the phone. "The good policeman should never believe the thing until he can prove it. But I do. I believe you. Anyway, I will keep the phone. Maybe I will have good news to text you soon."

After a quick glance over his shoulder, he began walking backward.

"Wait," Pia said. He stopped. "I have two experts with me. Jonelle was an MP in Iraq and Afghanistan; she's investigated many murders. Same for Marty. I'd like to offer their services for the investigation. They can help—"

"It is the generous offer, but improper to accept before we clear your name. Even then, impossible for Le Capitaine. She already has the black mark for losing al-Jabal. Also, she is the outsider who would bring in more outsiders? No. This cannot work. But merci."

"You never told me what happened," she said.

"The last two, executed in the street behind the bank. Each one separately. First Monsieur Wölfli, then perhaps some minutes later, Monsieur Affolter."

"How awful. Are they tied to Marot?"

"The same weapon, but this gun is common. The only thing we know is that the victims were all at the party. Madame Bachmann left suddenly, just the few minutes before the first murder. Wölfli and Affolter went home later, with everyone else."

"Didn't they have police protection? Wouldn't they be worried after what happened to Marot?"

"We alerted them after Madame Bachmann was killed," he said. "Neither man was home, and their wives knew nothing—only that they spoke to each other and left on urgent business. Before we discover their bodies, it was thought they were meeting Madame Bachmann's family."

"Any video cameras around here?"

Alphonse pointed across the rooftops. "One there. Too far, no doubt."

"No cameras at Bachmann's?"

"No."

"You know what that means?" Pia asked.

"Oui. They know the city."

"No, it means they were—"

"I have told too much already. You see?" Alphonse held up his hands. "This is why Le Capitaine does not trust me with you."

"Sorry." She looked away. "But why did they come here without bodyguards?"

"The guards are normal for you, not for the banker of Geneva," he said. "It is the shame. It was the executioner shot, in the back of the head. They were beaten first."

"Why kill them like that? Why take them one at a time? Why not bomb the building?"

Alphonse shook his head and held out his hands, palms out.

"We do not yet know if it was al-Jabal. All we have is the odd clue— none of the bankers have the cell phone with them. Au revoir." He disappeared behind the ambulance still wedged in the side street.

Pia called Agent Marty to escort her back to the hotel. While waiting, she stepped around the ambulance and watched as three men loaded a black body bag.

The killers had gotten that close to their victims yet tried to shoot her in the dark, standing forty yards away? Someone would have warned the bankers about the murders of their friends. They would have been vigilant. There were video cameras. And the phones—everyone carried a phone.

Then it came to her: a theory that explained the phones. Should she tell Alphonse?

CHAPTER 8

21-May, 8AM

"THEY'RE KILLING A SECRETS TRAIL," Pia said.

Agent Jonelle scraped the bottom of her bowl for the last spoonful, ate it, and dropped the spoon in the bowl. "You're right—Greek yogurt is great."

"Double the protein, half the sugar," Pia said. "What about my theory?"

"It's possible," Jonelle said. "You'd need to see the phones to prove it. If you're right, the killers tossed them in the river, and we'll never know. Doesn't matter—it's not our case."

"Why not retribution?" Marty asked.

"What do you mean?" Pia said.

"Bankers for Syria's Assad had prices on their heads at one point. If these people were hiding funds for the wrong dictator, it could have gone badly."

"If it were something they knew about, like banking for a dictator, they'd have been more cautious," Jonelle said. "Especially if they were in some conspiracy with Marot. They'd have hunkered down somewhere after his killing. Instead they went to their offices in the middle of the night without calling the police. They didn't know what it was—they were just finding out."

"Like I said, Marot told Bachmann something that shocked her enough to leave the party," Pia said. "She confirmed it and texted Wölfli; he called his guy, whatshisname. None of them were sure about it, so they didn't tell the police. Maybe it made them look bad. After each murder, the killers read the texts, looked at the call log, and knew who to kill next."

Marty nudged Jonelle. "Told you she was sharp."

Jonelle shot him a look. "Is that how you kept this job for the last three years? Just kiss her ass all the time?"

Marty jabbed his index finger in the air. "For thousands of years, ass-kissing has proven to be the most effective way to keep a job."

Jonelle scowled and turned back to Pia. "Tell me about the girls again."

"The old-money families in my school thought they were cooler than the scholarship athletes I sponsored. Jealous, whatever. So they'd grab a girl from Wyoming in the bathroom, send a racist text from her phone to the Mexican from California and have a laugh. Thirty minutes later they'd grab both phones and erase the texts. No proof."

Jonelle shook her head. "High-class private school, huh?"

"And you thought you had it tough when the Mara Villas and the Crips shot it out in your school's parking lot," Marty said.

"What, now you're kissing my ass?" Jonelle said. "Put a sock in it, soldier—I need to think."

Marty leaned back, folded his arms.

"OK," Jonelle said. "Let's say that makes sense. But the bankers were looking for something at the office, something not on their laptops or accessible from home. What were they worried about?"

"Pirates," Pia said.

Her agents looked at her, puzzled.

"This is about the pirates in Cameroon who hijacked the *Objet Trouvé* and those other ships," she said. "Marot wanted to talk to us about them, and now he's dead. His killer was carrying matches from a hijacked ship. I'm guessing Geneva International, whatever it's called, was involved somehow."

"Possible," Jonelle said. "But how? Why?"

"I don't know yet. Got any ideas?"

Jonelle shook her head and glanced at her watch. "Meeting time. Let's go."

★ ★ ★

TEN MINUTES LATER, PIA READ a brass plaque outside Banque Marot's front door that said it was built in 1412. They went to the fifth-floor executive lobby, where she paced in her hand-tailored business suit with matching pumps. Agent Marty took up a position where he could see every possible approach. Jonelle sat in a gilded chair. The velvet wallpaper had a fleur-de-lis pattern, the chandelier sparkled with antique crystal. Banque Marot had accumulated some significant wealth over the last six hundred years.

A secretary came in and offered coffee. She pointed out the window at the Saint Pierre Cathedral across the courtyard and said it dated to 1150. She dropped two newspapers on the coffee table, promised Mme. Marot would be with them in a few minutes, and left.

Pia took a chair, looked at the headlines.

The *Financial Times* of London read:

```
Sabel Security Leadership Change
Nepotism will work this time!
```

And *The Wall Street Journal* European Edition read:

```
Security & Soccer: Somehow Sabel Sees Synergy
```

Pia stood and paced, looked out the window, let an f-word slip under her breath. Dark and drizzle outside granted a poor view of the cathedral. She glanced at the artwork on the walls and sat back down.

"Have there been more resignations?" she asked.

"Twelve yesterday," Jonelle said. "Hundred twenty-three since you took over."

She stood up and looked out the window again.

A plump, impeccably dressed middle-aged woman entered the small lobby, clutching crumpled tissues. She dabbed at her swollen eyes and nose before she approached Pia with an extended hand. She gestured to chairs in a meeting room off the lobby.

"I'm Sara Campbell, our director general. It's a pleasure to meet you, Ms. Sabel."

"We came at Madame Marot's request," Pia said. "And to extend our condolences."

Ms. Campbell nodded again toward the meeting room a few steps away.

"She's still talking to the police. She should be out in a few minutes. We're going to close the office for the day, send everyone home. It's such a shock."

"We don't want to keep you from anything," Jonelle said.

"No, no." She sniffled and wiped her nose. "It's good to see fellow Americans again. Please, have a seat. They just finished questioning me. I wanted to talk to you. Thank you for what you did last night."

Sara dropped into a gilded chair on the far side of a finely inlaid mahogany table. Pia and Jonelle took chairs opposite her. Marty stood near the door, feet apart and hands clasped in front of him, his field of vision taking in the hallway and the room at the same time.

Sara eyed his nonthreatening yet commanding presence for a moment.

"I see why Monsieur Marot wanted to hire your firm," Sara said.

"I hope this isn't rude," Jonelle said, "but we don't know *why* he wanted to hire us. That is, he only sent us an agenda, no explanations. Could you tell us what he wanted? We expected to talk to him this morning to—"

Sara's eyes scrunched together, and the tissue came out again. Her shoulders shook for a minute. Pia reached across the table and patted Sara's arm. The woman relaxed, took Pia's hand and smiled at her.

"We thought we'd see him this morning too," Sara said. "I keep expecting him to step into my office—"

She gave in to the tears for a few more seconds. Pia felt a surge of empathy. Sara took a deep breath and lifted her head.

"What does a director general do?" Pia asked.

"Clément is—was—what we would call the CEO. He owns the bank and the client relationships, the strategy, but I run the operations, the staff, the investments. Like a company president or chief operations officer."

"Do you know why he called us?"

"He was worried. But I thought it was just drama of some sort."

"What was the problem?" Jonelle asked.

"Too much money."

Pia and Jonelle raised their brows.

"We're a private bank, family owned," Sara said. "We cater to Europe's finest families. We invest their money in growing businesses. Because of the numbered accounts in Switzerland, we sometimes attract undesirable investors, money from criminal activity. Clément was, despite common opinions of Swiss bankers, a highly principled man. We never knowingly took deposits from dictatorships or drug cartels, nor did we invest in them. That's why I can't imagine what happened."

Pia glanced at Jonelle, who shook her head. She leaned forward.

"Excuse me, I still don't understand. What happened?"

"We had too much money in the bank's central accounts, the money we reserve for losses and downturns. It was growing, and we had no idea why."

Pia and Jonelle looked at each other.

"Of course, if you don't know where your money is coming from, that often means one of your fund managers is dabbling in something illegal. Or it could mean you've got an accounting problem, or a rogue trader, or any of a thousand other things, none of them good.

"Clément hired me to run operations. I should have been the one to figure it out, but he wouldn't let me. He spoke to Sandra Bachmann at Genève Banque International but not to me. I'm an expert on international accounting, I have a Harvard MBA, and I spent ten years at Chase. He hired me because he wanted my expertise. Yesterday I pinned him down, and he told me about engaging Sabel Security. And look what happened to Sandra and Clément. Oh god, it could have been me. Should have been. But he wouldn't tell me..." She broke down in tears again. "Why wouldn't he tell me?"

Pia sensed a presence outside in the hall, and a polite knock on the open door followed. A thin figure in a black suit slipped past her and moved around the table. The son.

She stood and reached her hand across the table. He was a couple of inches shorter than Pia and slightly built. He'd gelled his hair into a short faux hawk. Appropriate for his age but awkward under the circumstances. His sleepless eyes were hollow and empty. She fought an overwhelming urge to make him feel better.

He shook her hand lightly as he introduced himself in French: "Philippe Marot."

Philippe patted Sara's back and said something in French that sounded soothing.

Pia introduced herself, then Jonelle and Marty. No one knew what to say next. Philippe looked at them with great sadness and nodded toward the door. They took their cue.

Pia pushed back her chair. "I'm sure your father was a great man. It was a terrible loss."

Philippe forced a smile and said something in French.

Without waiting for a translation, Pia blurted out, "I know how you feel. When I was little, my parents—"

The wrong thing. At the worst time. She wanted to claw her words back. Marty and Jonelle stared at her. Philippe's face was a blank slate. Her hands came up as if offering something, then dropped.

Philippe spoke in French.

Marty said, "He says his mother is waiting for us."

Jonelle touched her arm, nodded toward the open doorway. Pia's mouth opened and closed. She walked out.

A few steps down the hall, Marty said, "What flavor shoe polish do you use?"

Pia said, "Shut up."

Jonelle ignored them. "Did it sound like she talked to the police about this?"

CHAPTER 9

21-May, 9AM

CAPITAINE VILLENEUVE CAME DOWN THE hallway toward them. She wore a fresh uniform, but her face showed the strain of a twenty-four-hour shift. An officer following close behind scribbled on a notepad as she dictated.

Pia greeted her with a tentative smile.

When Le Capitaine recognized her, both groups stopped. Le Capitaine offered a handshake and a smile. In French, Marty explained their imminent meeting with Mme. Marot. Le Capitaine said something back.

Marty turned to Pia. He said, "She says your alibi has been confirmed with the hotel's video cameras. With apologies for the intrusion, she wants to see our phones, Jonelle's and mine."

"Give them to her."

"Um… that could be embarrassing," Jonelle said.

Pia raised a brow.

"I might have sent some less-than-flattering texts about certain officers in certain investigations."

Pia shrugged. Marty and Jonelle handed their phones to Capitaine Villeneuve, who handed them to her uniformed officer. The officer fumbled his notepad under one arm and checked the phones.

Villeneuve looked at Pia and spoke a stream of French that took Marty by surprise. She stopped as suddenly as she'd started. In the silence, the officer checking the phones chuckled while staring at Jonelle's. All eyes turned to him. He cleared his throat, handed the phones back to Marty and Jonelle, and shook his head at Capitaine Villeneuve. She turned to Marty and made one last remark, then smiled and nodded at Pia.

Marty only nodded. The police went past them.

"She wants us to leave the city because she cannot guarantee our safety with al-Jabal on the loose," Marty said.

Jonelle watched as Le Capitaine turned into the meeting room they'd just left. "And?"

"And she pointed out that we show up wherever assassins and corpses are found. Plus something about American vigilantes."

Pia turned to Jonelle. "You were right. We're on her turf and pushed our luck a little too much."

"Ah, you are here." Mme. Lena Marot stood in the hallway ahead of them. She motioned to an open door. "Please. Come."

Pia and Jonelle walked into the spacious office while Marty took up watch in the hall. Mme. Marot gave Jonelle a once-over look and frowned.

Jonelle stepped back. "I'll be out in the hall if you need me."

Pia scrutinized Lena Marot. The widow wore flat black, from her pillbox hat to her shoes and purse. She seemed composed yet still haggard and weary.

"The idioten let him escape," Mme. Marot said in her thick German accent.

"I heard," Pia said.

"And now three more. I have summoned bank security. Compared to you they are nothing. But they will have to do for now."

Pia followed her hostess across the office.

"You are so brave," Mme. Marot said. Tears filled her eyes. "The polizei are incompetent."

She shrugged, took a deep breath, and swung her arms out, showing off an office the size of two living rooms. She said, "Philippe's office. It has good views of the mountains, more than he deserves. He tried to ski professionally after college but his father brought him to the bank. Clément made him start at the bottom but gave him an executive office. Always he spoils the son."

She motioned to two chairs around a table beyond a large, elaborately carved desk. As they took their seats, Pia noticed family photos on a shelf, some battered hockey sticks in one corner, a pair of shiny skis in the other, a view of the cathedral from the windows, and distinctive artwork covering the walls.

"I didn't know Philippe worked here," Pia said. "He looked like he was still in college."

"Ja, two years ago he graduated."

"Do you work at the bank too?"

Lena Marot laughed. "My love is the opera, the music. Business, numbers—they are not for me."

"Do you know why Clément wanted to hire us?"

"No. He never told me the bank's problems. All week he worried but never said a word. When I saw you at the party, I remembered you. You played the World Cup in Germany and the Olympics in London. And you captured the killer. No wonder Clément wanted you. A young woman from the good family. Sabel, it is Nordic?"

"Swedish. It means 'sword' or 'saber', something like that. But I'm not—"

"You have good bones, solid structure. You are the Valkyrie, the Morrigan."

Pia had no idea what that meant.

Mme. Marot smiled at her, looking her over as if expecting something to happen. Pia had known fans to fantasize a whole conversation and future relationship before an introduction, but Lena Marot seemed to have some specific topic in mind. She leaned forward, took Pia's hand, and stared at her for a long, awkward moment. Tears again filled her eyes.

"They let him go. The killer. You will catch him again? For me? You can?"

Pia looked over her shoulder, but Jonelle was outside.

"I'll do my best. I promise. Unfortunately, Capitaine Villeneuve suggested I leave Geneva."

"She likes to be top dog, the one in charge. You are a threat to her."

"Doesn't matter. She is top dog."

Mme. Marot swatted the air with contempt. "She is a climber. The best mountaineer we could hope to have. But you are the one to catch killers. I have seen you play many times. In the game, the players are like an opened book to you. You frighten them, knowing their play before they make it, knowing their thought before they think it. You have the tiger's eye. Even in darkness you see your prey."

Mme. Marot smiled. "You can do this, ja?"

As Pia smiled back, she realized something had transpired. "Are you saying you want to hire Sabel Security?"

CHAPTER 10

21-May, 10AM

"FREE?" AGENT JONELLE SAID. "YOU told her we'd do it for free. Are you kidding me?"

"Yes, I mean, no. No kidding, yes free. She's a suspect—you said so yourself. So is everyone else around here. Besides, these guys tried to kill me." Pia's hands went up. "I want these guys, and I don't want to answer to anyone."

"She wants to pay us," Jonelle said. "That's OK. It happens every day at nail salons, grocery stores, movie theaters. Someone wants a product or a service, they pay money for it. And I've lowered her on my suspect list. She made sense for the first murder but not the others. If it turns out she did it, and we get a conviction, she still has to pay for our service."

From the suite's vestibule, Agent Marty said, "I'll go find a bellman."

He disappeared.

Jonelle said, "Pia, you have eighteen hundred employees working for you who struggle to put their kids through school, pay for healthcare, and put food on the table. Those people are counting on you to—"

"I'll reimburse the company, OK? I'll pay for it. I want independence on my first job. This whole thing stinks, and I think integrity is important." Pia paused. "Besides, Lena Marot gives me the creeps."

"OK. You're buying with your money. That works this time. But in the future, you have to understand. My father didn't give me a Lamborghini when I turned sixteen, and he sure as hell didn't give me a billion-dollar company when I turned twenty-five."

"Don't go there—I heard that crap every time I made the starting lineup. *Her dad bought her the starter spot.* No one said that when Alex Morgan took the field, because she earned it. So did I, but when your father's rich, no one cares how good you are. Shovel it on someone who cares."

"I came to work for Alan Sabel a decade ago, with ten years of military training and experience on my resume. You earned your starting position on the soccer field the same way. But that's soccer. At Sabel Security, you don't even know what we do. You have too much to learn. And you have to do it fast, or a whole lot of people are going to lose their jobs."

"I'm not doing layoffs."

"Not your call. You saw those headlines. *Nepotism will work this time*—that's what the business community thinks when they hear about the new Sabel Security. If our clients lose their confidence in us, they won't hire us to rescue their executives in Columbia or their truckers in Mongolia, and a whole lot of our employees won't have missions. If you don't have missions, you can't pay the employees."

Pia walked to the balcony, looked out at the drizzle. "Then I need a big win."

Her phone rang.

"This phone is most helpful, thank you," Alphonse said. "I'm catching up on witness statements. Some of them told me you jumped on a bench seconds before the killing and watched al-Jabal. They say it was as if you knew what he was going to do. Is this true?"

In a thousandth of a second, she thought about telling him the truth. She thought about telling him of the extortionist's demand for ten million dollars and the accompanying threat to murder ten-year-old Pia. And Alan Sabel's one-word reply: No. Which necessitated the hiring of off-duty Secret Service agents, the world's greatest experts at identifying assassins hidden among thousands of fans. Which led to the training and drilling of a child who was just as defiant as her father.

The extortionist was never caught and was still out there somewhere. As time went on, the Secret Service agents became the first Sabel Security agents. The intense operation they put together to keep one rich kid alive, day after day, became the hottest thing in executive security. She thought of telling him all this but simplified it.

"I saw his face," she said. "I could tell he was going to kill someone—I just sensed it. I lost track of him in the crowd and stood on the bench to see where he'd gone. I was going to stop him, but I was too late."

Alphonse said nothing for a long time. Then, "I see."

There was shouting in the background behind him. He put her on mute for a few seconds then came back on to announce in a rushed voice that there was an emergency. He clicked off.

Jonelle waited for an explanation. Pia shrugged.

Both their phones buzzed with an incoming text from Marty:

```
Sara Campbell shot at her house thirty minutes
ago. DOA.
```

Pia dialed her pilot. "Any change in schedule?"

"No," he said. "We can have wheels up five minutes after you board."

"On our way."

Pia dragged her suitcases into the hall as Marty and a bellboy arrived. Jonelle followed her out.

"Where we going?" Jonelle said.

"Lyon," Pia said.

"Why?"

"I worked it out with the pilots. Best way to get from here to Cameroon while staying off the grid and away from facial recognition systems is to drive to Lyon, take the TGV to Brussels, and catch a flight from there. They have to be there by one o'clock to make the Brussels flight. But they have to drive, and I happen to have a Gulfstream handy. Ready?"

CHAPTER 11

Lyon, France
21-May, Noon

PIA STROLLED ALONG ONE SIDE of the Gare de Saint-Exupéry train station, while Jonelle observed passersby from the coffee shop. Marty emerged from the lower decks, having scoured the platforms. He shrugged—nothing.

Pia kept her voice down as she spoke to her agents through her Bluetooth earbud. All three were linked through a com-call on their satellite phones. They checked the connector walkway to the airport, the escalators to the boarding platforms, the bathrooms, the shops. They checked cafés and bookstores. They checked positions along the concourse. According to their timing, if the killers came this way from Geneva, they were at least half an hour ahead of them.

They discussed the options again. Geneva's police had turned up their noses at the Lyon theory, though they admitted it made sense. They chose to deploy their limited resources on the obvious routes: by car to Berne or Brussels, by rail to Paris or Zurich. The Canton police checked every person going anywhere except the two back roads to Lyon. They admitted it was an imperfect plan, but it was all they could do. When Pia again offered her company's services, they reminded her that she wasn't completely in the clear herself and declined. Which left Pia, Jonelle, and Marty hunting killers in France with no official cooperation.

Slightly bored, Pia said, "Anyone want a Gini?"

"A what?" Marty asked.

"Gini. French lemon soda. I'll grab some." Pia trotted into a gift shop to find only three bottles of Gini left. She took them, turned around in the narrow aisle, and nearly fell over a wheelchair. It carried a young boy with deformed hands on the ends of short arms, his tangled legs beneath a blanket. She apologized and smiled at the father pushing him.

As she paid at the register, she saw the boy struggling to point at the refrigerator case. His arm reached in the vague direction of the empty shelf of Gini, and she heard sounds of exasperation. The father consoled him with a hand on his shoulder. The cashier handed back Pia's credit card. Pia slipped it away, picked up one of the Ginis, and whistled at the father.

When the man looked up, she tossed the drink in a slow underhand arc. While it was still in midair, she grabbed the other two drinks, turned, and walked out. She gave one to Marty and the other to Jonelle.

The three of them resumed watching the thin crowds streaming to and from the train platforms. With four escalators, they took turns wandering the concourse before returning to a static vantage point. Marty was on the airport side, Jonelle in the middle, Pia farthest away at the bookstore.

She wandered past a rack of tourist brochures, picked up one that described the station's wild architecture and flipped through it. The roof that soared overhead was designed to represent a bird in flight, its steel wings arched over a central corridor to represent rounded wings in mid-flap. The station ran perpendicular to the tracks below. Four regular train tracks and platforms five hundred meters long flanked two high-speed tracks—an arrangement that allowed the Paris-Marseille train to pass at three hundred kilometers per hour, or 174 mph. Over the top of her brochure, she spotted a familiar face.

Katyonak Yeschenko, third wife of Mikhail Yeschenko and one of the guests at last night's tragic party, approached from the airport crosswalk. Seeing her reminded Pia that she could ask Mikhail about the *Zorka Moscoq*. But why was Katyonak traveling commercial flights? Even for the plaything of a Russian oil baron, that was wrong. She eyed Katyonak and spotted a bruise on her arm and another on her neck. She winced.

"Katyonak?" Pia said as she approached. "What are you doing here?"

Katyonak stopped and paled. She clicked her fingers and pointed at Pia.

A short, over-muscled man stepped around her. He planted himself between them. Pia recognized the man for what he was: an overbuilt weightlifter with no fighting experience. Fighters, like farmers and steelworkers, have layered muscles—hundreds of small support muscles defined with chiseled clarity. Gym rats have overgrown power muscles, impressive but nowhere near as useful. She leaned around the broad man and locked eyes with Katyonak.

"I like your shoes, Manolos?" Pia said. Her words were met with a cold look. "Are you OK? What happened to your arm?"

Katyonak pouted and turned in profile.

"I need to speak to Mikhail," Pia said. "Can you give me his number, please?"

Katyonak didn't speak, didn't move.

"You go now." The muscleman stepped within striking distance.

Pia's eyes moved to him for a moment, then back to Katyonak.

"I need to speak to Mikhail about his ship, the *Zorka Moscoq*. I know how to find the pirates who stole it."

Katyonak uttered something petulant in Russian.

Muscleman growled at Pia. "You go now, or I beat on you."

"I beat on you?" Pia's brows rose as she considered him. She moved her left foot forward, bent her knees slightly, and cocked her head to the side. "I don't have a problem with you. I'm trying to help Mr. Yeschenko find a ship. OK?"

She saw his hands and thought they were about the same size as Katyonak's bruises. Not conclusive evidence by any means, but an alarming coincidence. When she lifted her eyes back to his, his eyes flared. He pulled his fist back like an amateur. Pia watched him. His fist came forward with all the power he could put behind it. His upper body never moved. She bent her knees and dropped four inches. His fist grazed the top of her shoulder. His momentum carried his center of gravity over his front foot. Pia rose, twisted her torso, and banged her shoulder against his. Off balance, he staggered sideways to the wall. He steadied himself with one hand and looked back.

"Hey, no need for violence," she said. She held her hands up, palms open. "I just want to talk to Mikhail about his ship."

Muscleman threw another left with all his might. Pia slipped her left shoulder to the right. His fist skimmed across her back. She unwound her core with a right cross, landing the heel of her hand in his temple. He staggered back, his skull banging off the wall with a thud.

"Call him off, Katyonak. I don't want to hurt him."

The Russian woman's hands flew to cover her horrified face. She said something in Russian. Muscleman's eyes glazed over. He leaned back against the wall. Bystanders gathered around, wanting to offer assistance but unsure who to help.

Pia said, "Katyonak, if anyone sees what a lousy bodyguard you have, you'll be in danger. Tell everyone to back off, then call your husband. I need to talk to him."

Katyonak did as she was told, handing her phone to Pia after the bystanders left.

"Mikhail, this is Pia Sabel. We met at the Chelsea-Arsenal game last fall. I'm calling about a ship of yours, the *Zorka Moscoq*."

Mikhail Yeschenko said, "How could I forget? You are an amazing player. You must try out for my Moscow team. I think you could be a starter there. Someone has to show those boys how game is played." He laughed. "I do not know shipping details, but I will have someone look into it and get back to you. The *Zorka Moscoq*?"

"Yes. Thank you. By the way, you need to hire Sabel Security. I just put down one of your men without breaking a sweat."

Laughter rolled through the airwaves. Pia pulled the phone an inch from her ear.

"He is not her bodyguard. Give your father my regards."

Pia squeezed her eyes shut for a beat. Her lips formed an "Ooo" that she didn't voice. She clicked off the phone and handed it back to Katyonak.

"What is it?" Katyonak said.

"Um. He knows about…" Pia slid her gaze to indicate Katyonak's companion.

Katyonak paled and swallowed hard.

"You're in a tough spot," Pia said. "Mikhail is going to dump you, and this guy is violent. You probably think you can still make it all work out. When it falls apart, call me. I'll help you." She pulled a business card from her purse and pressed it into the young woman's hand. "I'm serious. I'll help."

Pia turned to muscleman, "If you ever hurt my friend again, I'll find you and then—I beat on you."

Katyonak gave her the Russian double-cheek kiss and walked away. Muscleman gathered what little dignity he could and followed her.

Through her earbud, Jonelle said, "You sure jumped to a lot of conclusions. Maybe Yeschenko is behind this. Just because he's a friend of your father doesn't make him clean."

"No way."

"Why?"

"Russian money is all pirated money, but they bank that inside Russia. Banque Marot would be his safe money."

"Pia, you can't—"

Behind her, Pia heard yelling. Through her earbud she heard Marty in a heated discussion with someone. She looked up the concourse in time to see him cuffed by two gendarmes. Jonelle rose and crossed to him as two more gendarmes stepped in front of her, spun her around and cuffed her.

Marty's stream of French broke into English for Pia's benefit.

"I have no bombs. You can search me. Your caller was playing a prank."

Pia's heart rate picked up fast. She took measured strides to the bathroom beyond the bookstore and listened to their discussions on the com-call. Jonelle provided a calm, reasoned response in English. An anonymous caller had identified Pia's team as terrorists with bombs. Jonelle gave them permission to search her but ignored questions about Pia's whereabouts, saying only that Pia often worried about her jet's refueling.

Apparently the killers were there and had spotted her first, maybe while she was distracted with Katyonak. Marty and Jonelle, concerned for Pia's safety, would have watched her instead of the concourse. That didn't seem likely. They were too professional. But they were half-distracted. Which meant the killers were disguised and close enough to identify all three of them.

The gendarmes had sidelined her team, leaving them center-concourse with their hands cuffed. If the killers wanted to start shooting, they'd never get a clearer shot. Unlikely they would kill anyone in police custody, but these two had killed in public before. She had to find them.

Pia leaned her head around the bathroom entrance and saw her people escorted down the concourse toward the airport terminal. She felt eyes watching her and looked left to see the tall accomplice staring at her. His hair, dyed black, was still spiked, but his thin goatee was gone. Instead he wore a cheap prosthesis on his chin. Twenty yards to her left, a group of three adults with two children and a stroller passed between them. Spiky-hair used them as a shield to approach Pia.

Which meant the other killer, al-Jabal, must be behind her.

She turned and found him, disguised as an old man complete with hunched posture and a cane. The eyes, piercing and cold, gave him away. He was thirty yards to the right. The tip of a knife protruded from the long sleeve of his raincoat.

Her chances were best with spiky-hair. He might underestimate her.

Might.

She slipped the gun from her purse and charged forward at a dead run, screaming for help as she ran. She pointed her gun at Spiky-hair only to succeed in scaring the family into a state of frozen panic. Spiky-hair stepped wide of them, putting her directly between him and al-Jabal like a runner caught between bases. She aimed at him. He pulled a gun from his sleeve and took aim. She fired. The dart caught his coat. If she stayed for a second shot, he might get one off first. If he missed, the family would be in danger.

She ran.

The only way out was down the empty escalator in front of her. She flew down it three steps at a time, with a long way to go. Boots clumped on the stairs above and behind her. He'd have time to aim before she reached the bottom.

She vaulted onto the chromed center rail that separated up from down, took three running steps on it and jumped. Landing on her butt, she began a long fast slide.

Sparks flew off the metal near her hand.

A bang reverberated through the platform area.

She rolled left then back right as she slid, and jumped the last three feet. Staggering a few steps, she fought to get her balance while putting as much distance between her and Spiky-hair as she could. Then she remembered—the brochure said the platform was five hundred meters long. She'd started at the middle, taken a long escalator, and was now looking at the last two hundred meters of covered train station. A long distance for a runner. Not for a bullet. Beyond the station, she could see miles of beautiful French countryside, flat as a pancake with nowhere to hide.

To her right lay two train tracks in a lowered bed and a concrete wall that ended fifty meters away. She looked left—nothing. Ahead—nothing. She looked back. Spiky-hair was coming into view on the escalator. She kept running, but no hiding place appeared. Her only chance was to cross the rail bed, get behind the concrete wall, and shoot back.

Another bang rattled the building, scaring the daylights out of her. Bystanders screamed.

She jumped off the platform and into the track bed. Steel rails were bolted to concrete railroad ties. She jumped a rail, lost her balance, stumbled the next four steps before hopping the next rail. A puff of dust preceded another bang by an instant. His third shot, five left if it was a Sig Sauer. She swerved left, back right, then turned on the afterburners in a straight line. The timer in her head calculated how long it would take him to line up his fourth shot. She jerked right three feet. Another bang. Four left.

Shrieking police whistles erupted from the concourse above them. The gendarmes were on their way. She needed only thirty seconds or so to escape Spiky-hair. He needed only half a second to line up another shot.

She faked another swerve right and crossed the rail back to her left. With another antelope leap, she darted back right. The wall ended another ten meters ahead. She ran straight for three strides, knowing he would start shooting faster under pressure. She ducked left and right, but the next shot didn't come. She stole a glance over her shoulder.

Spiky-hair had followed her into the track bed but landed with less grace and was picking himself off the ground. She was going to make it to the wall.

In two strides she cleared the corner, put on the brakes, and planted her body against six inches of concrete. She moved into position and peeked around the edge. Spiky-hair was up and running, fire in his eyes. Her aim was fair, not great, her weapon less accurate than his and with a lot less range. She would wait.

Her feet felt the rumbling first. The ground shook beneath her toes, vibrations tingling from her shins to her knees, rising to her quads.

The northbound Marseille-Paris was coming in.

She glanced left. She was standing on the TGV's high-speed pass through track. Four hundred tons of France's finest engineering was headed her way at three hundred kilometers per hour. It entered the tunnel at the far end. She did the math: five hundred meters at three hundred km/h meant six seconds before she would join the grasshoppers on the TGV's aerodynamic nose.

She poked her head back around the wall. Spiky-hair was less than six seconds away. At speed, the train would pass in half a second, providing no cover. She had to keep running and hope Spiky-hair gave up, or stand her ground and pray for a miracle.

Pia opted for both.

She stepped out from behind the wall, aimed, fired, and missed. Spiky-hair looked up. Stopped and aimed. Pia ducked back as a chunk of concrete turned to powder. The train was bearing down. She could make out the engineer driving it. Time to run. She reached around the wall, exposing only her hand, and fired blindly to slow her pursuer. Then turned and ran.

The track bed used raised concrete ties to absorb some of the vibration and spare the track bed excess wear. Spikes and bolts held the rails to the ties. The design left a gap of three inches between the rails and the bed. Pia's foot caught the gap and she fell face first into the track bed. Her knee hit hard. Her chest hit the far rail. One hand jammed into the gap under the other rail. Instant panic flooded through her.

The noise grew to an alarming pitch as the train approached. The air pressure rose fast. The ground shook harder.

She could not tell the source of her problem for one whole second.

Enough time for the train to travel eighty-three meters. Most of a football field. Pain shot from her knee to her brain. She tried to spin in place, but her foot held fast. Realizing the problem, she backed up an inch and tugged her foot. Not enough room. She backed up another inch and tried again. This time her foot came free.

She flipped onto her back and looked at the oncoming train. Close enough to see the engineer's eyes wide open, along with his mouth. The train's horn blasted a shockwave of sound. She buckled in the middle, did a power sit-up, and flipped up into a standing position. A common maneuver on the soccer field. She leapt backwards four feet. Just outside the rail. With a second leap, she was clear of the track. Her head came up. Spiky-hair was rounding the corner at full speed. His eyes, filled with rage, locked on hers.

The train passed in front of her, nothing but a blur of steel for a quarter of a second. Then it was gone. Spikey-hair was gone too.

In the next instant, her eyes were full of the blowing dust and grit that swirled in the currents behind the train. She coughed and spit and blinked and blinked and blinked. As her vision cleared, the sound of shrieking steel assaulted her ears. The Marseille-Paris TGV screeched in a desperate attempt to stop. Given the weight and speed, she estimated it would take at least one kilometer.

Pia turned and ran for the far platform. As she reached the edge of the tunnel, she checked the gathered travelers for al-Jabal before crossing the tracks. Not there. Everyone faced the train and the shower of sparks flying out from under it. She placed her hands on the platform, swung herself up and walked to the escalator. No one looked her way.

At the top of the escalator, a gendarme waited. Far down the concourse, three others emerged from the other platform's escalators. Pia presented her wrists to the officer.

"Let me guess," she said while he cuffed her, "al-Jabal got away?"

CHAPTER 12

Potomac, Maryland
23-May, 5AM

PIA SLAMMED RAPID PUNCHES INTO the double-ended bag, an eight-inch ball suspended at shoulder height between the ceiling and floor with elastic straps. Her blows were a mix of uppercuts, hooks, crosses, and jabs that landed with blinding speed. Barefoot, she wore black spandex shorts, a white sports bra, and pink boxing gloves. Each punch sent the bag reeling away, only to be pulled home by the elastic, where her following punch sent it flying again. Despite the erratic motion, she never missed. She concentrated on each blow, calculating distance, speed, and placement in an instant. Her breathing intensified. Her punches grew tighter, faster, stronger. Her trainer sat in his wheelchair, tracking the blows with a hand-held tally counter. He called them out in twenty-fives: one-fifty, one seventy-five, two hundred.

She became vaguely aware that Agent Jonelle had entered the gym at the far end.

Her trainer said, "Thirty seconds. Finish strong now."

Pia pounded faster. The bell rang.

"Three forty-two," her trainer said. "Must be the jet lag."

She stepped back, touched one glove to the vibrating bag to stop it. Sweat dripped down her brow and face, her shoulders and back and legs. She tugged the Velcro and pulled her gloves off, stuck them under her arm.

Panting like a racehorse, she faced Jonelle. "Water?"

"No thanks," Jonelle said. "What did you want?"

"Did you like the spa day?"

"It was a very nice gift. Thank you. I appreciate the new suit, too.

Your tailors are amazing." Jonelle turned around, showing off her new business suit. Her face remained fixed, no smile. "You didn't need to do that. Firing at the killer was just me doing my job. But Pia, it's five in the morning. Why did you call me in here?"

Her trainer tossed a water bottle at Pia. Without looking, she snapped it out of the air. Pia unscrewed the cap and poured half the water down her throat, then locked eyes with Jonelle.

"We didn't get along all that well in Geneva," she said.

"We got things done. You came home in one piece. Don't worry about it."

"Dad told me you asked to be reassigned."

Jonelle winced. "Don't take it personal. I'm just not interested—"

"I have a plan to stop the resignations."

"Glad to hear it. You're not mad?"

"I need your help to make it work. I'd appreciate it if you'd hear me out, listen to the offer." A bell with a different tone rang. Pia held up her index finger between them. "Right after this next round."

Jonelle glared at her. "If you want to have a serious conversation with me, postpone the workout and let's talk. Otherwise, reschedule the meeting."

Pia thought for a minute.

"OK," she said. "I want you to be my mentor. You'll effectively run the company but transition the role to me as I learn."

"I asked to be reassigned."

"Dad had you playing babysitter. This is different. I want you to help me."

Jonelle tightened her crossed arms.

"It takes a lot of training." Pia waved her arm around the gym. "I know how to listen to coaches. For the first year I trained here, Coach Billy wouldn't let me punch anything until I could duck everything they threw at me. I have the discipline it takes to be the best. I want you to teach me, coach me, make sure I'm on a gold medal path. I intend to be a champion in the world of security, Jonelle. I decided that when I swam the Rhone. Oh. And there's a large incentive plan."

Jonelle's eyebrows rose.

"A million for each anniversary. One million on the first anniversary, two on the second, and so on for five years."

Jonelle gasped. "Fifteen million?"

Pia nodded.

"How long do I have to think this over?"

"Until Colonel Grant comes in for his interview."

The bell rang. Pia tried not to look at the bag.

"How much control do I get?" Jonelle said.

Pia shrugged.

Jonelle walked ten steps away. She came back and started to ask a question. She stopped, turned, and marched toward the door. Thirty feet away, she stopped and headed back to Pia.

"I hate it when rich people use money to get what they want," Jonelle said.

"I want the best. Is that so bad?"

"I take it Alan told you how much I make," Jonelle said, "and you set the bonus high enough that I couldn't say no. We both know it's five times as much money as your father offered. And I'm sure Alan will have me back if I'm not happy. So we both know I'll take the job."

Pia tried to hold back a big smile. She said, "Thank you. I have a company-wide video conference scheduled to introduce your new role. I'd like to change your title. You left the military at the rank of major. I'd like to call you the Major, to differentiate you from all the other agents. I hope that works for you. We'll finish the conversation at my office."

Pia drank another bottle of water as Jonelle walked away.

Major Jonelle Jackson stopped near the door. She asked, "When was Colonel Grant coming in?"

"Don't know, haven't scheduled him yet. Do you have his number?"

CHAPTER 13

Bethesda, Maryland
23-May, 9AM

PIA OPENED THE VIDEO CONFERENCE to her employees.

"Life is not fair," she said. "How I got this job wasn't fair. We can always complain about how someone got a promotion, whether he stabbed people in the back or she slept her way to the top. What really matters is what that person does with the job, what actions she takes. What gains are made under her leadership. I ask you not to judge how I got here but how I execute my responsibilities to you and our customers. To ensure I do the best I can, with the best advice possible, I've promoted Agent Jonelle Jackson to be my primary advisor. From now on, everyone will refer to her as the Major."

The two of them handled questions from the others about the company, Pia's leadership, and the Major's role until the questions ran dry. Pia wrapped it up with a personal commitment that echoed her Olympic commitment. The Major stepped in and closed the meeting. The video blinked off. The screen retracted into the ceiling.

For a while, the Major was silent.

"Yeah, I know what you're thinking," Pia said. "It was a good speech. A good pre-game show, now it's time to make something happen."

The Major nodded.

"So the next thing is to pick who I need with me in Cameroon."

"You don't assign people to a mission," the Major said. "Sabel Security doesn't work that way. Your employees get a small salary, a little more than the Army, but they get to choose which mission they take. We post missions with a goal and a bonus structure, the agents get to determine the risk versus the reward then sign up for the ones they like. If no one wants to take the mission, we tell the customer he needs to put up a higher bonus or adjust his goals. Some do, some don't. But it works. When rebels kidnapped geologists in Columbia, the mining company offered a big bonus. Our people rescued the hostages and split the money. To attract the top people on your mission, you need to post a bonus and a mission brief."

"This is the part where being a spoiled rich kid helps—"

"For the bonus, maybe. But money is worthless if you get killed. Agents only join missions with a clear, achievable goal and a reasonable expectation of survival. That would be where the mission brief comes in."

They worked on the brief for two hours before posting it. It listed a one-week goal and a large bonus, with details promised in a video conference to follow shortly. The Major sent a text to ten agents she thought appropriate for the job, asking them to consider it.

"Alphonse sent me an update on what they've learned," Pia said while they waited for responses.

"Does le Capitaine know he's talking to you?"

"Doubt it. I've just asked him a few things. As, um, friends."

"Uh huh. Um-friends. She's not too keen on you inserting yourself into her investigation and that could get him in trouble."

"That's what he said. Anyway. al-Jabal is traveling under the name Badawi al-Jabal, a Syrian poet who died thirty years ago. The airport in Brussels identified him getting on a flight to Douala, Cameroon. Unfortunately, they were working from a cell-phone picture taken at the party. Didn't get him identified until today. Everything is pointing to the Niger River Delta on the border between Nigeria and Cameroon."

"Smart police work, Pia. What about the time line? Why are you in such a hurry?"

"All the ships on Marot's agenda were commandeered and never seen again. The pirates strike every seventy-five to eighty-five days, like clockwork. It's been seventy-nine days since the *Objet Trouvé* was taken. We have a week to find them or wait another three months."

"And when you find them?"

"Find out who funded them. Dad says it's about money laundering.

Pirating ships is easy—getting cash out of them is hard. That's what makes this operation much more dangerous than Somalia."

"So this is probably a squabble between pirates and bankers. Was Clément Marot the one laundering money? Or did he expose a conspiracy at Banque Genève International?"

"Sara Campbell said Clément was researching the problem," Pia said.

"First thing you have to learn about criminals is they never tell you the truth. She might have been honest, she might have been the one the pirates were really after. Until we can verify one way or the other, nothing she said is fact."

Pia nodded.

The Major paced. "What if Sara Campbell was working the pirates, alerted them to Marot's snooping? He'd already told Bachmann, so they went down the chain until they killed them all."

"Why Sara, then?" Pia said. "Wouldn't they still need her?"

"Pissed them off, maybe. She was supposed to keep it under control. Hard to say. Criminal conspiracies aren't rational organizations with a clear hierarchy. They're a loose confederation of guys who don't trust each other. One thing goes wrong and criminal gang turns into a cauldron of trigger-happy paranoia."

"Why did they want to kill me?"

"They think you know something. Do you?"

Pia shook her head. "Only that I can recognize al-Jabal."

"Who's Capitaine Villeneuve questioning? Who are the suspects?"

"Alphonse didn't say, but I'll ask."

They turned their attention to the mission team and sorted through the agents applying to join the mission. They trimmed the list to six and set up a video link.

Pia dropped the LED screen from the ceiling and positioned the camera.

"Most women who leave the Army want to fall in love with a guy, pump out some babies, vacation in France, have lunch at Spago," the Major said before they started. "Normal women aren't looking to take a gun into the jungle in Cameroon. And yet you have one woman here, highly qualified, who's volunteered to do just that. She's good, but not exactly normal."

Pia smiled. "My kind of girl."

The Major shook her head.

Pia shrugged and started the video meeting. With everyone online, she briefed them on events from the shooting of Marot to al-Jabal's escape in Lyon. Putting a map on screen, she noted that Cameroon was on the Gulf of Guinea, had about the same land mass and population as California, with one hundredth the economy. The average Californian made sixty thousand dollars a year, the average Cameroonian six hundred. The team would fly into Limbe, in the English-speaking Southwest Region. The rest of Cameroon spoke French. Pia had engaged an investigator from Douala to gather intelligence in remote villages. She hoped for some good leads when they arrived. She took a roll call for volunteers.

"Agent Marty," she said, "are you interested?"

"You know it." He smiled. "No one tries to kill my boss and walks away."

"Agent Jacob?" She addressed the bald fireplug of a man on her screen. "You in?"

"Heck yeah, I'm in. First thing they taught me in basic training—never pass up a chance to brown-nose the brass. Besides, I never shot anyone on that side of Africa."

Pia glanced at Jonelle who shrugged then moved on to Agent Eric.

"No way. I'm surprised at Jacob, he knows better," Eric said. "Pardon me for saying so, Ms. Sabel, but you're way out of your league here. You're going into a territory so hostile your brain will freeze up. Your body reacts to danger by shifting all the body's oxygen to the brain. Your coordination, your muscles, suffer from the lack of oxygen. That's why you fumble things when you're scared. Soldiers train under live fire specifically to deal with that problem. Civilians don't. You've never had live fire training. You've never dealt with that much adrenaline—"

"You've never driven your way through Sweden's defensive line."

"With all due respect, ma'am, it's not funny. The Swedes might be tough, but they weren't trying to kill you. You're going to get killed. And worse, you're going to get our teammates killed. I'm out."

Pia drew a deep breath. "Yeah. Well. If you're right, I'm leaving instructions to have you promoted for your keen insights." Her voice slowed and lowered. "But if you're wrong and any of us come back—shrink when you see us in the halls."

The others stifled laughter and leered at Eric in the video windows. Someone repeated the word *shrink* with a snarl. Agent Eric shrugged and shook his head.

Pia moved to Agent Miguel, buzz cut, short, square, average-looking. He said, "In."

She waited a couple beats, decided he had spoken, and moved on to Agent Tania. Of mixed race, she formed an exotic mystery with angry eyes. Her enigmatic face hinted Asian, Native American, African, or maybe all three. But her glower was uniquely hers.

"I grew up on the edge of Brooklyn, the wrong edge," Tania said. "I've seen plenty of rich bitches like you. But Jacob pulled my ass out of a burning Humvee after an IED blew it twenty meters. He's worth dying for. Anywhere he goes, I go. But Eric's right, you're untrained and that makes you dangerous. I wouldn't cross the street to save a snotty punk like you. Not one step. Just so you know where I'm coming from."

"That's your problem, not mine. The minute it interferes with the mission, you're fired."

Agent Tania sneered and turned a shoulder.

Agent Benjamin was already shaking his head when she called his name.

"I'm with Eric on this one," he said. "Live fire is no place for on-the-job training. You go to boot camp, do a tour of duty in the Korengal Valley, then call me."

"You heard what I told Eric," Pia said.

Last up was Agent Ezra. Obviously the oldest, he had a gray crew cut, deep-set eyes, a square grizzled face. He could have played a bad guy in any gangster movie.

"I've half a mind to side with Eric and Ben on this, but I've got two problems," he said. The first is, I just have to know if you can really do it. The second is, I have no intention of *shrinking* if you do. Count me in."

Pia thanked them and set a wheels-up time for next morning. A planning and review session would take place onboard. She clicked off the video conference. The Major stared at the map of Cameroon, biting her thumbnail.

"Worried?" Pia asked.

The Major took a deep breath, turned to Pia and tightened her lips.

Pia said, "I only play to w—"

"Yeah, I've heard the sports talk. The rah-rah. It's good stuff." Her cold hard look felt like a slap. "But Eric's right. There's a huge difference between taking a corner kick and dodging a bullet. You wanted a success under your belt, so you blew the starting whistle. Your next play could end someone's life. So let me ask you—worried?"

CHAPTER 14

Limbe, Cameroon
25-May, 3PM

THE CHOIR SAT DOWN AND a layperson began reading from the Bible. Pia leaned toward the old man next to her. "Bishop Mimboe, what is your position on ordaining women for the priesthood?"

He smiled at her, mischief in his face, then answered with resonant vowels and hard consonants. "My dear Ms. Sabel, Africa and America face different challenges. Very different. Let me give you one example. The other day, an important man came to me and inquired about converting to Christianity and joining the Anglican Church. He asked me how many wives would he have to let go if he joined?"

Pia sighed and sat back in her chair. Her eyes wandered back to the church service in progress. A full mass, ordered by the bishop to consecrate her generosity, was underway. When the police in both Geneva and Lyon panned her visa application to Cameroon, she'd reapplied to visit the Anglican school funded by her charitable foundation. Because this was only her second visit to the country, the diocese had turned out in droves, despite the short notice. The congregation was ecstatic and treated her like royalty. Most ecstatic was the diminutive, bishop sitting next to her. His hair streaked with gray, his black skin aged and weathered, he had the smile of a cherub and movie-star charm.

She relaxed and joined in the rhythmic singing and chanting. After all, it would only be an hour or so.

When they finally came to the sermon, the bishop kept it swift and funny.

"My beloved people," he said as he wrapped up, "we must change.

We must change our troubled souls. Somehow, we must find forgiveness in our hearts for the horrendous foul Pia Sabel committed against our beloved Adisa Ngandy in the Olympics." He looked at her and winked. "I know Ms. Sabel's aggressive play challenged the faith of many parishioners. How could a loving God allow such an injustice? Yet the Bible teaches us: God's love falls like the rain, equally on the good and…" he looked a Pia and shrugged, "the others."

He called her to the pulpit and introduced her. She wore the latest mid-thigh dress from Ghanaian designer Aish Obdubi, featuring African geometric circles in green and turquoise and cut in a western style. She made brief remarks about investing in hope but made no mention of the foul. When she finished, another priest came forward and continued the service.

Back in their seats, the bishop leaned toward her.

"Ms. Sabel, I understand you were violently baptized in Geneva a few days ago. Praise be to God you emerged. When we emerge from the waters of death, we are changed. Sometimes for the better, sometimes not. Tell me. Do you still harbor anger toward those who persecute you?"

Pia stared at the altar without answering.

"Is there something in Cameroon that troubles you?" he asked.

Pia glanced at him sideways, saw a new intensity in his eyes. "Troubles me?"

"Your mind is working on something outside this place. Your heart is not with us now."

Pia bit the inside of her lip. She wondered if perception was something he'd learned on the job or with age. She said, "I'm here seeking justice."

"Your visit is a blessing to Cameroon and the church. Whatever troubles your heart troubles us." His voice dropped, his eyes narrowed. "There is a difference between justice and revenge, Ms. Sabel. And both belong to the Lord. Leave it to Him and you can find peace."

She shot him another sideways glance. He was serious, but so was she. Serious about finding a killer and exposing a conspiracy. His look made her reflect on her mission. Why was she in Cameroon? Was she really trying to solve a murder? Or was it a vainglorious mission to prove herself? She thought about it and resolved her questions.

"We're in the same business, Bishop—we both strive for peace. You strive for spiritual peace, I strive for physical peace. The people of Cameroon need both."

"Then your work makes mine easier." He patted her knee. "Seek spiritual peace first and your burden will be lighter."

She smiled and put her hand on top of his.

After the service, the choir and clergy recessed out of the church with Pia in their midst. She stood a head taller than the bishop. In a way, she felt protective of him. Yet she sensed he was the kind of man who'd give his life rather than take a life to protect others.

For years psychologists lined up to tell her father that Pia's risky behavior and reckless drive to succeed stemmed from the desire to have saved her mother's life. Were they right? One of her parents' murderers was already dead, and she'd find the other soon enough. She lived with that part just fine. The other part, though, the question that ate at her day and night: If she could go back in time, would she have given her life to save her mother's?

They stepped outside. The sun glowed like a pearl in the hazy sky and the humid air left dew on her skin as if to save itself the effort of raining. The choir sang and chanted ahead of them as they walked. She reached out and held the bishop's hand. The school she funded lay across a wide dirt road. Three buildings of classrooms, a dormitory for abandoned children, and a meeting hall were clustered around a soccer field.

Agent Ezra stood watch on the far side of the road, his weathered face a formidable presence. His eyes, hard and humorless, noted everyone in the crowd. The Major trotted alongside the procession, falling into step with Pia.

"The team cleared the hotel," the Major said. "We're meeting your investigator, Monique Tsogo, in an hour. She turned up something. Agent Jacob hired a speedboat and went up the coast to get a feel for the delta. He says the mangrove swamps are big enough to hide a battleship."

With a quick glance at the bishop, Pia nodded and continued the tour of the school. By midafternoon she'd seen the church, the school, the grounds, and just about everyone there. She sidestepped an invitation to watch the girls' varsity soccer team play Yaoundé Catholic the next evening and politely refused an invitation to stay in the convent. She finally broke free and made her way to the Hotel Seme Beach.

Limbe had dirt roads with no street signs or traffic lights. There was little motorized traffic, mostly pedestrians and bicycles. As they drove through town, Pia saw children playing soccer in a dirt lot. A couple of crooked sticks at each end formed goals. Their ball was made of socks stuffed with old rags. They played barefoot without shin guards. An adult shouted at them from the sidelines.

A few minutes later, the cab turned into the hotel's guarded entrance and crossed the bricked courtyard. They got out, and Pia pushed Miguel back to the cab. She pulled out a stack of hundred Euro notes and gave it to the cabbie. Miguel waited, staring at her.

"Go to the nearest soccer store and buy everything they have—shoes, socks, balls, nets, everything. Take it back to that field, and give it to the kids. Make sure they distribute the stuff as evenly as possible. Miguel will verify."

The cabbie said, "Who should I say gave them these things?"

"A friend."

Miguel grabbed the door handle and stopped. Before he got in he said, "Must be nice to have a lot of money."

"How much you have is not important. It's what you do with it that counts." Pia looked at the ground and breathed out. "I have a long way to go."

Pia turned to the hotel. She could feel Miguel staring at her as she walked.

A two-story main building, the hotel had tiled walls dotted with small windows. A portico with four folding chairs and a feral cat greeted them. Mildew permeated every interior space—in corners, mold bubbled out from under the paint. Clean and tidy, for Africa.

The rooms overlooked a picturesque private beach on one side and views of Mount Cameroon on the other. Agents Marty and Tania had chosen the middle of three bungalows on the beach for Pia. Tania walked in first, checked the corners and closets, and opened a window to a warm salty breeze.

Tania pointed to a pattern of mold in the corner. She said, "Is this good enough for your highness?"

Pia stared at her without speaking for an uncomfortable time. Pia tossed her bag on the bed. She looked at the bare desk, the small tube TV on a tiny stand in the corner. Finally she said, "If you don't like your room, I'll trade with you."

Tania scoffed. "Don't try to win me over, bitch. When the shooting starts, you're on your own. I wouldn't cross the street to lay down cover for you."

Pia pulled a tracksuit out of her bag, eyeing Tania the whole time.

"You mentioned that once already. You have a specific complaint this time?"

"Yeah. I got something specific. You really expect us to use those stupid darts? No hollow points? No armor piercing rounds? All we got is darts with no range and no stopping power?"

Pia stepped over to Tania, towering over her by several inches. "Sabel Security no longer uses deadly force as a first option. That was my first order when I took over last week. We have conventional ammunition as a last resort. No exceptions."

"Oh, there're exceptions all right. The bad guys fire the exceptions. If you'd ever been in a real firefight you'd know that."

Ezra stepped into the room, stood behind Tania. His craggy face softened.

"People in this part of the world wear lightweight clothing," Pia said. "Not a lot of body armor. If you nick a guy with a 9mm round, he can still shoot back. If you nick him with a Sabel dart, he's down."

Ezra put a hand on Tania's back. "Trying to get fired, Tania?"

"She's just testing me," Pia said.

"We made a mistake, Ez-man," Tania said. "She brought us out here in the middle of nowhere with nothing to find. Those fuck-tard pirates are probably using one of the tankers as a base out in the ocean somewhere—"

"Not unless it's invisible," Pia said. "Yeschenko's people called me— they patrolled the Bight of Bonny for weeks after the *Zorka Moscoq* was taken. They only thing they found was a fishing trawler. The people he sent said the attacks had to come from the mangrove swamps in the Niger delta. Look at a map. It's the only option."

Tania's scowl faded.

"C'mon kid," Ezra said with a friendly shoulder rub. "Switch your watch with Marty before you say something you'll have to apologize for."

"No apologies required if you speak your mind," Pia said. "I'd rather have outspoken employees than a bunch of suck-ups."

Ezra raised an eyebrow. "Then in all honesty, Ms. Sabel, I have to be outspoken too—without a doubt, you're the smartest, best-looking boss I ever worked for."

Pia laughed. Tania spun away from his hand and went outside.

Pia and Ezra glanced around the room, then at each other.

"Never mind her," Ezra said. "She doesn't loosen up until the shooting starts."

"Eric was right," Pia said. "I've never been in a firefight. Got any advice?"

For a long time the old soldier looked like he was about to speak but didn't bring his eyes up. After a full minute, he met her gaze and let out a long breath. He said, "When a soldier commits to his mission, the first thing he does is figure he's already dead. Every breath he draws after coming to that realization is a special breath. Every decision he makes is more focused, more important, more sacred." He looked at her intently. "Every day I'm alive is like a gift from God."

"Kind of depressing," Pia said with a small, nervous grin.

"We don't go to war to win it. We go to stop it."

He glanced around the room, one last visual sweep, nodded at her and left.

Pia sat on the bed and stared out the window for a long time. Children ran on the beach, birds flew by in the air, waves rolled in and rolled out. What had she gotten herself into?

The Major came in with a short, thin woman wearing a colorful African dress and matching gele, headscarf. The investigator, Monique Tsogo. She explained in excruciating detail how many fishmongers she'd spoken to, how the road from Batoké to Idenao was bumpy, how the road ended there and she had to hire a boat to Bekumu, then walk to Bamusso.

Then she described a villager from deep in the delta who was willing to work with them. Money meant little to the remote tribes, and the villager wanted help with a problem as payment. They'd meet her up the coast in the morning.

After Monique left, Pia turned to the Major. "The boys who've been following us, do we know who sent them?"

CHAPTER 15

25-May, 4PM

"You saw them?" the Major said.

"I've been followed before," Pia said. "Used to be overzealous fans or someone ticked off about a foul. Guess things are different now. Who are they?"

"Tania and Marty pushed them around a little, talked to them, took their pictures. They were embarrassed but not deterred. They just kept a little more distance."

"Let's follow them," Pia said. "I'd like to know who sent them and why."

"They've been making calls on cell phones."

Pia's eyebrows went up. "Can we jump the frequency?"

"Miguel is our electronics expert, he has a cell phone scanner."

When Agent Miguel returned from distributing soccer gear, he gave her a hand-sized device and showed her the basics. As they went over how it worked, he changed the subject for a second. "The Sabel Foundation gives out millions in charity, why make the soccer gear anonymous?"

Pia said, "When you know the source of your good fortune, you can always ask for more. When you don't, you take very good care of your gifts."

An hour later, in running shorts and a tank top, Pia dropped a soccer ball at her bare feet. She dribbled her way onto the beach with a Bluetooth earbud in her ear. Connected to that were both her phone and the eavesdropping receiver in her runner's pack. Tania followed. The Major drove up the coast road. Marty and Miguel rotated off watch and headed for the hotel bar.

Pia's two shadows looked concerned about the group's splitting up but made no calls.

She dribbled up the beach at a warm-up pace, the brown sand squished between her toes like soft silk. Tania did her best to keep up. Patches of scar tissue on her legs covered most of one thigh and half of the other. The rewards of serving her country.

They left the populated section of the beach.

The boys followed, though not quite at Pia's speed.

A couple kilometers out, Tania stopped. She said, "OK, I get it. You're an athlete. Now can we jog at a normal pace?"

Pia huffed. "That was just a warm-up. What's your 10K time?"

Tania stopped running, put her hands on her knees. "I dunno, under fifty minutes probably."

"Air is up here," Pia said stretching her chin skyward. "Never bend down when you're out of breath."

Tania stood up straight. "What's your time?"

"Thirty-two or thirty-three, usually."

"Look, we're way ahead of the boys. Isn't this good enough?"

Their favorite spies had fallen so far behind they were merely figures in the distance.

Pia took off again, dribbling the ball. Tania whined and took off after her. A stand of dense trees and brush grew close to the water, obscuring the way ahead. Rounding a bend that cut off visual contact, Pia stopped and hid among the foliage. Tania followed her into the small peninsula of jungle, panting profusely.

"Can you see them?" Tania asked.

"Yep, they're arguing. Tough spot we put them in—do they follow us into an obvious trap or stay under cover? Now they'll have to use the phone."

She worked the receiver to isolate the boys from the thirty-two active calls in the area. Pia scanned until she came on something with a beach breeze blowing in the background, an unmistakable whoosh across the microphone every few beats. Wanting confirmation, she squinted to see if the lips synched up. But they were too far away for certainty. The tall boy held the phone to his ear. He turned around. Immediately she heard the change in wind on the monitored call.

She had them.

"Can you tell what they're saying?" Pia handed the earbud to Tania.

Tania glared at her. "What, you think I'm part African so I can speak Zulu or whatever the hell that is? Is that what you're saying?"

"You're more African than I am, but that's not what I meant. It doesn't sound like a Bantu dialect."

"Bantu? Oh, is that it? They speak Bantu?"

"Dialects south of the Equator are usually based on Bantu, the way French and Spanish are Romance languages. It was in the mission brief."

"Yeah? Well, fuck Bantu." Tania grabbed the earbud and shoved it in her ear. After listening for a few seconds, she dropped it back in Pia's hand.

"Sounds like Cajun or something."

"You're right. Pidgin French probably. Dammit."

"Did you ask the Major about Bantu?" Tania said. "She's all African."

"Get focused."

Tania huffed. She asked, "Is that a record button?"

"Hope so, I pushed it a few minutes ago."

"So how do we find out who they work for?"

"I don't know," Pia said. "They didn't follow us as far as they were supposed to." Pia peered through the bushes, then back at Tania. "Let's ask them."

Tania rolled her eyes but jogged down the beach toward the boys. Once she'd passed them by a hundred meters, she turned around and ran back toward them. At the same time, Pia ran toward them from the other side. The boys were in their late teens, slightly built and scrawny. They wore pastel slacks and button-down short-sleeved shirts to blend in with the hotel guests. Their heads swung back and forth between Tania and Pia like fans at a tennis match.

With no one else in sight, they decided to make a break for it.

Running for the hotel, they charged at Tania. Twenty yards out, she pulled up short and raised a hand. They didn't even slow down. She glanced around, then pulled a gun out of her waist pack. The boys stopped in their tracks.

The taller one narrowed his eyes and bent into a fighting stance. The shorter one stepped sideways, splitting her aim. Neither of them saw Pia coming up behind them faster than they could have imagined.

Her slide tackle took down the short guy and distracted the tall one. Tania stuck the gun in his right eye.

Pia's target scrambled to his feet. Seeing the situation, he pulled up two fists and growled at her. She smiled and shook her head.

"We only want to talk to you," she said.

The taller boy said something that sounded vaguely French.

Pia looked at him, "Do you speak English?"

"Hell yeah they speak English." Tania kicked the taller boy. "They spoke to Marty. Ain't that right, skinny boy?"

The short boy lashed out with a kick to Pia's midsection. She twisted right, his foot glancing off the back of her thigh, then unwound with a right cross that connected her open hand to his temple. His head spun over his shoulder, his body following in the twist. He collapsed on the sand.

"Holy shit!" Tania said. "Did you kill him?"

Pia looked at Tania and the tall boy, their eyes wide, faces shocked. She shook her head and said, "He's counting sand while he sorts things out."

On cue, the shorter boy spit sand and rose on his elbows, then on his hands and knees. He flopped around and sat in the sand shaking his head. Slowly, his eyes rose to Pia's.

"All I want to know is who hired you to follow me," she said.

The tall one glared at his friend. "No talkin dem to da lady, abi."

Pia turned to the tall boy. "You talk to da lady, abi."

He squinted at her and shook his head.

"We ain't getting anywhere with these guys," Tania said. "Can I shoot 'em?"

The whites of his eyes bulged out. Pia nodded and Tania popped a dart into the short boy. He fell over. They turned to the tall boy.

"No, no, no." He waved his hands in front of him as if swatting away flies and backed up. "No bosses for we. Dis tins happens for anoder raison."

"What was that?" Tania asked Pia. "Was that your Bantu?"

"No, sounds like Pidgin English. I think he said he doesn't have bosses for a reason. Guess that means he doesn't know who's in charge."

"Who was he calling then?" Tania waved the gun at him. "Hey, you. Who were you calling then?"

"Not knowing. Call for we side, she answer."

Pia drew her gun and pulled the trigger.

"Yeah," Tania said, "he was getting boring."

"He was saying he just called in and spoke to someone without knowing who." Pia patted him down.

She found a phone in his pocket and pressed the redial button. Three rings later, a woman's voice offered a quick and curt *allo*. The voice sounded familiar. Pia waited, hoping the woman on the other end would repeat the greeting or ask something, anything that would help her identify the voice. Without another word, the woman clicked off. Pia called her back. This time the woman played Pia's game—she picked up the call but said nothing.

After a couple beats, Pia said, "This is Pia Sabel, who are you?"

On the other end, Pia heard a surprised intake of breath. The line went dead. It had to be someone Pia knew, or she would have responded with "wrong number" or made some lame excuse for the boys. That didn't narrow it down much—people speaking French included the maid, the bishop's wife, guests at the hotel, and countless others.

She copied the phone numbers involved and returned the phones to the boys. She and Tania dragged them into the jungle, then propped them against a tree to keep their airways open. They administered the injectors.

"How come you hit that guy with your hand open?" Tania asked. "I thought you were a boxer or something."

"With gloves on, you're protected," she said. Pia made a fist and pointed to her knuckles. "Lots of little bones in there. If you're street fighting without gloves, use the heel of your hand or your elbow. Fewer broken bones that way."

Satisfied the boys would wake up safely in a few hours, they wiped the sweat from their brows.

"Interesting solution." The Major stepped from the dense foliage an arm's length away.

"HOLY SHIT, Major!" Tania shouted. "You scared the crap out of me."

"Reassuring to know you're guarding the boss." The Major turned to Pia. "You've now shown an adversary what kind of weapons we use and how willing we are to use them. Nice. Remember when you asked me to be your mentor?"

"Yeah."

"Remember when we came up with a plan to interrogate the boys: lead them to me and let me use my twenty years of experience to question them?"

"Um."

"What happened to the plan, Pia?"

CHAPTER 16

26-May, 3AM

THE ROOM SWIRLED AROUND PIA before coming into focus. It was dark, nothing familiar in sight. Her dream still echoed in her head, her mother saying, *You hired the Major. Why don't you listen to her?*

Pia shook her head, pushed herself out of bed, stretched and glanced at the clock. Three hours of sleep. She looked for a light switch. A silhouette outside, backlit by moonlight off the ocean, caught her eye.

Her breath stopped. It looked distinctly human but short. Either someone crouched or was seated on the porch. She reached for her gun on the nightstand. When she reached, whoever it was moved. Was it one of the boys from the beach? She couldn't tell which way it faced, in or out. Were they watching her? Or looking out to sea? Impossible to tell. Who had watch at this hour, Jacob or Ezra? Didn't look right for either.

She tightened her hold on the gun and considered her next move. Opening the sticky wooden door would alert the lurker. Darts couldn't penetrate the glass. Bluff? Scare him off?

She stepped closer to the window. A board creaked under her foot.

The figure outside spun into a standing position, gun drawn. For a full second they aimed at each other. Then the figure relaxed, lowering the gun.

"Jesus, Pia," the Major said. "You scared the crap out of me."

"We're even, then." She started breathing again.

"The manual says you don't sleep much, but I didn't expect you up this early."

"What are you doing out there?"

"I sent Marty in and took his watch overnight. Did I wake you up?"

"No, come in, Major." Pia opened the door. "I was just going to check out what our experts back home could learn from the phones."

"You can call me Jonelle when we're alone."

"I call you Major out of respect. Doesn't matter who's around."

The Major bowed her head a moment. Then she said, "There's one thing that kept me up, Pia. You brought us to Cameroon because of a pack of matches and a bus ticket. I thought we were wasting resources. Now I realize you were on to something—you hit a nerve somewhere. Those boys might have been cheap amateurs, but someone sent them to watch you. Which means you have us in the right place."

Pia stared at her for a beat. "Thank you, Major. I appreciate that."

"It also means we're in greater danger than I thought."

The Major nodded and walked outside to keep the watch.

Pia's phone buzzed, caller ID showed Dad. As much as it pained her, she let it roll to voicemail.

She pulled up the report. The boys' phones originated in Vienna. Someone had converted them for use in Africa on an anonymous pre-paid plan over the MTN network. The phones had no GPS location capability. The woman who answered could have been anywhere from Ghana to Gabon. The two recorded conversations between the boys and their handler revealed nothing but whining about the tedium and lack of things to report. They wanted to leave.

They got even less from the woman's end of the conversation: *Allo* and *Non*.

Pia slumped back in her chair and heard the Major's words echo in her head. *What happened to the plan?* Caught up in the euphoria of domination, she'd picked up on Tania's impulsiveness. She darted the boys because it seemed like fun, like something within her power to decide. It was irresponsible. An opportunity lost.

She picked up her e-reader and went outside. The Major returned, sat in one of two chairs next to her and watched the beach. Moonlight between the clouds occasionally lit a wave, all else was blackness.

"What are you reading?" the Major asked.

"*The Memoirs of Jack Reacher*." Pia looked up from her book. "Hey, he was an MP too. Did you know him?"

"I was a new recruit, he was my CO. Worked for him on and off over about five years. He taught me everything I know."

"Did really he do all this stuff?" Pia held the book up.

"Never read the memoirs. But if he said he did—he did. That's for damn sure."

"Pretty violent guy."

"He never hurt anyone who didn't have it coming. Keep reading, he's a good role model."

She put the book down. "I need a plan for today."

"You have great instincts, Pia. Have confidence in that. But, in front of the others, everything has to come from you. I'll only jump in to prevent a serious mistake. Now, let's start with the goal."

They talked for thirty minutes. When they were done, Pia changed into her running shorts and shirt, grabbed a pair of water runner shoes, and headed back outside. Ignoring the Major's security protests, she did her ten-kilometer warm-up. In the dark, with only a small headlamp for guidance, she had a chance to clear her head and plan her day. Thirty-five minutes later, she was back in the hotel's gym lifting weights.

When she finished, she found a text from Alphonse: call me.

"I was not certain when you wake," he said.

"I told you, I'm an early riser."

"I like that in the woman."

"Easy there, Romeo," she said. "Hey, I found two teenagers following me yesterday." She explained the phone source and the French woman's voice.

"Vienna?" he said. "Perhaps stolen from tourists? Or is that where the pirates live?"

"Their attacks came from a pretty nasty area of swamps and jungles. No electricity or running water, so they probably live somewhere else between attacks. But Vienna? Kind of land-locked for a bunch of pirates. Anyway, we're heading up the coast for some recon. Hopefully, we'll know something by this time tomorrow."

"We have found little on our end. Capitaine Villeneuve has ordered me to interrogate the wives. She thinks perhaps there was the love triangle. But, this is not possible. It would have to be the love pentagram."

Pia laughed. "Orgy, maybe? You know how wild bankers are."

"It makes me ill to think. Mme. Marot is difficult to question. She is superior, only speaking to le Capitaine, and even then she is quite rude. Sandra Bachmann lived with the sister who knows nothing of banking. Eren Wölfli's wife, Ramona, would be the suspect in my mind. She has the questionable past, some arrests before she married Wölfli. But why kill so many? It makes no sense. Sara Campbell's husband, drunk at every interview. Reto Affolter's wife, Antje, was most devoted."

"Did you find anything on the accomplice?"

"Affolter's murder in the parking garage was on video, but there is not much to see. Two men beating him before shooting him. Faces are not visible." His voice perked up. "Oh, and the gendarmerie in Lyon has made identification of your attacker. A soldier from Norvège, no past, no records. He went to Cameroon a year ago and came back the day before the killings."

"Sounds like assassins to me."

"Even le Capitaine admits you could be correct about this. Is your offer to have Sabel Security help us still open?"

"Absolutely. I'm already trying to find them, may as well join forces."

"I will mention it again. She is most insistent now that I find something new."

"What about the money at Banque Marot?"

"Quoi? What money?"

Pia relayed what Sara Campbell had told her about having too much money. For a while, Alphonse was silent.

"This is most interesting," he said. "It is unfortunate that she was killed before…"

As his voice trailed off, Pia understood the implication.

"You should go, Alphonse. Follow up on that one."

"Oui, au revoir."

She'd expected the police to make more headway, at least a few clues for her to follow in Cameroon. So far, they were living up to her original assessment of them. Were they ever going to start investigating?

CHAPTER 17

26-May, 6AM

AS THE SUN ROSE INTO another gray haze, Pia showered and dressed for the day in black compression shorts, sports top, and her water runner shoes. She joined her agents and Monique Tsogo on board the *Limbe Explorer*.

They headed north, swinging wide around the massive Limbe tanker pier, where two tethered tankers were being filled with crude oil.

Captain Whittier, the *Limbe Explorer's* proud captain and a California expat, insisted on giving Pia a personal tour of his Dvora class patrol boat. Capable of forty-five knots should Pia wish to pay for the extra fuel consumption, the twenty-seven-meter boat had a low radar signature and a draft of only one meter. Captain Whittier beamed as he showed her the open-air bridge up top. Below was the main control room, an armored pilothouse that allowed him control in adverse conditions. They had enough supplies to last three days, plus a water filtration system. Four Zodiacs were stowed for side trips.

Captain Whittier rattled off several oil companies as his primary clients. He said, "Their geologists and oil hunters often required the *Limbe Explorer's* speed for escape in case of attack."

"Attack from whom?"

"This isn't the Great Lakes, Ms. Sabel. There are desperately poor people living in this region."

"Have you been attacked?"

"Oh no, ma'am. But I've left in a hurry quite a few times. Don't worry, if I see anything dangerous I'll get you out of there before the shooting starts."

Pia managed not to ask, *What about getting into the shooting?*

Instead, she looked around at the decks and the thick metal shielding. She asked, "Bullet-proof?"

"Grenade-proof."

Sunrise broke over Mount Cameroon into a cloudless sky. The early fog burned off quickly, leaving a hot unfiltered sun. The smell of warming beach and fish filled the air. She watched the endless jungle pass by and felt the salt-water breeze rough her skin like fine sandpaper.

They stopped off the coast of Idenao to pick up Calixthe Ebokea, the villager from the delta. She had a triangular face and sharp eyes that assessed everyone with quick, stabbing glances. Gray streaks peeked out beneath her gele and she wore a dark dashiki and leggings with threadbare sneakers.

Shaded from the intense sun by a large awning, they grouped around a table with a map in the center they weighted with handguns laid on each corner.

As Pia joined her agents on the spacious aft deck, Monique glanced up.

"Calixthe is from Bekumu, here at the end of the river," the investigator said. "She says the pirates are deep in the mangroves in this area." Her hand swept over a featureless area to the north and west. "She can lead you to their general vicinity, within a mile. But she wants your help first."

Calixthe showed them where a river ran parallel to the coast for nearly ten kilometers before turning into the ocean. A wide stretch of land and mangroves separated ocean and river.

"Slavers," Calixthe spoke with a hard voice and an African cadence. "Europeans with big promises. They say our women will have jobs in Belgium or France or Denmark. The women are forced into prostitution. These men have been here before. We know their lies. This time they come to Bekumu and take many women by force. I come to Limbe yesterday but the authorities, they do not listen. The police work only for bribes. You help me get the young women back. Then I help you find the white men you seek."

"Not a problem," Tania said. "How many men?"

"Three, maybe four."

Pia held up a hand and eyed her people quickly. No one spoke. She turned to Calixthe.

"Where are they?"

"Here, an abandoned village called Boa." She pointed to a bend in the long coastal river.

"How long ago?"

"A week."

"Where are the men from your village?" Pia asked.

"Mostly at sea. They work the drilling rigs for two weeks, maybe three. Others are out fishing. They will not be back for another week."

Pia nodded in the direction of the wheelhouse. Monique led Calixthe away, giving Pia privacy with her team.

"Perfect," Tania said. "We do a good deed and get—"

"Whoa," Jacob and Ezra said at the same time.

"Bad idea," Jacob said. "Really bad."

Pia frowned. "Why?"

"We need to keep focused," he said. "We stick to our mission, obtain our goals. Traffickers in drugs, guns, women, whatever, are not our problem. We start down that path and every village will want us to run off their criminals. We'll have to pull a coup d'etat and run the country."

"Ezra?" Pia asked.

"What he said." Ezra pointed at Jacob.

Pia looked to Marty next.

"I say it's a win-win," Marty said. "We take down some slavers and we have jungle swag. Villagers all over the delta will love us. This is something we have to do."

Pia read the faces of the others. Miguel, indifferent. The Major, waiting for a decision. The others had spoken.

"Three or four men in the jungle," she said. "How dangerous is it from a tactical standpoint?"

Jacob rubbed his jaw. "A couple of us do a quick recon to verify the target, shouldn't be a problem. If she's right about the numbers. If she's wrong, we could be in deep."

"Risk for the recon trip?" Pia asked.

"Low," Ezra said. "We swing around wide, in and out in a couple hours."

"If recon shows three men, ten hostages, what's the risk of going in?"

"Still low," Jacob said. "Tania can take down three men after an all-night party. I've seen her do it. I just don't like straying from the mission."

"I can live with it," Ezra said.

"We should stick to the plan," Jacob said. "Get the pirates. Find 'em and take 'em down. None of this save the world crap. That kind of thing gets you killed."

"We're doing it," Pia said. "We can't buy information so we have to work for it."

Everyone stared at Jacob. He shuffled from foot to foot.

"Ah, screw it," he said. "You guys want to go, I'll go. Marty snipes, Ezra contains, Miguel and I take the recon."

"No," Pia said. "I'll work the recon trip with Miguel and Marty. Everyone else gets ready for a quick trip up river if and when we confirm the enemy numbers."

Everyone grunted agreement and headed toward the coffee bench. Tania watched Pia intently until Ezra handed her a cup.

Pia stepped to the Major, who leaned against the railing.

"You handled that well," the Major said.

Pia nodded and looked out to sea. "Thanks. Good idea?"

"No. I'm with Jacob—stick to the mission."

"Should I—"

"You should never second guess an order." She straightened. "Make sure you have it right the first time."

Pia went back to the map and looked it over. Her finger traced the river from its source near Bekumu, down the coast, until it swept into a broad P-shaped curve, with the P lying on its back. Boa stood at the top of the curve. From the village to the coast was three kilometers of open beach with a broad channel. A quick trip for the *Limbe Explorer* if the recon confirmed things, a quick evac if it didn't.

A couple yards away from her, Monique answered her cell phone. "*Allo?*"

The word caught Pia's ear. Had it been Monique's voice on the boys' phone? French-speaking Douala was less than forty miles from Limbe. She couldn't tell.

Monique handed out Egusi puddings wrapped in banana leaves—a spicy pumpkin seed mash with ground fish and meats, Cameroon's version of a protein bar. The group feasted, some more willingly than others.

The Major sat on one side of Pia, Ezra on the other. They watched the coastline as they passed. Small strips of beach glowed with white sand and dark trees leaned over the water between them. They chatted about the beauty of the coastline and the birds of Cameroon. Then there was a lull, each of them thinking about the day ahead.

"Could be some gunfire today," Ezra said. "We do everything right, the only people who will die this morning are slavers."

Pia and the Major nodded.

Ezra said, "Major, I know you've had to kill in the line of duty. Not easy, but you survived, you were trained for it. However you, Ms. Sabel... well, there are company rumors. Lots of variations but all of them similar. One in particular is pretty hard to believe. So I have to ask. Have you ever killed anyone?"

CHAPTER 18

Niger Delta, Cameroon
26-May, 9AM

MIGUEL PILOTED THEIR ZODIAC BETWEEN islands of mangrove and sand. Water, crystal clear in the shallows and stained the color of dark tea, flowed in the tangle of tidal channels. Rock and coral lay inches below the surface in some places, sand as smooth as china in others.

Following Calixthe's suggestion, they threaded their way to the river and bypassed her village to prevent any news of their arrival reaching Boa. They went upstream from Boa, in the opposite direction from where lookouts might keep watch on the river's mouth. Once they reached the main part of the river, they hugged the shore. They stopped when they came to an overland trail between the villages. After they dragged the Zodiac up into a spot where it wouldn't be seen, they strapped on their gear and headed out. Pia tugged on her Kevlar vest unsure if she'd ever get used to it. Calixthe led at an easy run.

Half a kilometer in, the mangroves gave way to lush jungle. Daggers of sunlight stabbed through the canopy, flashing off Calixthe's back like a strobe as she ran. Something bothered Pia at the back of her brain, as if she should recognize a danger but wasn't clear about what it was. Were her nerves fraying on her first mission? She shook it off and ran.

There was more open space between the trees and bushes than Pia expected. Pillars of trees supported an arched canopy a hundred feet above them, as if she were in a gothic cathedral. Miguel and Marty kept close, occasionally checking the rear for followers. While they ran, Calixthe told them she'd sent young boys up this same path to spy on the slavers, and in twenty trips they'd encountered slavers only three times. She was confident they'd remain undetected.

As they neared Boa, packed dirt and clay turned to sand and pebbles under their feet. Lava flows formed rock walls in places. Glimpses of a cliff face loomed above them, visible from time to time through the tree branches. They climbed over a lava flow as tall and wide as a city bus and continued until the dirt and jungle suddenly stopped. A pond of hardened lava blocked the way forward, its swirls and currents permanently embedded in cold black stone.

Calixthe pointed across the flow.

"From here we can climb the cliffs or go through the jungle."

"Open country up there." Pia said. She looked at Miguel and Marty. "You two find some high ground, triangulate your views, let me know what you see. Calixthe and I will get in close on the ground. Keep in touch."

She tapped the Bluetooth earbud of her comlink.

Miguel started to object, but Marty tapped his shoulder, tossed his chin at the cliff and headed out at a jog. Miguel shook his head but caught up with Marty.

Pia checked her waist pack. It held her Glock and three spare magazines. Two magazines held darts, one held hollow points. Nine shots per magazine. She slung an M4 over her shoulder with one magazine carrying thirty 9mm darts. No lead.

Calixthe looked her up and down, then disappeared into the jungle. Pia followed.

A few minutes later, Marty reported in. "In position now. I have one large clearing straight in front of you and another half a kilometer north. No movement."

Miguel's voice came next: "Same."

Pia tapped Calixthe. "How close are we?"

Calixthe answered by drawing back a large leaf. Beyond it lay a wattle-and-daub hut. Beyond the hut, a clearing and a fire pit. Farther out were a couple more huts peeking between the foliage. Calixthe motioned Pia to follow and moved to the right. A hundred meters farther, she crouched and pulled back a fern. A large hut on short stilts sat across a dirt courtyard. Five smaller huts surrounded it. A twenty-meter perimeter, cleared of vegetation, gave them a view of the village.

In the center, two white men in shorts sunned themselves in rickety lawn chairs. One was short and round, his big gut visible through his open shirt; what little hair he had left fell in an unkempt halo around his ears. The other was taller and pale with a full head of dark hair and a trimmed beard. Big-gut pushed fifty while Tall-guy looked younger, maybe thirty. A large bottle of booze was on the ground between them.

Pia waved Calixthe back, deeper into the jungle. Calixthe followed, then stumbled. A bird took off. Pia crouched and watched the men with her hand on Calixthe's back, holding her down. Pia's heart pounded so loud in her chest she was sure the men could hear it. But the men didn't even glance up. After a full minute, Pia started breathing again and helped Calixthe to her feet. She glanced around to find what tripped her guide but saw nothing.

Fifty meters deeper into the jungle, Calixthe pointed to a large stand of bamboo with an opening like the letter C, but big enough for several people to stand in the center somewhat hidden. Matted grass in the middle indicated an animal den of some kind.

Pia took her earbud off mute and discussed the situation with Marty and Miguel in tense whispers. They repositioned themselves on the cliff until they could see the huts and the white men. Neither saw evidence of women held against their will. In fact, they saw no women at all. Pia would have to move around the clearing to gather more information.

She and Calixthe circled the huts twice. Still no sign of the captives. The women must be held in the large central hut. They had to get a look inside.

"They are in there," Calixthe whispered. "I told you."

Pia silenced her with a finger and shook her head. They crept back to edge of the clearing and watched as Marty fired a conventional shot. The loud report echoed through the jungle, setting off birds and monkeys. The two men leapt to their feet. A boy wearing shorts and a faded shirt came to the doorway of a hut.

"What the bloody hell was that?" Big-gut asked.

"Hunters?" Tall-guy said.

Big-gut turned to the boy in the doorway.

"Oi, Delany. What the hell you doing there? Your watch now, yeah?"

Delany, possibly twenty, small and skittish, fled into the jungle. Pia watched him disappear. Calixthe touched her and pointed. Pia held up three fingers, meaning three targets. Calixthe shook her head and held up four. She pointed in the opposite direction from Delany's route.

"Elgin Thomas would do a cheeky thing like that, you know," Big-gut said. "Send a man round back to see if we're watching both sides." A nervous laugh. "Bugger us both for it, he would."

Tall-guy looked down at him and frowned. Big-gut picked up the bottle and chugged three or four ounces. He offered it to Tall-guy, who shook his head and squinted into the jungle.

Pia's panic level ratcheted up a notch. She felt an immediate danger, but what? She tugged Calixthe and they withdrew to the bamboo again to consult with Marty and Miguel.

"We think there are four of them," Pia said.

Marty asked, "Sure enough to bet your life on it?"

CHAPTER 19

26-May, 10AM

CAPTAIN WHITTIER STEPPED UP TO Major Jonelle Jackson.

"Your friends all set, then?"

"They're doing well." She pointed to a ship some distance out to sea. "What kind of ship is that?"

"Deep sea trawler. A bit unusual for these waters—too shallow here, I'd think. They were approaching but stopped out there. Can't imagine what they'd fish for here. I hailed them but they've not responded."

"Do they have a radio identifier, what do you call them, MMSI?"

"They'd have to respond for us to find out." Whittier laughed and went back to his pilothouse.

The air was so still not even the smell of salt rose from the ocean. Sunlight glinted off the small choppy waves. It forced her eye to flick and twitch. Jacob read a book, Ezra paced the deck, and Tania stared at the map still laid out on the table. The Major joined her, keeping an eye on the trawler.

"Hey, Major," Tania said lazily. "Ever wonder why Pia Sabel looks nothing like Alan Sabel? I mean what's up with that? Is that 'cause rich people are always marrying their cousins? I mean you know they ain't gonna pollute their precious gene pool with the likes of you and me."

"Don't try dragging me into your hate-the-rich problem. Alan Sabel created twelve thousand jobs, including yours. He earned his money. What are you looking for on the map?"

"I don't like it," Tania said. "The layout's wrong. The more I look at it, the more it looks like a trap."

The Major watched her.

"Look at this." Tania pointed to the river's path. "Boa is a lousy place for human traffickers. Supposedly, they bring girls out of the villages and hold them here. If that's the case, then a couple of pissed-off natives could take care of the problem in a heartbeat. There's only one way in or out overland. You stand anywhere along this path and ambush the slavers when they come along. If you don't want to do it on land, you've got the same thing on water. Only one river."

The Major waved Monique over to join them and had Tania repeat her observations. She said, "Monique, how much background did you get in this area?"

"Slavers have been a problem in Bamusso, Mbongo, Liwenga, places like that for years. This is nothing new. The authorities can do little because usually the slavers trick them or drug them and take them to Nigeria through Mundemba or across the Niger River. When I was making inquiries, Calixthe was in Idenao and contacted me. Her story is fairly common. And if the slavers bring them down the trail to Boa, they would enlist the men in Bamusso to help them. In the jungle, human life is a commodity like copper. Not like gold."

Monique wandered away and sat down, fanning herself with a magazine.

"I still don't like it," Tania said.

"Lots of things not to like around here," Ezra said. "Like that trawler. One man in the wheelhouse but they have four Zodiacs on deck."

"Ready to launch?" Tania asked.

"Not exactly, but not stowed either."

"You guys finally figure out there's something terribly wrong with this little side trip?" Jacob said from his seat across the deck.

"OK, Jacob," the Major said. "If you're the self-appointed genius, what do you recommend we do now?"

"The recon team finishes up and we get the hell out of here."

The Major nodded. "Not as dumb as you look. Of course, that was Pia's plan all along."

She pushed her earbud in a little farther and checked the sat-phone connection.

"Recon team, this is Major Jackson. We have too many anomalies out here for comfort. Give me a sit rep."

"Marty here, Major. Pia and Calixthe are too close to the hostiles to report but they can hear you. What anomalies?"

"Deep sea trawler standing half a klick off to one side. And Tania has some problems with the layout. We're concerned about exit strategy."

"Understood." Miguel's voice reported in. "I've got another concern—large clearing just off the village. Tarp covering something big. I'm thinking a large supply depot."

"Supply depot?" Ezra chimed in. "For human traffickers? Might be more of them than we thought."

"Hang on," Marty said, "just got a text from Pia. She heard something. The men on the ground are waiting on someone named Elgin Thomas. Sounded like they expected him any minute."

"Decision time," the Major said. "Have we found what we're looking for?"

"No women in sight," Miguel said. "None."

After a long silence, the Major said, "Yeah, that's not right."

Pia spoke up. "I'm in a bamboo shelter and can talk for a few seconds. We're going in now. Take these guys down with darts, check the huts for the women, turn them loose and get the hell out of here. They find their own way back home and the three of us grab the Zodiac and head for the boat. Everyone good?"

Another long silence followed as each of them thought through the consequences.

"If you put them to sleep and find no one in the huts, no harm done," Ezra said. "I like it. Let's do it."

"Shut up, Ezra," Tania said. "I'm not dying in some backwater for nothing. Let's think this—"

"I told you getting off track would screw things up," Jacob said. "We never should have—"

"Quiet!" Pia said. "Not a discussion. We're going in. Follow me."

"Good timing, Ms. Sabel," Marty said. "The lookout, Delany, is moving toward your position. Maybe he's just on patrol, maybe he knows where you are. Looks intentional to me, though. He's two hundred meters northwest of you and headed straight to you. You head back to the big hut, Miguel and I will intercept him. We'll link up near your last position and go in together."

"Let's move," Pia said.

The conference line went quiet. The Major looked at three anxious faces around her and put her phone on mute. She said, "Anyone know how we ended up with the most dangerous position being taken by the least experienced member of the team?"

"You mean," Ezra said, "how the hell did we let the boss take point?"

Jacob turned back to his book, his eyes scanned the mangroves not the pages. Ezra walked to the bow and scanned the horizon with binoculars. Tania stared blankly at the map.

"What's the big deal?" Tania asked. "She wanted her pampered little white ass out in the jungle. Guess where it is?"

CHAPTER 20

Boa, Cameroon
26-May, 11AM

PIA'S PANIC LEVEL REACHED A new high. Why did Big-gut mention a pirate by full name? Why did Delany change course? There was only one answer. She cursed and led the way through the undergrowth. After a few meters, she motioned for Calixthe to go ahead. As soon as the older woman slipped past, Pia pulled her Glock. She pressed the muzzle between the guide's shoulder blades.

Calixthe froze. Pia leaned forward, her lips nearly touching Calixthe's ear. "Hand me your gun, slowly."

Calixthe gave it to her, hand trembling, face full of pain and shock.

"How did they get to you?" Pia asked.

Calixthe relaxed a little and shook her head.

"I'm really pissed off right now," Pia hissed. "Tell me or I dart you here. If they win, they'll find you and do whatever they want. If I win, I'll come back for you and make you cough up some answers." She paused. "And I'm going to win, Calixthe. I always win. So talk to me. You've got four… three…"

"They know me," she said. "I have been coming around, threatening, begging them, anything. Two days ago they caught me drawing the layout. I wanted to offer the authorities an advantage. But the slavers came to Bekumu and took our girls."

"How many are there?"

"Just the four."

"Can I believe that?"

"Yes," Calixthe said.

"Who is Elgin Thomas?"

"Chief, boss, captain. They expect him today."

Marty's voice came through Pia's earbud. He said, "Thanks for keeping your comlink open."

"You take down Delany," Pia said. "I'll wait for you twenty meters short of the bamboo. I'm guessing that's where they planned to ambush us."

"Agreed. Great place for a crossfire."

Pia turned to Calixthe. "Walk in front of me, that way. This time don't trip."

They headed back toward the bamboo circle and looked at it with different eyes. She pulled Calixthe behind a bush and shoved her Glock into the woman's ribs. From her new vantage point, she could see half the circle. She waited until she saw Big-gut and Tall-guy sneaking between trees from opposite sides of the growth. The two men peered into the bushes, eyes and guns trained on the bamboo.

Through her earbud Pia heard two darts. Marty and Miguel had finished off Delany.

Big-gut had probably been drinking a lot, so Tall-guy was her biggest threat. She moved Calixthe to a better position, keeping twenty meters from the bad guys. Too far, considering her inaccurate darts and her lack of live-fire experience.

Nerves turned to fear. And fear began taking charge. Pia's hands shook. Sweat dripped from her forehead. She left Calixthe where she could keep her eye on her and crept through the shadows until she was ten meters behind Tall-guy. A missed shot would cost her the element of surprise and put her in a gunfight with an experienced soldier.

She took another five silent steps. Too far away and she'd miss for sure. Too close, and he'd hear her coming.

She fired three shots. First one missed. Second hit his shoulder. Third hit his neck. Tall-guy dropped face first.

"Hey, Günter, what you doing, mate?" Big-gut shouted from the bamboo's far side.

Either the man was a moron or he was baiting her. More likely the latter. Even drunk he wouldn't give up his position. She tiptoed back and knelt next to a fallen mahogany tree. Her eyes scanned the shifting shadows. One down, but she'd lost track of Calixthe and Big-gut in the process. A shiver of fear crawled across her skin. A few steps away, something caught her eye. She looked at it, leading with her gun. Nothing. She moved forward a few steps, hopefully away from the ambush.

Big-gut rolled out from behind a tree, his Sig Sauer directly in Pia's face.

"Got you, you fucking berk." He looked her up and down. "Say, you're a big strapping lass, aren't ya?"

Fear overtook her like a giant wave, all at once and unstoppable. She shook.

His eyes were clear, his nasty breath had no trace of alcohol. Pia looked for an opportunity to strike but saw none. She stepped closer, holding her hands up.

"Stop right there." He tossed his nose up. "Now let the gun swing by the trigger guard and hand it over, nice and slow."

She did. He took the gun, slipped it in his belt.

"Keep your left hand out while I relieve you of this M4. Make me nervous and I'll put a hole in your head."

He slipped the strap off her and dropped the machine gun on the ground.

"Some shoulders you got there. You one of them transgender fellas?" He laughed and pressed his pistol into her ribs. "Now put your hands on top of your head, nice and slow."

She did.

He motioned for her to turn around.

She did.

He yanked the Bluetooth earbud out of her ear and tucked it into his own. He pushed her forward, pressing his gun barrel into her back. They marched toward the huts.

Pia scanned the jungle for any sign of Calixthe. Nothing. She could only hope the older woman was looking for a weapon or waiting for Marty and Miguel.

Inside the courtyard, Big-gut edged her toward the larger structure. She pushed through the rug-covered doorway into a stench of mold and rotting meat. Her eyes adjusted slowly to the gloom. Eight bound and gagged women, ranging from six or seven to seventy or older, squatted in the center. Sixteen eyes rounded with fear. To the left a trap door stood open, waiting to swallow them up at any moment. Her muscles tensed and her nostrils flared.

Furious, Pia spun around. Big-gut smacked her face with the gun. Her eyes focused on the barrel.

"Don't get cheeky," he said. "Yes, the safety is off and I've chambered the first round. One squeeze, my little darling, and your miserable life is over."

"Why didn't you shoot me back there?"

"Shut up! Speak without permission again and I'll put a bullet in your bloody knee."

Pia felt oddly calm. More angry than scared. Her mind ran through scenarios: if she spoke and he lowered the gun to shoot at her knee, would she have time to knock him out before he pulled the trigger? Maybe. Maybe not.

A young guy of mixed race, maybe sixteen, ran in the room and stopped an arm's length from her. Shirtless and shoeless, he wore True Religion blue jeans and looked vaguely familiar. Angular chin, wedge-shaped face, sharp darting eyes. The women cowered at the sight of him. He looked Pia up and down and smiled.

Big-gut turned his back and peered outside. He said, "Where's your bloody captain then?"

Pia watched the young guy. He pulled twine out of a bag hanging on the wall. A bottle of pills fell to the floor. Big-gut barked a stream of obscenities at him. Young-guy scrambled to put the pills back, then approached her with the twine. She brought her hands off her head, bringing them to shoulder level while keeping her eyes on Big-gut. She sensed a nervousness underneath the man's bravado. She guessed he was waiting for reinforcements.

"I'm not gonna shoot you if you answer my bloody question, you stupid git. But I'll blow your toes off if you don't. Where and how many?"

Young-guy motioned with his hands, wrists together, holding them out to mimic handcuffing. She shook her head as if she didn't understand. He repeated the motion. She leaned in a little closer, cocked her head, and slid her left foot forward. She dropped her left hand to her waist. Her hands remained too far apart to tie up. The boy looked displeased. She bent her knees slightly, coiling and tensing every muscle in her body. Slowly, she drew her left hand back and made a fist. He repeated his motion indicating how he wanted her hands.

"Where are they and how many?" Big-gut bellowed.

"Two others. They were five minutes behind me."

"Yeah? You're just a scout, eh? And where's Calixthe then?"

Young-guy stuck his hands out again, exasperated.

Pia exploded off her back foot with an uppercut that raised him off the ground and pushed the air out of his lungs. Before he could recover, she threw a right cross that shoved him backwards into Big-gut's arm, forcing the gun outward as he fired. The women yelped and cried in their gags. Pia landed two lightning-fast body blows into Young-guy, pinning him to Big-gut and both to the door jamb. Big-gut swung the gun toward her, his eyes red with rage. Another uppercut banged the boy's head backward into Big-gut hard enough to hurt them both. She twisted her body core to the left and landed her elbow in Young-guy's face. He fell. She spun herself out the door at the same moment he fell, tripping her.

She rolled across the courtyard and landed on all fours, leapt to her feet and ran. Big-gut twisted around the door jamb, aimed and fired. A split second later she heard him trip over the same body. In his physical condition, he wouldn't pop to his feet. Pia fled around the building's backside, across the cleared space, into the darkness of the jungle. With every step she checked her nervous system for any indication of a wound and felt nothing. Fifty meters into the jungle she slipped behind an ebony tree and collected her breath.

Now what?

CHAPTER 21

26-May, 11:30AM

PIA SABEL WANTED TO THROW up. Instead, she swallowed hard and shivered, a small tremor that grew into a full body spasm. She fought to get herself under control. Her heart pounded so hard it hurt. Every part of her body was slick with sweat. Every instinct in her told her to flee this dangerous place. Those last sixty seconds back there had been pure luck. She'd never survive another round. Despite being fitter, stronger, and quicker than Big-gut, he had a lot more experience and was far more ruthless. Worse was the fact that she'd led her team into the trap. Their lives were at stake because she fell for Calixthe's treachery. If she wanted to be a leader, she needed to lead her people to safety immediately. It was the responsible thing to do.

Set against all that were the faces of the bound and gagged women in that stinking hut. They haunted her, enraged her. Morally, she saw no option but to charge once more into the fray. Yet her natural desire for self-preservation ordered her to run. A decision she could easily justify by saving her people. If she could ask them now, would Tania and Marty change their minds? Would they vote for a retreat to safety right now, knowing they could come back later, better armed? In a trembling state of panicked confusion, Pia fought her conflicted impulses. The pleading, terrified faces out of the youngest girls, innocent six-year-olds, flooded her conscience. Would the pirates let them live through the afternoon?

She had to go back. No question.

She fumbled her sat-phone out of her pack, shut down the Bluetooth connection, and held the phone to her ear. Silence.

"I'm out. Got away." She took a breath to steady her voice. "I've shut off the Bluetooth so the hostiles won't hear. We should have a clear line now. There are two of them in the big hut. Eight girls and women are in there bound and gagged."

She heard movement to her left.

She dropped to one knee and laid the phone on the ground. Between streaks of light and shadow, she searched for anything that moved. Sunlight bounced unpredictably. Air currents turned leaves here and there. Something moved toward her. Miguel or Big-gut? Marty could be out there somewhere. Maybe there were more hostiles.

Pia drew the gun she'd confiscated from Calixthe, dropped the magazine out, and checked the load: sleeper darts. They were quiet, but would the greater range and stopping power of lead be worth the noise? Probably, but the chance for collateral damage was too great. No sense accidentally hurting the women she came to save. She slipped the magazine back in and scanned the shadows again.

"Pia." Sounded like Miguel. "At the edge of the clearing now. No sign of hostiles."

Bugs and birds chirped and squeaked and called. A human voice on the phone was out of character against the jungle's background noise. Anyone nearby would have heard it and recognized it for what it was— Pia's phone.

She left it on the ground and slid backwards five meters into a wall of ferns.

Something in the corner of her eye caught her attention. A shadow crouched among the shadows to her left. The harder she stared, the more confused the shadows became. One shadow blended into another. More shadows layered on top of those. But the one that caught her eye, the one that she stared into until her vision blurred, had a shape. The shape of it scared her. It was definitely human. Someone was out there. The shadow carried a stick, held high in striking position. Calixthe? Delany? Marty? Young-guy? She wanted a target but this shadow presented nothing discernible.

The figure rose, fully silhouetted, and flew to the ebony tree in full attack, raising the stick high like a club. Pia aimed carefully and fired three shots.

Calixthe dropped to the ground.

Pia stabbed the antidote injector into her leg and checked her breathing. She grabbed the phone.

"I'll be there in a second. Have you found him?"

"Pia, stay," Miguel said.

Her temper flared until she remembered the Major's words in Geneva: S*tay behind us, not in front of us.* No doubt Miguel and Marty were ready to shoot anything that moved. She stayed.

After two motionless minutes, she decided that closer would be better. Just in case they needed her help. She slipped from one tree to the next, a watchful glance tossed in every direction as she went. At the bamboo stand she saw her M4 lying on the ground. She slipped her Glock in her waist pack, picked up the heavier gun, and moved the firing switch to three-round bursts. She dug her spare earbud out of her pack, joined it to the phone and squished it in her ear. She double checked that her new unit was connected and Big-gut's was off. She listened to the comlink. Marty and Miguel were silent. Good.

After a careful look around, she moved on.

Everything vibrated with light and shadow and sound and movement. She tried to sense the enemy presence. Tweets and beeps and scratches filled her ears, the noise of the jungle continued undaunted. A distant chimpanzee, a nearby cricket, a noisy bird. She tried to hone in on anything man-made. Her skin picked up cooler air currents near the bushes and muddy places, warmer currents where the sun streaked through the canopy. Her nose picked up the scent of animals she'd not noticed earlier, village dogs maybe. Among those natural scents, the faint scent of soap from the hotel—Marty.

Her eyes were wide open as she searched for movement in her peripheral vision. She was the assassin now, stalking her prey. She knew the look she'd seen on others was the look she wore herself at this moment.

Motion to her left. She snapped her head to see Marty staring down his M4 twenty meters away. Her heart wound up ready to burst. She felt incredibly light, but not in a good way. Marty scowled at her and pointed. She pointed toward the huts, turned her rifle that way and stalked forward.

Marty went ahead, one eye on the ground in front of him and one eye sighting down the barrel. His posture became her model. Pia pulled her M4 around, looked down the sight, aimed it at everything, then lowered it and slithered to the next tree. Her heart pounded in her ears to the point of distraction. Her nerves jangled with electricity, as if she'd found the light socket with her fingers. Yet she moved forward. She thought about Big-gut's breath. No alcohol meant the bottle of booze he'd chugged earlier was just for show. Calixthe had already admitted she told them Pia was coming. So why had Big-gut faked it? Why lure her in when there were only two men and a couple boys? Why hadn't he killed her when he had the chance? Why did Young-guy look familiar?

At the moment she figured it out, gunfire raked a stand of trees to her left. Marty dropped to the ground. Pia did the same. Her brain shut off every extraneous thought and detail. On her earbud she heard Marty's voice.

"Pia, you OK?"

"Yes, shots came from your left."

Three shots echoed through the trees and Miguel's voice came in.

"Darted him. Looks young."

"That leaves Big-gut," Pia said. "I'm going for the hut."

The Major broke into their call. "We're bringing the boat up river. It's shallow, so we'll drop a Zodiac to pick you—"

"NO!" Pia said, her voice low but fierce. "It's a trap. They want to draw you in. DO NOT COME UP RIVER. That's an order."

No one spoke.

Pia jumped up and ran for the hut. Marty stayed near the perimeter, covering the jungle. Miguel popped out of the jungle fifteen meters away and followed her in. She jumped the steps, threw herself through the entrance, rolled onto the floor and to her knees in a firing position. Miguel stayed outside. His gun swept the village. Then he charged inside behind her.

The women were gone. The hut was empty except for a few things pushed against the walls. A camp stove on a table, six beaten-up stools, a shelf of dry goods, a stack of plastic containers. A backpack hung from a hook.

"Talk to me," Marty said.

"Empty," Miguel said.

"Not exactly," Pia said. "We have his medication."

She pointed to the center of the room. A large Muslim prayer rug lay on the floor. She pointed to the backpack on the wall. Miguel squinted at her, unsure what she meant.

"Keep watch outside, Marty," Miguel said. "The boss is up to something."

Pia rose and rifled the backpack. One bottle of Lithium and one of Dantrium, each half full.

She showed them to Miguel, who shrugged.

"Someone's a psycho," she said loudly. She walked toward the rug. "Lithium in this dosage is for total schizophrenia. There's a rare but deadly side effect that requires Dantrium. I saw it in a clinic I sponsored in Suriname. Without Dantrium the patient's muscles lock up like rigor mortis. Then his brain goes back to the schizoid state, making a bad condition worse."

She tugged on the prayer rug, pulled it up. The trap door came up with it. A wooden ladder disappeared into the darkness below.

"Hey, Big-gut," she called down, "did you know Cameroon is a predominantly Christian country? Using a Muslim prayer rug to hide your trap door was just as stupid as leaving your medication up here. Think Elgin Thomas gives a rat's ass about your problems? Think Elgin Thomas is going to disrupt his timeline to get you more meds? I mean, c'mon, he already left you behind because he can't trust your scrambled brain. Ready to work with me?"

From deep inside the hole came the brief but hopeful sound of the bound women struggling to free themselves, then the silence of a struggle lost. Pia clenched her fist. She said, "Hey, Englishman. You got a name?"

Silence.

She looked back at Miguel, "See if there's a flashlight or something around here."

He produced one from his pocket and she panned it around the hole. Deeper than she thought, with six tunnels that radiated out from the bottom of the ladder. She sat back on her knees and thought. The tunnels could come up somewhere else, in another hut or another part of the village. Or he could be stuck in a dead end with eight hostages. Going after him was the only way to find out.

"Marty, check the other huts and around the clearing. See if this tunnel comes up somewhere else. I doubt it, but keep an eye out. Miguel, stay topside."

On the phone, the Major said, "Trouble out here. The trawler just deployed four Zodiacs, two of them heading up river to your position. The other two are heading directly for us. They've just launched a RPG and missed us. Get out of there on the double."

"I'm freeing the women," Pia said. "Miguel, fire enough to push him back."

She flew to the ladder and slid down into the dark.

The last three things she heard before her comlink lost connection were:

The Major, "NO! Miguel! Do not let Pia drop down that hole."

Ezra, "Don't worry about us, Tiger. Do what's right."

Miguel, "Too late, want me to go after her?"

CHAPTER 22

"JESUS CHRIST!" THE MAJOR SLAMMED her fist onto the table. "What the hell is wrong with that girl?"

Tania shrugged and dropped a magazine of sleeper darts out of her M4. After a long stare at the Major, she slammed in a thirty-round magazine of parabellums. "I'm not dying in this hellhole to save that bitch. She dove into a hole in the ground like a moron—that's her problem. We clear out of here. Soon as we have Miguel and Marty on board. Jacob was right, we should have left the slavers alone."

"Think, Tania, think! The spoiled rich kid figured it out." The Major grabbed a magazine of bullets and made the same swap. "Maybe you can too."

"What?"

"There never were any slavers."

Tania glared at her and slipped on a Kevlar vest. She threw one to the Major and stomped away.

Two Zodiacs approached at high speed, head on. Whittier turned the boat left, only to have the Zodiacs split up to circle wider. The Major checked her deployment: Ezra stood on the bow, Tania on one side slightly aft, Jacob on the other slightly forward.

The Zodiacs bounced over the waves. Even close up they'd make difficult targets.

"Run 'em down!" Ezra shouted over his shoulder, then pointed at one of the small boats. "I'll take these guys out."

The *Limbe Explorer* veered right, then swerved back to the left as a rocket-propelled grenade, RPG, flew over the Major's head and continued out to sea. The *Explorer's* propellers hadn't yet hit full speed when one Zodiac attacked.

The Major stepped into the pilothouse and saw Ezra glaring through the heavy glass at Whittier. He gestured again at the boat on the left and took up a position in the prow with his body wedged into the v-shaped railing. He kept his aim as steady as he could while the deck bounced beneath him.

She went back on deck and watched through a portal as Ezra rattled off the first shots at the circling Zodiacs. They returned fire. Ezra took careful aim, expecting the boat to rise on a small wave. He aimed above and in front of the coxswain and squeezed off a three-round burst. A man rose in the midsection and fired back. Another stood with the RPG. The Major aimed at him and the Zodiac turned away. The RPG went vertical, exploding high above them.

Tania knelt behind the gunwale and leaned around the armored wheelhouse. Aiming for the inflated rubber hull, she fired a burst. The Zodiac caught a wave and bounced out of range. At the same time, the *Limbe Explorer* turned hard as the engines cranked to full power.

While the Zodiacs had no speed advantage over the *Explorer*, they had the advantage in acceleration and maneuverability.

"On the right, on the right!" Jacob shouted over the rumble of the engines.

The Major joined him, sighting down her M4 as the second Zodiac swung into position on their newly exposed flank. As the bigger ship struggled to regain speed after the turn, the smaller craft leapt their way. The *Explorer's* decks leaned into the turn, the edge of the deck nearly level with the waves. The Zodiac ran straight at them and bounced up the gunwale. She turned and ducked but the pontoon banged her hard in the shoulder. The impact knocked her to the deck before the Zodiac slid backwards into the sea.

She flipped over and emptied half her magazine at the retreating attackers only to have the boat's rocking deck throw her aim downward. Wasted ammo. She scrambled to the safety of the gunwale. The pirates were coming about for a second run. She crabbed a few feet aft, rose to her knees and fired again, then ducked back below the gunwale. Multiple wakes from all directions made the boats bounce and rock unpredictably. She popped up, looked around, dropped back to the deck. The Zodiac carried four pirates, two wounded and two still standing.

To cover her, Jacob fired from a gun port behind the wheelhouse. A wave rocked the *Explorer*, spoiling his aim. The Major popped up and opened fire while Jacob stepped out from behind the armored wall.

One pirate dove overboard, fleeing the hail of bullets. The Zodiac came at them again, ramming the bigger ship a second time. Two men still aboard leapt onto the *Explorer*'s deck. One fell, landed on his back and fired his rifle at Jacob.

The Major shot the pirate in the back.

Jacob went down clutching his side.

The other pirate ran for the pilothouse, but Tania saw him coming. Closing too fast to shoot him, she slammed her gun into his groin and swept her feet under his knees. He fell. She fired three rounds into his chest.

An explosion rocked the boat at the bow. Tania looked around the pilothouse.

"Ezra's down!" Tania shouted.

"Jacob's down," the Major said.

She scrambled to Jacob, saw he was alive, and looked at the Zodiac. Flames engulfed it, but no one stood on the small deck. Two heads bobbed in the water. She resisted the urge to shoot them.

Tania crept forward of the pilothouse and out of the Major's sight.

Jacob grabbed her hand with an iron grip and pulled her close.

"I'm hit," he said. "Just below the vest." He gasped and struggled for words. "Nothing life-threatening. Get Ezra. Get Ezra!"

"Tania's getting him," the Major told Jacob. "Take it easy."

He nodded. She checked the pirate nearest her, still alive and groaning. She pulled her Glock full of darts and popped him.

"Ezra's hit bad," Tania called out. "RPG got him. Sank the boat on this side."

The Major looked overboard and saw the shore receding quickly. She jumped to her feet and stormed into the pilothouse. She said, "Turn this boat around and take us up river. NOW!"

"Are you out of your mind?" Whittier said.

"Do it now or I swear to god I'll do it myself. My people are back there."

Whittier glanced at his first mate, who shrugged. Monique Tsogo cowered in the corner, shaking her head and mumbling incoherently.

"Seven men tried to board my ship!" the captain said. "They have F470s, for crissake. Those are military Zodiacs with self-sealing chambers. Eight men went up river in those and you want to go after them? Lady, I don't know who you—"

The Major pulled the charging handle on her M4 and stuck the barrel in his chest.

"I'm Major Jonelle Jackson, Sabel Security. Those men are pirates who commandeered the *Objet Trouvé* last month. They're heading up river to slaughter three of my people. You take me up there or I leave you bleeding on the deck and make your mate the new captain."

"All right, all right!" Whittier shouted. "But you're the pirates now. You're stealing my goddamn ship."

He turned the boat.

Satisfied they were on course, the Major pushed his throttle over to full.

"Major," he said when the course stabilized, "you'd better have a look at your man out there."

She stepped out of the pilothouse and made her way forward. Tania knelt over Ezra, gripping his hand as pain spasmed through his body. His eyes stared skyward. The Major knelt beside them.

"You're going to make it, you old bastard," Tania said. "Hang in there. Stay with me."

"Legs burn...." Ezra said through clenched teeth.

The Major looked over his wounds, mostly on the back of his legs. Thank god he'd ducked when the grenade went off, but he was losing a lot of blood fast. She checked his head and shoulders, applied pressure to several areas, but arteries in his legs spurted blood onto the deck. She tore a strip from her T-shirt for a tourniquet, wrapped it around his leg, pulled it firmly and tied it off. She tore a second strip from her shirt. Tania grabbed it from her and slipped it around his other leg.

"Two inches above the wound," the Major said.

"I know where it goes!"

Tania pulled the tourniquet tight and tied it.

"The bleeding will slow because his veins will contract," Tania said, "but that only lasts a little while. We need to get him to a hospital."

"Tania, we have to get the others."

Ezra grabbed Tania's arm, pulled her close to his face.

"Get them…. I'm not…" He gasped and blood spilled out of his lips. "I'm not…"

He choked. His body shook and twitched.

"Hang in there, Ezra," Tania said. "Hang in there and I'll kiss you all over when we get back."

Ezra smiled. His face turned pale. Blood spurted out of his legs despite the tourniquets. His eyes went blank. He tried to speak but only coughed up more blood. His body shook violently again. Black bile came out his mouth. Then he was still.

Tania screamed a long, wordless scream, then stood and screeched with all her might at the trawler, "Fuck you! I'll kill you all!"

The *Limbe Explorer* slowed and made a wide sweeping turn in the river's channel.

Tania dropped to Ezra's side, and slid her arms under his shoulders. She pulled his lifeless form into her lap and hugged him. After a minute, she rose and pulled his body backwards off the foredeck. Tears streamed down her face.

The Major picked up Ezra's feet.

"Leave him alone!" Tania shrieked. "Leave him alone! He's mine. Go get Jacob." She dragged Ezra's body back behind the pilothouse to the safety of the armor-plated structure.

The Major ran around the other side to find Jacob propped up against the railing. The first mate mopped his wound with a fist full of gauze from a small first aid kit.

"Sorry, ma'am," he said. "This is all we have."

"I'll be fine," Jacob said. "Just…nailed my hipbone. Maybe something inside, intestines or spleen. Hurts bad. I'll live. How's Ezra?"

She shook her head. Behind Jacob, Tania sat on the deck with Ezra's body in her arms, running her fingers through his gray hair as she stared out to sea.

Jacob clenched a fist and pounded the deck.

"Like a death wish standing out there. He knew better, goddammit."

The Major nodded. "If they'd gotten any closer with that RPG..."

"Yeah. He saved us."

"I see them!" Whittier shouted from inside the pilothouse. "Three hundred meters, one ashore, the other coming about."

The Major stepped into the small room and followed his pointing finger. One Zodiac was beached and empty. The other was halfway through a turn that would set them head-on and closing the distance fast.

Tania stepped in behind them.

"Ram them," the Major said. "I'll blow out the rubber and sink them."

"Aim low," Tania said, "metal skirts around the top. Took me a couple shots to figure it out. Get them, I'm going ashore. Looks shallow enough to swim from here."

"Are you crazy?" Whittier said. "They just killed one of your men and wounded the other. You go out there and they'll kill you. There were four men on that boat, another three right there."

"Yeah, Ezra sent their RPG to the bottom of the Atlantic. All they have left are the AK47s. The Major can handle those schoolboys out front. I'll take down the rest."

"We'll hold here until you call in," the Major said. "If you can get the recon team into their Zodiac, head down river and we'll cover the retreat. You get tangled up, head up river and try making your way out through the mangroves. We can pick you up out there."

Whittier slowed. Tania stepped out and jumped overboard into thigh-deep water. Her M4 and a belt with three extra magazines held overhead, she waded ashore while the *Limbe Explorer's* engines engaged. It gained momentum and flew at the other Zodiac.

The Major stepped around the pilothouse, stopping near the leading edge. The river was rough where the wakes of the boat chopped it. She aimed low and fired.

A man in the Zodiac's bow returned fire just before the smaller boat wheeled around and away at full speed. The Major aimed for the engine but missed as it swerved.

Whittier yelled, "Hang on!"

The *Explorer*'s gears ground and groaned. The bow dipped, the stern rose, and the boat stopped. A second later, the Major realized they were backing up. She ran around the pilothouse and stuck her head in the hatch.

"Shallow water, they're trying to lure us upstream to ground us," Whittier said. "We have a shallow draft, only three feet, but they have less than a foot. There's a sandbar right there."

She followed his finger and saw the river's bottom. Even a landlubber could tell the depth was a matter of inches. They stood off four hundred meters, at the outside edge of the M4's effective range.

The Major said, "Get me as close as you can, I'm a pretty good shot."

She climbed onto the upper control deck, where shattered Plexiglas littered the floor. A quick crab walk got her to the forward bulkhead. She peeked over the edge. Four men hunkered down in the metal covered raft. Light armor, homemade. They counted on Sabel Security using M4s, which didn't have enough penetration to clear a thick piece of steel. She pulled a scope out of her waist pack and attached it to her M4. Without a chance to calibrate it, she'd have to dial it in on the fly. She found her first target at the back, most likely the boat's coxswain. She fired.

The shot was high. She adjusted the scope and tried again. This time they were hugging the bottom of the boat. An arm extended upward and she tried to hit it. Her bullet bounced off sheet metal slung over the outboard motor. Close, but not good enough.

The arm had been twisting the throttle forward. The Zodiac was a moving target. Now the game began in earnest. She jumped over the bulkhead and lay down flat on the pilothouse roof like a sharpshooter. She held her weapon tight and fired three quick shots. None of them hit flesh. As she dialed in another, leading the target by a hair, she saw one of the men rise up and spray bullets in her direction.

Whittier gave the boat a jolt of power, enough to tip the bow upward, then slammed the engines to full stop. Just enough to allow the armored pilothouse roof to give the Major some protection. A trick that would work once.

The Zodiac charged again, swerving left and right as it came. It's bow high, the wake behind it churned the otherwise peaceful waters. This time three men stood up and sprayed bullets at the *Explorer*.

The Major leapt over the control deck bulkhead and slid down the ladder to the main deck. Once inside the pilothouse she stopped to think.

"They're trying to get around us," she said. She and Whittier watched their approach. "They'll have a better time firing at us from the back end."

"Right, and we're in a narrow channel here. Not enough room to turn around."

"Then throw it in reverse, that should keep us parallel long enough for me to shoot a couple of them. Increase our odds if they do get behind us."

"Holy shit," Whittier said, his mouth and eyes open wide. "Are you serious?"

"Do it!"

She stepped back to the armored gun port Jacob used earlier and looked through it. Limited line of fire, but it might work. At least she wasn't on the open seas with a wave-tossed deck. She leaned around the outside edge and measured the progress. The *Limbe Explorer* was gaining speed and the pirates were still unaware. The gap was about a hundred-fifty meters and closing. The *Explorer's* drives, built for going forward fast, complained loudly at the reversal. She stepped back to her gun port, strained to see forward as far as possible, and waited.

Nothing came.

She stepped back out and looked up river. Nothing in sight. Wrong side.

She ran to the opposite gun port. Bullets pinged off the armor. She took her position and aimed. When they flew by, she flipped her switch to full-auto and emptied her magazine into the boat.

One body fell overboard.

Whittier called out, "Did you get them?"

CHAPTER 23

Boa, Cameroon
26-May, 12:30PM

MIGUEL EMPTIED A MAGAZINE OF darts to cover her descent. Pia rolled into the tunnel on her right and held her breath. Big-gut had to know she was there, but he must not know exactly where or he'd have shot her. So long as she was silent, he couldn't shoot without giving away his position. It came down to a game of stealth. The first to make a mistake would die.

One hand tightened around her M4. The darkened flashlight dangled from her wrist. Other than a dim shaft of light at the ladder, the rest of the pit was pitch black. She felt her way back into the ladder room, a round pit roughly ten feet in diameter. She hugged the wall to prevent even a remnant of light from touching her. She found the edge of the neighboring tunnel, then stopped for a second to consider what she needed to do.

Trick him into giving away his position.

But first, stop trembling. She took a few deep breaths and let them out slowly. As soon as her breathing was back to normal she reached around the wall and aimed the flashlight into the dark recess of the tunnel. Only her hand was exposed, her body still in the dark. She had no need to see down the tunnel. Only to let him think she was going in. She clicked the flashlight on for a split second. One flick was all it took.

Three bullets came from deep in another tunnel. If she were in tunnel number one with number two on her left, numbering around the circle he was in tunnel number five. She would be slightly behind him as he emerged. Perfect.

She scooted over, backed into tunnel number six and aimed at where

Big-gut would emerge. She flicked the switch to full auto. She put her phone on mute and whispered into it.

"I'm hit, I'm hit! Somebody get down here."

Cautious footsteps approached from Big-gut's tunnel. She raised her M4 and sighted down the barrel. She heard the sound of someone trying to duck-walk but was too fat. She heard his shorts rubbing together. But there was the sound of four feet. Someone was with him. Pia guessed he was shielding himself by placing at least one woman in front of him. A real gentleman.

Pia cried out in pain and made a thrashing noise.

He emerged from the tunnel pushing a bound woman in front of him, his gun pointed at her head. He crouched behind her as he came into the dim light of the ladder chamber. Pia fired a single shot. It missed. Big-Gut ducked and felt the back of his head—the shot had been close.

Pia said, "Hands up or the next one goes through what's left of your brain."

He dropped his gun and raised his hands. He froze for a moment then bent down, reaching for his left ankle. Before Pia could yell at him, a gang of angry women poured out of the tunnel behind him. They leapt on him and pounded him with their bound hands. They kicked him with their unbound feet. They yelled obscenities at him through their gags. Pia flicked on the flashlight.

"OK, ladies, I think he's had enough." She pressed her gun barrel to his forehead.

Everyone stopped moving.

"Hey, Miguel. Drop down here with a couple knives and help me free these women."

Miguel slid down the ladder and cut one woman loose, then handed her a knife to free the rest. He patted down Big-gut, found a knife, a radio, and a snub-nose in an ankle holster. Miguel went up first, to hold a dart gun on the captive. Pia sent Big-gut next and followed him up the ladder. Topside, Miguel slapped plasticuffs on him. The first of the freed women came up.

"We have a problem," Miguel said. "Four of his pals are coming inland right now. We think we have a five-minute lead on them, no more.

Another three are blocking our river escape but the Major's whittling them down."

Pia turned to the freed women. "Who speaks English?"

Two women raised their hands.

"OK, I need your help. There are three bodies outside, a woman, a man and a boy. They've been put to sleep and won't wake for a couple hours. Tie them to a tree and leave them. Make sure you can see them from a distance. Can you make your way back to Bekumu on your own?"

They nodded.

"We'll draw the bad guys our way. With your help, we can all get out of here."

The women thanked their liberators profusely until Pia told them to get moving. Miguel and Marty stared at Pia, who poked Big-gut with her rifle. She said, "You and Calixthe have just the one boy?"

"I'm not talking to you," he said.

She held up the bottle of Lithium. "Is that because the voices in your head are such great conversationalists?"

He lifted his chin.

"Have it your way, genius. March in front of me five paces, or I'll dart you and tie you to a tree like your pals."

The sound of distant gunfire echoed outside. A few bursts—impossible, in this dense jungle, to determine distance or direction. The four of them headed out at a quick clip with Big-gut at gunpoint.

Marty scanned the trees while they marched.

"Hey, where's Calixthe?"

Pia said, "She's one of them."

"I thought she was a conscript."

"Calixthe didn't want to stop in Bekumu because they've never seen her before. Then she tripped and fell on nothing but air. That was to tip off the bad guys. I accidentally gave her that excuse about being forced into it, but later she tried to sneak up and club me."

Marty said, "Everybody wants to do that."

Pia punched him playfully.

"Reckless, going in that hole," Miguel said. "Those women could have been acting too."

"I thought about that. They were all ages, including several grandmothers. Can't imagine what pirates would want with them. They looked like real villagers and cowered at the sight of these guys. Didn't look like acting."

Marty said, "The pirates thought we were all going to walk into that bamboo hut and get killed?"

"They only needed one of us," Pia said. "They kill or torture one and the boat comes up river. Once the boat was in the river, they planned to bottle us up with the Zodiacs, turn it into a kill zone."

More shots echoed through the trees. They picked up the pace.

"Tania's got them on the run," Marty said. "She's a one-woman army since they got Ezra."

"What?" Pia stopped.

"Sorry, you were down in the hole," Marty said. "Ezra took a lot of shrapnel." He shook his head. "He didn't make it."

"Dammit." Pia bit her lip. "He was a good…"

She didn't try to hide tears slipping out of the corners of her eyes. After giving her a moment, Marty patted her back.

"Need you to suck it up, boss. We grieve later," Miguel said after a minute. "We can't avenge Ezra if they gun us down."

Pia nodded, wiped her eyes with the back of her hand, took a deep breath.

They ran on.

"Why did you have the women tie up the pirates?" Miguel asked.

"Psychology," she said. "We can't take them with us. So it shows how little they mean to us. Like throwing back the little fish."

Marty said, "That's cold."

"And it'll slow them down."

Big-gut stopped running. "Thomas'll just gun 'em down for failing. You've given them a bleeding death sentence."

"Are you serious?" Pia said. "Your pals would kill them instead of untie them? Either you're bluffing or you picked your leader badly."

Big-gut looked away.

"Get moving." Marty pushed him forward. "He's lying. Why would they waste the ammunition?"

Pia looked at Miguel, who shook his head and followed Marty. Pia thought about the situation. If Big-gut was bluffing, there'd be no harm. If he was serious, there'd be a lot of deaths, for which she'd be responsible.

She stopped. "I can't let Elgin Thomas kill those people. I'm going back to help Tania. You two get this guy into the Zodiac and bring it down river. I'll meet you on the beach."

"No way," Miguel said. "You go with Marty. I cover Tania."

Marty said, "Hey, both of you free up Tania and I'll meet you south of the village. I can handle lard-ass, no problem."

Pia and Miguel turned and ran toward an area just south of the village. When they got close enough to follow the gunfire, Pia tried her phone.

"Tania, can you hear me?"

"Shut up, bitch," Tania said.

Pia rolled her eyes.

Miguel smiled at her. He pushed his earbud in tighter and said, "Tania, two hundred meters east of you and moving in. Where do you want us?"

"Fifty meters west," Tania said. "I'm shooting lead, aiming east."

They moved out, watching the light and shadows.

Pia's mind wandered. This was the most dangerous situation she'd ever been in. She'd had that same thought three times in the last few days but each new situation presented an escalated level of danger. Eric was right about her lack of experience. Eric... She stumbled.

"Focus!" Miguel said.

She nodded and moved on.

They moved between the trees, snaking their way into the fight. The crackling sound of gunfire echoed through the jungle. Every bug and animal had gone to ground in the hope of staying alive. Even the trees refused to sway. Other than the eerie snap of bullets every minute or so, the jungle was silent.

Miguel pulled up behind a tree and yanked Pia behind him. He motioned with fingers, two hostiles on the left and two on the right. He would take out the left and Pia would stay behind the tree. She shook her head. He shrugged and motioned for her to follow behind him. She watched the right flank, half hoping to shoot someone.

Instead, a barrage of gunfire sent them both to the ground. An indiscriminate burst aimed in their general direction. The element of surprise was lost. Pia crawled backwards to a large tree and tried to locate the enemy. To the right, beyond several trees, she saw two men trotting toward them.

Her glance connected with a pair of hateful eyes.

al-Jabal.

For all her talk of joining her mother in the afterlife, the idea that this murderer could be the one to send her there made her both furious and afraid. She focused on the anger. She pulled her gun around and fired. He ducked. She missed.

"Tania, Marty will be due south with a Zodiac in three minutes," Miguel said. "How deep are you?"

They heard her fire a three-round burst.

"I can get there, but I'll be coming through the two on your left," Tania said. "If you can brush them back, that would help."

"Two on the right," Pia said, "closing in on us. One of them is my friend from Geneva. I'll hold them. Miguel clears your path and we should be good to go."

"We're counting on you, boss," Miguel said.

He left.

Pia peered around the trunk in the direction of her nemesis and saw bark flying in front of her face—the sound of gunfire reached her an instant later. She backed around the other side and instinctively ducked back an instant before another cloud of bark disintegrated. They had her pinned down. Their bullets could make the distance but her darts couldn't. She cursed herself for her overconfidence. She ran in the opposite direction, using the tree to shield her retreat.

She wove back and forth, putting plenty of trees behind her, then pulled up behind a fallen log and squatted. She listened. They were slow, but they were definitely in pursuit, crashing through the underbrush and jumping small ferns.

The first to emerge from the darkness was a stranger. She aimed at him and considered the distance. One shot would give away her position. She couldn't afford to miss. He ran on, disappearing behind a stand of saplings. Then he re-emerged, light flashing off his face. He stopped. This was her chance—damn, she wished she'd had more training with an M4. She aimed and pulled the trigger.

He dropped.

Knowing al-Jabal would pinpoint her in a second, Pia ran back in the direction Miguel had gone. Gunfire erupted but nothing near her exploded. Al-Jabal was firing in anger. Good. Angry people don't think straight. Sometimes they channel that energy into working harder, faster, smarter, but Al-Jabal wasn't that smart—she hoped. A large termite mound offered her cover. She slid behind it, caught her breath, and crawled up. Peering over the crest, she searched the jungle in every direction. He could come from anywhere.

The trees and air were still, the jungle silent. Out there in the shadows lurked Marot's killer. Something moved. She felt al-Jabal's presence, sensed his anger at seeing her in Cameroon. She scanned the trees, the shadows, the open spots. Something moved again. On her left. Was it in the shrubs? Behind the tree? A flash of clothing in a sunbeam, a moving fern. He'd gone that way. Should she follow? Make a noise and draw him in? Or should she keep the high ground, a tactical advantage?

CHAPTER 24

26-May, 1PM

ON HER EARBUD SHE HEARD Miguel announce that his targets were fleeing south. The escape route was clear. Tania and Miguel headed for Marty's Zodiac. Pia checked her sat-phone's compass and figured al-Jabal must be east of her, the others south. Everything in her wanted to track him and dart him, but that was a dangerous game against a dangerous man. She'd wait for another day, another time. She slid down the mound and trotted due west.

In a hundred meters she found the river but not Marty, Miguel, or Tania. She ducked back to a secluded place and checked in via phone. Her GPS tracking showed them upstream two hundred meters. She began trotting in their direction while Miguel came to meet her. Twenty meters later, something caught her eye.

Someone in the trees. She planted her feet and jumped backward seconds before bullets shredded a bush in front of her. She dropped to the ground and rolled in tall grass. Not knowing the direction, she dared not stand. At the same time, she couldn't stay in the open. Rising to a crouch, she ran for a clump of trees, turned her back to one, and looked in all directions.

She saw him.

Only a few meters away, he scanned the shadows down his rifle sights, looking in the wrong direction. If he turned thirty degrees, he'd stare straight at her.

She raised her gun, then froze. Beyond al-Jabal stood Tania, her hands raised in surrender. Al-Jabal would take no prisoners.

But he was too far away, out of range for darts.

Sometimes a bluff is all you need. She flipped the switch to full-auto.

Pia shouted, fired for effect, and ran straight at al-Jabal.

Surprised and confused, he turned, dropped to the ground. Tania fired, missed him but hit his gun. It spun out of his grasp. He scrambled for it.

Pia's darts flew unaimed and off target as she ran. She stopped, aimed, fired. Too far, another miss. He picked up his gun. She ran, bounding left and right to avoid his fusillade. Tania ran ahead of her, calling and pointing the way. After a few meters, Miguel came alongside and the three of them dove into the Zodiac on top of Big-gut's comatose body.

Marty cranked the throttle and sped down the river. A sharp bend ahead promised to shield them from al-Jabal's AK47, if they could get there in time. Only Tania had bullets that gave her the range to shoot back. She fired her last three rounds just left of al-Jabal. The killer fired back, his bullets streaked up the river. Marty cut back to the right and found another line of bullets hitting the water immediately in their path. They all tensed, waiting for the bullets to hit someone or burst the pontoons.

Nothing happened. Marty swerved again.

"Out of ammo." Miguel pointed at al-Jabal, who threw his gun on the ground. "They always think they have movie-star guns."

Pia pulled her magazine out. One dart left in the mag, one in the chamber.

Tania stood up and waved to al-Jabal.

"What happened to our hostage?" Pia asked.

"He started shouting," Marty said, "tried to alert his men. So I darted him. What do you want with this loser anyway?"

"I need information," Pia said and pointed at the darted captive. "This guy will trade for it because I have two things he needs. Badly."

Rounding the bend, they found the *Limbe Explorer* dead ahead, churning the water and stretched across the river sideways. Marty hailed the Major on the phone.

"We ran aground trying to turn," The Major said. "The other Zodiac went down river. We're not sure if they went to block the mouth or get back to the trawler for reinforcements. You stay there. Captain Whittier hopes to have us out of here in another couple minutes. We'll lead with the armor. Whittier doesn't want to bring you aboard until we're clear of the sandbar—too much weight. We're already sitting ducks if they come back."

"Any sign of the coast guard?" Pia asked.

"At least two hours out. Hey, captain says we're almost free. Stand by to follow us out to sea."

The *Limbe Explorer* began rocking and churning. It turned ninety degrees in the river. Once straightened out, it began accelerating forward. Marty stayed back, center of the channel. As the *Explorer* gained speed, he allowed a larger gap between them. The big ship lumbered up to forty knots and left the jungle behind. Open sands on the left and a wide beach on the right looked to be clear of hostiles. Only a few tiny islands remained between them and the open ocean.

"All clear," the Major said. "Like they've gone home."

"Mangrove islands, could make good cover," Miguel said. "Plenty of those."

Out in deeper water, the *Limbe Explorer* slowed. Miguel and Tania kept their eyes on the islands while Marty guided the Zodiac alongside the ship. Monique and the Major attempted to pull Big-gut's dead weight over the railing, but he was too heavy. Miguel pulled, Marty and Pia pushed. With the toughest angle topside, Marty jumped over the railing and grabbed a hand.

"Here they come," Tania called out. "Dammit! They were waiting for us."

Marty, Miguel, and Pia stopped tugging and looked out to sea. Fifteen seconds away, a Zodiac sprayed a rooster tail as it headed straight for them.

Tania called to the others for extra magazines—the Major had emptied everything on board. They had sleeper darts and handguns. Marty tossed one magazine to Tania. Miguel's was empty. Pia had two darts in her M4, one in her Glock, plus two magazines in her pack.

Miguel yanked their hostage one more time and finally got him half over the railing.

"What am I gonna do with darts?" Tania shouted. "I'm about to face down a rubber boat and all I got is quarter-inch needles? How about a harpoon? Does Ahab have one of those? Fuck."

Tania stormed to the back of the Zodiac, cranked the throttle over, and headed out to meet the enemy head on. Pia knelt in the bow, trying desperately to train her M4 on the approaching pirates. Their boat bounced, the pirate boat bounced, her gun bounced.

"Hey!" Miguel shouted from the *Explorer's* deck. "Get back here!"

Tania pulled away, her eyes on the enemy. When she finally looked at the only passenger onboard, she did a double-take.

"Holy shit! I got the rich bitch too?" Tania said. "And you can't aim worth a damn? Get back here and take the helm, dammit. We need someone up front who knows how to use the ammo. Get your ass over here."

Her attitude made Pia's skin crawl, but her logic made sense. Pia dropped the M4 and took the helm.

"Run straight at them," Tania shouted above the engine noise. "That worked for you in the jungle, scared that guy for a second, let's see if it works again. Oh, and, uh, thanks for saving my life."

Tania staggered forward, knelt, and rattled off a few shots. Nothing hit. They held their fire. The gap closed fast. Both boats bounced over the waves. Both groups eyed targets in the other boat—then they were on each other. Tania rose on her knees and fired. Nothing.

Pia swerved to avoid their first salvo. The other boat mirrored her move at the same time. Pia's boat bounced up and crashed down over the bow of the pirate boat. Tania was tossed into the enemy boat and landed on a pirate. Her gun flipped into the ocean.

Pia ran up the pontoon onto the other boat. She chose to fight the man grappling Tania first over the unarmed coxswain. Tania did not appear to be winning. A man with sun-bleached hair and leathery skin rose to his feet, one arm around Tania's waist and a knife under her chin. Tania's eyes were wild with anger. The blade bit into her skin, ready to slice her throat open. The pirate eyed Pia.

"Put the gun down or I cut her," he said.

She did.

"American, huh?" Pia asked.

She put her hands up and steadied herself, her left foot forward. She bent at the knees, rolling with the waves. He eyed her, then glanced behind him. The coxswain tugged on a rope looped across the floor of the boat. Pia felt something tug at her ankles—probably the rope—but kept her eyes on the pirate. The instant he glanced at the coxswain, she launched her attack. Three violent jabs hit home, the first to his windpipe, the second to his right eye, the third to his temple.

He ducked her blows and slashed out with the knife. His method was a crude swipe, typical of a fighter who counted on an opponent's fear instead of any technique or form. She knew she could win this one. She ducked and came back up with two fast body blows. Tania rolled right as a wave pushed the pontoon into her shin. She tumbled face first over the side with a scream that was silenced mid-syllable when she hit the water.

Stunned, the pirate managed to slash at Pia with the knife again. She stepped back and felt the coxswain at her feet but didn't look down. She'd have to finish them off one at a time. She feigned a left hook. When his knife slashed in that direction, she smashed his throat again with a right cross. His knife came back too late, slashing at the open space left by her retreating fist. He swiped again, across his body. She stepped closer, trapping his knife arm against his chest. In the split second he needed to pull his arm free, she let loose a barrage of blows into his throat followed by an uppercut. Unable to breathe, he reeled in pain and dropped the knife. She spun left and slammed her elbow into his head. He crumpled in a heap on the pontoon.

Pia felt a hard tug at her ankle and looked down.

A slipknot in a rope led from her ankle to the outboard motor. The coxswain threw the motor overboard. The rope zipped over the pontoon. Pia reached for the fallen knife. The sinking motor pulled the slack out of the line. Her fingertips touched the knife. The knot tightened on her ankle and yanked her overboard.

No knife.

She flew into the water as the line went taut. She turned and dove straight down, swimming for all she was worth, trying to get ahead of the rope. If she could catch some slack, she could untie the knot before the dead weight dragged her to the bottom.

This far out, Pia figured the bottom could be anywhere from forty to a hundred feet. The motor hit bottom and the line jerked against her ankle. She was closer to the ocean floor than the air above.

Pia reached for her foot and felt the knot. She could see little more than light and dark at this depth. No detail at all. The surface above was barely visible through a brownish-green haze of water. The ocean pressed in on her from every angle. It pounded her ears and squeezed her body—her muscles felt the weight of a thousand tons of water. Already she longed for air.

She wrenched the rope. The knot had to be simple because the coxswain had tied it so quickly, yet she couldn't figure it out. It was just a tangled clump of rope, swollen by salt water and yanked tight by the weight of the engine below. She cursed herself for not watching the man more closely. She drew on the knot—too tight. She'd need to use fingernails. She felt the shape of it, trying to imagine which direction she should pull each piece of rope. After some effort, she thought she had it right and dug her nails in.

Her lungs were complaining about the lack of oxygen, that same burning sensation she'd felt in Geneva—only this time she was in much deeper water with much greater pressure. She felt the knot loosen a hair and tugged with renewed energy. All her veins and arteries burned. The weight on her chest and abdomen squeezed the life from her. Even her spinal cord felt crushed. Her eardrums pounded. *Fight the panic, panic burns oxygen.* She felt the knot loosen another hair. She tugged harder. She kicked her foot. Bad idea—the knot pulled tight again. She tugged and regained the lost ground but precious time was slipping away. Then another piece of rope slid almost imperceptibly. Another loosening. How many more before she was free? She had no idea.

Her lungs demanded air.

Above her she heard a boat zoom away, leaving a wake behind it. Had one of the pirates survived and stolen her Zodiac? The coxswain. Tania had shot up his engine and he lost his gun. That's why he tossed his motor overboard.

Pia's hopes dimmed.

The knot wasn't loose enough to free her foot.

Would the Major come looking for her? Was Tania up there somewhere? Had any of them even seen where she went under? She didn't care. The only thing she wanted was air, just one sweet breath before she drowned.

The knot finally pulled loose.

She tugged her heel through the loop only to have it snag on the ball of her foot. Loosening the knot a little more, she pulled it free and began her awkward ascent. Above her, she could see a dim circle of light through the murky water. Or was tunnel vision setting in?

She swam, moving her arms with the efficiency practiced in Geneva. Yet the surface stayed far away. Too far. Her vision narrowed to a small spot. Swimming was an effort that required oxygen and she had none left. She'd spent it all fighting the knot. The water was heavy. Dense. She was much deeper this time, had been under much longer. Stroke after stroke, she headed to the top and yet the top was no closer than when she'd started.

The burning sensation in her lungs was replaced by a pleasant sensation. Being held tight in the ocean's embrace seemed comforting, relaxing. Wonderful, now that she thought about it. She began to feel light. She could float the rest of the way up. Maybe even light enough to float into the sky. She felt sleepy. And the ocean made a soft pillow. She forgot about the surface. She forgot about al-Jabal and Jonelle and Dad and Tania and Alphonse and everyone else. She even considered forgetting about soccer. If she lived, could she play in the World Cup one more time? But then, nothing matters once life is over.

And there it was—a dim shadow crossed the light above her. A silhouette hovered, graceful and beautiful, like an angel swirling down into the depths to carry her home. Home to a better place.

"Mom?"

CHAPTER 25

Bight of Bonny, Cameroon
26-May, 2PM

THE LIGHT STUNG PIA'S EYES. Her body rolled to one side and a hundred gallons of water spewed out of her. More water than one stomach could possibly hold. Nearby, noisy voices argued. Strong hands grabbed her, tugged her into the light. A figure blotted out the light for a moment—a familiar figure. Hair slicked back in a low bun, dark skin, penetrating eyes. Those eyes stared at her and everything in the world stopped for a moment. The voices stopped and the waves slapping against the boat stopped and the rocking sensation stopped.

Then they all started again, louder and closer than before.

The figure above her laughed, her mouth opened wide, showing white teeth, pink gums. Two hands clapped together followed by the roar of a "Hallelujah!" Someone else laughed long and honest and sustained. The laugh went on, stopped for air and continued. Other voices whooped and yelled. And when it finally ended, hands clapped again and again.

She knew the voices. She knew the laughter.

The Major looked down at her and smiled. Then she looked at someone else and said, "One more time, Miguel. Just to be sure."

Miguel placed two hands on her abdomen and pushed down firmly, then rolled her onto her side. More water spewed out, a good deal less this time.

The Major stood, her arms outstretched to the blue skies above. "Thank God!"

"Thank..." Pia could only croak the one word. Her stomach flipped over. Speaking was not going to happen right now.

"Save your strength," the Major said. "Besides, it was Tania who pulled you out."

Tania's face, hair dripping ocean goo, came into Pia's line of sight.

"Yeah, you thought colored girls from Brooklyn couldn't swim, huh. Well, this one went to the Y, baby. Brooklyn Mako Swim Team for eight stinkin' years!"

"Thank…" Pia's croaked again. Her hand flopped out weakly toward Tania but missed and fell back to her side.

Tania picked up her hand and squeezed it between both of hers. She said, "You saved my life twice in one day, girl, so I owed you one. I'm beginning to like you. Heck, Ezra only saved my ass once."

Agent Marty leaned into view, his left arm wrapped in a bloody towel. He said, "Thank God you're alive—I did NOT want to call your father."

Pia smiled on the edge of a laugh. "Thank…"

"Don't talk," The Major said. "You drank half the Atlantic. You'll be very sick this afternoon. You'll have diarrhea."

Pia's eyes snapped to the Major and zeroed in.

"Just the messenger," she said.

"Jacob and…" Pia struggled.

"We're on our way back to Limbe now. Jacob caught a round in the hip during the first assault. The last bullet fired in this whole thing snapped one of the bones in Marty's arm. Ezra … you know about Ezra."

Pia shook her head, rolled onto her side, and threw up more sea water.

"The Coast Guard is chasing the trawler out to sea," the Major said. "They're in a race for Nigerian waters. They'll try to make the open Atlantic. Try to get some rest."

"Call … Yeschenko." Pia gasped and gulped air. "He … has people."

"Whoa. You want me to call in the Russians? You know that's a death sentence for all of them, right?"

CHAPTER 26

Limbe, Cameroon
26-May, 5PM

PIA WAS FULL OF SALINE, electrolytes, and soft foods when the hospital released her. Bishop Mimboe and his wife had come to visit. They prayed for her, invited her to the evening's festivities at the school, and again offered accommodations at the old convent on campus. She took them up on it: with half her agents gone, the convent offered better security.

But first she had to interrogate Big-gut at her hotel.

Pia sat down in the bungalow with the Major, who filled her in.

"His name is Conor Wigan of Manchester. "Name checks out—prescriptions, papers, other places. Miguel has him fed and waiting outside. We told him he gets a sleeper dart every time he makes noise or pisses us off. We didn't mention him to the Coast Guard."

"And no medications?" Pia asked.

"Not yet. He's overdue for the Lithium."

"Bring him in," Pia said.

"You sure you're OK? You still look a little green."

"Getting better."

Miguel brought him in, checked his plasticuffs, and seated him. Miguel stood at ease next to Pia's chair, the Major sat off Pia's side, and Tania took the watch outside.

"You can't hold me here," Conor said.

Pia pushed a pill halfway across the small table. Lithium.

"I don't want you going nuts while we're trying to reason with you," she said. "Now, the Dantrium is another story. Tell me what happens to you if I toss the bottle out in the ocean."

"You're not that kind of person."

"Normally, no. But a few days ago I watched a friend of yours kill a friend of mine. I followed him to Cameroon, and right when I was closing in on him, you came out of nowhere and tried to kill me. So tossing your medications in the ocean and leaving you tied up somewhere for forty-eight hours isn't going to keep me awake at night. Knowing your nervous system is locking up is not my problem. Knowing you can't eat or drink, much less walk away from the police, isn't going to keep me up at night either. See, if I was a mean person, I'd call your enemies and tell them where to find you."

Conor's lips trembled. He clenched his fists on the table.

"Could I have a glass of water to take my pill?"

Miguel handed him a paper cup half full of water. Conor took the cup in one of his cuffed hands, tossed the pill back and drank.

Pia said, "We have to help each other, Conor. You tell me a few things and I'll help you get what you want. That is, if you want Calixthe, your son, and your medications. Do we have a place to start negotiations?"

In a quiet voice, he said, "You planning on turning me over to the bloody police?"

"Depends on how much I like you in the end. Right now, I'm thinking that would be the best thing for society. The idea of having you locked up for life in a nice jail cell where you can't kill anyone has its appeal." Pia leaned across the table. "If you help me, I might consider turning you over to the Swiss. Their jails are clean and tidy. You might even get a fair trial. If you turn out to be really nice and you give me information that leads to al-Jabal and whoever paid him to kill my friend, well, I might give you a five-minute head start before I call the police."

Conor stared at her, his droopy red eyes pleading, his mind working hard. Pia tapped her fingernail on the table between them.

"All right," he said. "We have a deal. But who is this character you're looking for? The killer."

"He used a fake passport with the name of a long dead Syrian poet, Badawi al-Jabal. He's about this tall, had a trimmed beard but shaved it, and mean-looking eyes."

"Never heard of him."

"Too bad. Looks like you have nothing to give me then." She rose, turned to Miguel, "Call the police. Let them know we found one of the—"

"Hang on! Let's not be hasty. Syrian, you said?"

"He used the name of a dead Syrian. Said he was from Tangiers. He had a friend who ran a dress shop in Geneva called Marrakesh. Anything ringing a bell?"

Conor pursed his lips, shrugged, shook his head.

"Did I mention the *Zorka Moscoq* is owned by a friend of mine?" Pia said. "Mikhail Yeschenko. He's Russian. Owns an oil company. Hired a bunch of Russian sailors to look for the people who stole his ship. One phone call and they're here, Conor. Word is the Russians are old-fashioned about piracy. You know what I mean? Ropes and yardarms, that kind of thing. So, last chance, I'm looking for a mean-looking guy from Morocco, used to have a beard. Seen him?"

"You must mean Mustafa Ahmadi. Stupid twit, that one. Crazy, too."

Pia stayed still.

"He jumped into the business with too much cheek and not enough sense, got us all into this mess. Stupid little suck-up."

"Start at the beginning," Pia said. "We know you've been commandeering oil tankers and selling them. We know your outfit worked pretty well for the last eighteen months or so, a clean operation for the first three ships. Then things started going wrong. Second ship, three sailors died. On the last couple ships, murdering sailors seems to be the new rule. Then my friend was murdered by one of your crew. Fill in the blanks here. Who runs the operation? How many are involved? How did the killing start? Why kill Clément Marot and Sara Campbell?"

He shook his head. "No, you got that all wrong, mate. Uh, ma'am. See, I'm not involved with those people. I'm not one of them. I'm just a poor working man living in Limbe with my wife, raising our son best we can. I worked the oil rigs in Nigeria before my health got me in a bit of trouble. Then this old mate of mine from the Army comes to town, has a crew and some big plans—"

"Name?" the Major asked.

He glanced at Pia. She shook the Dantrium bottle at him.

"Elgin Thomas was his name in the Army. He's going by something else now, passport and everything. I forget his new name. Anyway, he has these plans—"

"You forgot his name?" Pia said. "You expect me to believe his name was Elgin Thomas and you *forgot* his new name?"

Conor blinked his big red-rimmed eyes.

The Major said, "OK, let's go with Elgin Thomas for now. Go on."

"Well, Elgin has the crew and the boats. He's funded by le Directeur. Don't ask, 'cause I don't know. Neither does Elgin. Just a voice on the other end of the phone."

"Le Directeur sounds French," the Major said. "Is it?"

"Yeah, yeah, they were always talking in French, le Directeur and Elgin. I never took to the frogs, you know. Bloody awful language by my reckoning. Anyway, Elgin had this plan and he wants me and Calixthe to watch the coast for him. He never told us what he was planning but we figured it out easy enough. Limbe's only business is filling up tankers and sending them on their way. One of them gets nicked and Old Elgin's been asking about it for a week, well, we get the picture pretty quick. So we ask him for a bit more … consideration, if you will. He gets snotty and takes our boy. Puts him on the crew. Just a lad. Now Calixthe and me's got to do whatever he asks."

"He kidnapped your son?" Pia asked. "And you let him?"

"Well, he did give us the extra consideration. Wasn't all bad. It's not like we're rolling in cash, though. Me outta work a couple years and all. Anyway, Elgin ropes us in—"

"Yeah, awful," Pia said. "But I don't care. Elgin runs the show. Le Directeur runs Elgin. Who has the money? How does Elgin get his hands on it?"

"Just want you to know how hard it's been, what with—"

"Just answer the questions," the Major said. "Our sympathy for you ran out when you started shooting."

Conor let out a long sigh and slumped in his chair.

"Le Directeur has the money. Elgin meets him, comes back with it. Cash. Lots of it. No one ever sees it all. He only comes round when you're alone. All he carries is your pay, not a dime more. You couldn't even rob him—"

"How much did he pay you in cash?"

"Me?" Conor said. "He'd give me about sixty million CFA every trip."

Pia exchanged glances with the Major. Conor smiled.

"What's that, about a hundred thousand Euros?" Pia asked.

He nodded. "Yes, ma'am."

"Where does he meet le Directeur?" the Major asked.

"Europe somewhere. Never told me nothing."

Pia shook the bottle of Dantrium.

"You don't have to threaten me, ma'am. You got one of your people killed today. That's not my fault. No reason to take it out on me."

"It is your fault," Pia said. "You set the trap. Your people fired a grenade. Remember, your medication is on the line here. Where does Elgin Thomas meet le Directeur?"

"Don't go on like that about the medicine, love. D'you know what happens to me?"

"I saw it happen once. The man almost died before the doctors figured out what was wrong with him. I don't care if that happens to you, Conor. Your little trap killed Ezra Goldstein."

He sighed. "Seemed like a German country. Austria, maybe."

They waited.

"Might have been Vienna. He's always talking about a place called Kaffehandels near the Vienna Opera. He's an opera man, that one. All that bloody shrieking."

The Major typed away on her pad and nodded at Pia.

"You finally told us something we can believe," Pia said. "There are coffee shops near the Vienna Opera house. We'll come back to that in a minute. Now I want to know what happened over the last few months. Why did Elgin's crew start killing people?"

"They're all a bunch of wild kids. Thought they were getting away with it, they did. Could do anything they bloody well pleased and no one would mind. Then the Malaysians were waiting for them. Turned into a bloody riot. Second go-round for the Malaysians and they were out for revenge. Hid in the holds. Battled it out below decks. Elgin's boys got pissed. Bloody shame."

"How many boys does Elgin have?" the Major asked.

"Enough, I guess. I've seen six or eight."

"We saw twice that many today," Pia said. "I'm not feeling good about the quality of information you're giving us, Conor."

"Well, I wasn't counting them. He doesn't bring them all in at once. Ten, fifteen maybe."

"Where does he find them?"

"He was a NATO liaison for the last decade. He knows men all over the world, knows the ones that'll bend his way. There's plenty will work for what he's paying. Latvians, Germans, Croats, Finns, Portugese, and more Filipinos than he could get rid of. Takes a couple from each country so they don't gang up on him. Runs a ship off, sends 'em home. If they did well and he trusts them, he'll call them back for the next one."

"And the banker?"

Conor put his hands up as if he were blocking a punch. He said, "I wouldn't know anything about that, ma'am. First thing I know, that twit Mustafa Ahmadi's talking all over Limbe. Says after he does a favor for le Directeur he's going to take over for Elgin Thomas. Like he had the brains to run the operation. He's the one chopped the heads off them Malaysians. Just a cold-blooded killer, that one. Nothing more to him."

"Mr. Wigan," the Major said. "Pia said someone killed her friend. Then she said someone killed Clément Marot. Then she asked you about the banker. And you answered. If you're just a poor working man from Limbe, how'd you know Clément Marot was a banker?"

Conor paled.

Pia leaned over the table and spoke quietly. "You can still redeem yourself, Conor. We need you to get le Directeur to meet you somewhere. How about the Kaffehandel?"

"You got it all wrong!" he said. "It's Elgin who knows the guy. I can't set up a meeting with him, don't even have his number. Besides, he'd be bloody pissed to find out I know he exists."

"He's probably right," Pia said. "I doubt Le Directeur would rely on a clown like this for anything important. We need to catch up with him and

Conor can't help us. Guess we give him the pills and turn him over."

"Hold on," the Major said. "I think he can tell us what Mustafa Ahmadi was bragging about when he was *talking all over Limbe*. Right, Conor?"

Conor's gaze shifted to every corner of the room before settling back on Pia. "Yeah, yeah. He was bragging 'bout a snuff job. A banker. I put it together's all."

Pia rolled her hand: go on.

"Mustafa said le Director called him directly because Elgin was soft. Said he could get the job done. Said he was gonna show up Elgin and take over the operation after."

"Were you surprised when he came back to Cameroon?" Pia asked.

"He's gotta get paid, doesn't he?"

"When's payday?"

"Couple days out yet. Elgin's meeting le Directeur tomorrow night."

Pia said, "I just asked you to set up a meeting—"

The Major grabbed her arm. "OK, here's the question that'll get you into Swiss custody instead of Cameroon. Where is Elgin Thomas right now?"

"Hiding out until he can catch a plane to Vienna tomorrow, I'd imagine."

"Where was he at nine this morning?"

"At sea, getting ready for the ambush."

"And where was he yesterday?"

"Don't know."

The Major nodded toward the door and left. Pia followed her outside.

"So le Directeur is the one laundering the money in Geneva," Pia said. "Elgin Thomas runs the pirate operation in Cameroon. Calixthe and Conor are what, lieutenants? Mustafa, al-Jabal, is bucking for promotion over Elgin. Do I have that right?"

"If he's telling us the truth. Criminals are stupid. He knows he's not bright enough to make up a whole lie covering everything, so most of what he told us is probably true. I'm guessing the only parts he altered were the ones he thought would save his skin. He's a lot closer to the action than he claims."

"Doesn't matter," Pia said. "Calixthe's the brains. She led us to him in a way that would let her look like a hero no matter who won the fight. Should've brought her back with me. Anyway, we turn him over to the police and try to find Elgin Thomas. He'll be heading to Vienna tomorrow or the day after. We can get him and maybe le Directeur."

The Major nodded.

"But le Director will be harder to catch." Pia paced the deck for ten steps, turned and came back. "Villeneuve should be ready to accept our offer to help by now. You and Miguel go to Geneva, watch the bankers. I'll take Tania and find Kaffehandels in Vienna. If I don't catch them both, you'll at least know who's missing from the banks in Geneva."

The Major looked at her a long time. Then she said, "That's a very good idea, Pia. If I take Miguel, that leaves you with Tania; you're going to need more help. When the shooting starts, she's the bravest. But she's got a screw loose."

Pia grinned.

The Major said, "OK, so you're two peas in a pod. I'll call our Berlin office, have them send a couple people. In the meantime, turn him over to the local police."

"We just promised him a ride to Switzerland."

"He'll want us to turn him over here. I'm sure he set up a get-out-of-jail bribe in advance. He'll be home before dawn. We put some trackers on him and we can find him if we need him."

"Why would we want to see him again?"

CHAPTER 27

26-May, 6PM

EVENING COLORED THE CITY WITH dusty golds, cool blues, burnt orange. The day's heat began to dissipate as Mt. Cameroon's long shadow made its way down the slope into Limbe. Two tightly packed minivans cruised through the dirt streets, passing clapboard houses with corrugated tin roofs. Mud, splattered from passing cars, covered the lower third of every wall in sight. Some houses were whitewashed, some painted, a few had glass windows.

They arrived at the chartered plane and gathered around Ezra Goldstein's coffin. Tania collapsed on the unfinished wooden box and wept. Major Jonelle Jackson stroked her back.

Everyone turned to Pia.

"A few words?" Miguel said.

The Major leaned close to her. "The ranking officer says a prayer or eulogy."

Pia swallowed. A part of leadership she'd never given any thought. She straightened, looked at her agents, put a hand on the coffin and took a long deep breath.

"Ezra was a hero. The old-fashioned kind like Hercules and Theseus. The kind you see every day without knowing it. He was the kind of hero who when he saw wrong, tried to right it. When he saw suffering, tried to heal it. He told me when he went to war, he went to stop it. That's what heroes do. We send Marty and Jacob home to bury him while the rest of us try to carry on in his place. We will carry Ezra's heroism with us as our inspiration. We *will* find them, Ezra. We *will* bring down the conspirators and stop their war."

Miguel said, "Amen," and bumped his fist to the coffin.

The ground crew loaded the body in the hold while a bandaged Jacob limped up the airstair. Pia caught up with Marty, his arm in a sling, and walked him to the jet. He'd been in charge of her personal security team for three years. His wound was the slightest but she felt it the most.

"Oh, hey boss," Marty said. "Can I have a day off? Just need a day to grow it back."

He wiggled his sling. Pia smiled.

"Marty said, "Too bad they restrict women in combat roles because Tania would have cleared Kandahar all by herself. But she has a short attention span."

"You think she lacks finesse?"

"That's a nice way to put it."

They walked a few steps in silence.

Pia said, "I didn't want anyone to get hurt."

"Don't blame yourself. We're all adults and we signed up for this. You're the CO, stand tall, keep your eye on the goal." He stopped at the airstair and looked at her. "I remember one time you told your injured teammates 'It hurts less if you win'. Well. Win it—bring those guys in and it'll better for me than the best pain pill in the world."

She gave him an awkward hug on his good side, then left.

Tania climbed into the minivan with her and they headed back into town. For a while Tania bounced up and down in her seat as if riding a pogo stick, humming. Then she stopped, dropped her head into her hands and cried. Pia reached out and patted her shoulder.

They disembarked at the convent next door to the cathedral. Both buildings dated from the late nineteenth century. The convent had twenty rooms but only four nuns lived there now, along with two high school girls who preferred the quiet to their dorm. Pia and Tania's room had two beds, one against each wall on either side of the door, and a desk with a lamp and a chair. Above the desk was a window the size of a large book, above that a bare wooden cross. The whole place smelled fresh and clean, no mold or rot or mildew.

They did a security check of the grounds with the sexton. The convent had a central lobby where Bishop Mimboe had stationed a sleepy-looking guard. There was one entrance that led to the cathedral. Another more obscure doorway led to the school's dining hall. Outside, three two-story buildings held classrooms. One had Sabel Hall written in stone above the door. Tania took a long slow look at it and whistled.

They ended the tour at the school's entrance, a narrow passage between two of the buildings. A ten-foot wall surrounded the rest of the property.

Pia spotted two familiar figures across the street.

The boys from the beach.

She took off running. They saw her and sprinted around a corner. Tania followed as best she could. Pia rounded the corner only to run into a large mound of a man. She bounced off him and he bellowed in pidgin English. She landed on her butt and jack-knifed back to a standing position. As she did, the boys shot past her on a pale blue scooter. They turned on the main street and were gone. Tania caught up as the giant waddled over to Pia to scold her again.

"Step back, fat boy." Tania drew a switchblade. "You heard me. That's it. Back up, asshole. You know those boys?"

The man said, "Haba! Hear word! Yawa go gas—"

"Yeah, whatever," Tania said. "Answer the question in regular English."

Pia tugged Tania's knife down, apologized to the fat man, turned Tania around and pushed her back toward the school. The big man yelled at them until they were around the corner.

Pia said, "If they're here—"

"We're in danger, yeah. But I don't get it. Who'd hire those little meerkats? The pirates, or what's left of them, would come themselves."

"We should ask them again. Set a trap. If I stay out in the open tonight and they see me, can you catch them?"

"Might work." Tania looked her over. "But the Major's never going to go for it."

Behind the school's main buildings was a soccer field sculpted out of a hillside. The gentle slope above it formed natural bleachers. Four large lights on poles poured illumination onto the grass. People milled around the field, at one end of which a crowd of people danced to a native drum quartet. Others served themselves from a buffet table.

Pia and Tania stood in the school's entrance. A low streetlight pushed their shadows far in front of them on the narrow walkway. Anyone coming through would be visible from anywhere on the field. They looked it over until they were satisfied.

"Let's do it anyway," Pia said. "You check this spot and I'll stay out in the open. If they want to spy on me—or shoot at me—they have to come through here first."

They joined the group and moved with the music, bouncing on their toes and swinging their hips. Tania kept an eye on the passageway between the buildings. Two slim boys could blend in easily if they made it past that point. So long as Tania kept sight of that passageway, they should be safe.

They filled banana leaf plates with Ndolé, a dish of stewed nuts, bitter leaves, fish, and prawns. They hiked partway up the hillside where they could see the school gate and passageway and sat to eat.

Bishop Mimboe, talking to a circle of people on the field, waved to them. They smiled and waved back.

"Thank you for saving my life," Pia said. "I never thought I'd be that close to death, never. I'm glad you were there."

"I saw you fall in, so I waited for you under the boats. Thought you'd come back up right away. Only you kept going down into the dark. I lost track of you, couldn't see you anywhere and I panicked. I started swimming down, looking around. Had a helluva time finding you. When I did, I saw you struggling. Then you just stopped." She shuddered. "No way was I going to lose you down there. It's like Gimu, man."

"Like what?"

"You know, Giri, On, Gimu, and Ninjo, the four corners of Japanese morality? No? OK, the Japanese have a code of loyalty and faith to those who help them in some way. It says that if you owe someone, like I owe you my life, you must be loyal until you can repay that debt of honor. So I had to save you."

"OK, so now we're even."

"You saved me twice. I still owe you one."

"Let's hope that doesn't come up again anytime soon."

They bumped fists and ate in silence for a long time.

Pia glanced at Tania and saw her struggling to hold back tears.

"Ezra was a good man," Tania said. "I went clubbing with him sometimes. Got to know him a little. Hooked up, you know, when there was no one else."

Pia put her arm around Tania's shoulder. She said, "He told me soldiers figure they're already dead."

"Yeah, he told me that bullshit too." Tania wiped her eyes with the back of her hand. "Not me. I go into battle figuring three of them are already dead—I just have to pick out which ones."

They chuckled nervously and watched the dancers for a while.

"How'd you end up in the Army?" Pia asked.

"My parents were divorced, living in small apartments in bad neighborhoods. Always struggling to stay afloat. My sister got into a gang, the Six Tre Folk Nation over in Flatbush. Seemed like someone beat her up or stabbed her every week. I didn't want any of that, so I joined the Y, the swim team, anything to stay off the streets. When I graduated from high school, I had a choice. I could get shot in the head fighting to keep my country free or get shot in the head fighting to keep my 'hood safe. I figured if I died in the Army at least my mother would get a flag."

Pia gave a little laugh. "Sorry, that just sounded funny."

"Not funny then," she said. "But I'm glad I can laugh now."

The drums ended and the evening hushed around them. Everyone that came through the passageway moved straight into the crowd and seemed to have a school connection. No one unusual, nothing out of the ordinary.

The players took the field with much fanfare for the home team. The Anglican girls played well against their aggressive opponents, Yaoundé Catholic School. The Anglicans employed Pia's favorite opening strategy: all players on defense, stripping the offensive drives and sending the ball deep into Catholic's eighteen-yard box, then letting the Catholics bring it back, running themselves ragged. A solid defense. If the Anglicans were fit and strong, the strategy would pay off late in the second half.

A few minutes into the game, the Major and Agent Miguel walked up the slope. The Major scowled at the Castel Beer parked at Tania's side and took a seat next to Pia. Agent Miguel kept watch near the field.

"The local police told me," the Major said, "someone named Elgin Thomas is booked on the morning flight to Brussels. Since we don't have any evidence he's involved, they can't do anything to stop him."

"What time does the connecting flight land in Vienna?"

"No connecting flight. He could be doing planes, trains, and cars to keep us from tracking him."

"He's using a different alias to get to Austria."

"If he's going there," the Major said. "Conor might have told us the truth, might not."

"But it fits. Geneva is an hour's flight from Vienna. Easy for le Directeur to get back and forth without raising suspicions or being seen. I think Conor was telling the truth, it's Vienna."

"Everywhere in Europe is an hour's flight."

"Go to Geneva like we planned," Pia said. "You can figure out who makes regular trips to Vienna and I'll track him down. With what we've learned, Villeneuve will be dying to work with you."

"I'd rather work with Alphonse," the Major said.

"He's going to meet me in Vienna."

"What? Why?"

"I got a text from Alphonse earlier. Turns out Mme. Marot is an opera fan and spends a lot of time in Vienna."

"Nine times out of ten the murderer is a family member—wait a second," the Major said. "Have you been telling Alphonse about our operations?"

"We've been sharing information."

The Major squeezed her eyes shut for a second. When she opened them she was glaring at Pia.

"Did you stop to think someone told al-Jabal—Mustafa—you were on that bridge? Did Alphonse know we were going to Lyon? How did Calixthe find out we were coming here?"

"No, or yes. I mean, no to Lyon, but ... I don't know. I might have told him about ... you think?"

"Yes, I think it's possible your boyfriend is trying to kill you."

"He's not my boyfriend. And he'd never do that! He's ... um."

"Too handsome to lie to you? You're thinking with your rosebud, not your head. He knew where you were every time, Pia. And so did Mustafa."

Pia shook her head, and watched the game. After a while she said, "He doesn't fit. What would he have to do with pirates and bankers? He spends his free time on ski patrol."

"Have our people in DC check his background."

"OK, but I still don't think—"

"Doesn't matter what you think. You don't tell an outsider about our ideas, our plans, our travel. Nothing. The Cantonale is not our customer. We don't owe Alphonse anything. Got that?"

Pia shook her head. "It's not him. Can't be."

"Dammit, it could be. Don't take risks with our lives. And you made plans to meet him in Vienna?"

"I figured we could help each other."

"I don't believe this." The Major looked at the sky. "Did you have a meeting place picked out? Did you tell him about Kaffehandels?"

"No. Villeneuve hasn't approved his travel yet."

"Call him back, tell him you're going to some other place. No, don't bother. You ride around in a Gulfstream with Sabel written across it, he'll find you anywhere south of the Arctic."

"So, I should work with him and watch him?"

"Like your life depended on it." The Major rose and walked down the hill. Halfway down, she stopped. "Are we clear?"

CHAPTER 28

26-May, 8PM

TANIA SAID, "TOO BAD YOU weren't in Afghanistan. Some of those al Qaeda guys were hotties—you could have given them our passwords, duty rosters, rotation schedules...."

Pia scowled. "I know Alphonse, you don't. He's clean."

To her surprise, Tania laughed. "Well, since you're going to hook up with him in Vienna you can pump him for information. Get it? Pump him—"

"Yeah. Ha ha ha."

The Anglican girls scored and the crowd jumped to their feet, shouting and singing and dancing.

Tania jumped up and joined the celebration. Pia stared straight ahead. The game continued but she watched without seeing the action. Her mind was consumed with thoughts of Alphonse. When they broke at halftime, the score was one-all.

A woman walked along the sidelines, looking over the crowd.

"Pia Sabel, you come to Cameroon and you don't look me up?" the young woman called with a smile in her voice. "Come out and play!"

It took Pia a minute to recognize Adisa Ngandy, midfielder for Cameroon's national team and Canon Sportif in Douala. People on the hill turned to look at Pia.

Pia waved at her then turned to Tania. She said, "Watch that passageway, Tania. This is when they'll have to move in close if they're coming tonight."

She wove her way down to join Adisa on the field. A cheer went up from the crowd when they hugged.

Adisa said, "They want us to play with them for the first ten minutes."

"Oh, that wouldn't be fair—"

"I went to Yaoundé Catholic."

"And I went to St. Muriel's Episcopal in DC," Pia said. "You're on."

An Anglican player loaned Pia her cleats and shin guards.

The ref blew the whistle and Catholic kicked off. Their first play, a diagonal pass to the outside, was followed by a quick back-pass to Adisa. Pia darted to defend against her rival, who sent the ball to the outside. Adisa blew past Pia's right, running onto a give-and-go from the outside mid. Pia wheeled around and gained on Adisa but not in time to stop a perfect pass to the top of the eighteen-yard box. The Anglican defense, surprised by the distance and accuracy, was caught too far forward. They ran between the ball and the net but they were out of position, in defensive disarray. Catholic's speedy forward drove into the penalty area, crossed to an attacking mid, and scored.

Pia's forwards kicked off and back-passed to their defensive mid. Adisa followed the ball like a racehorse. Her aggressive speed scared the intended kicker, who ran for the sidelines and lost the ball out of bounds.

Pia called, "Can you win it back?"

Her teammate nodded, stepped back from the sidelines, watched the thrower's eyes, and ran into the ball's path. With an extraordinary leap, she intercepted, headed the ball to her midfielder, and called for the back pass. On her second try she didn't let Adisa's charge scare her—she struck the ball hard and sent it to Pia.

Pia chested it toward the sideline as three defenders ran to hold her. One approached on the sideline, one covered the goal, the third moved in to stop the pass. A perfect defense. Pia tossed the ball from left foot to right foot and faced her tallest defender. She pointed to her head and the six-yard box. Her defender, after a second of shock, took off running while Pia drew Catholic's defenders into a tighter circle. When they were aligned in a perfect triangle, she began her run to the goal. Three players converged. Three feet connected at the same time. One foot pushed through. Pounding her way out, Pia popped the ball in the air and smacked it hard with her head, sending it fifteen yards.

Her defender was in position in front of the last defender and the keeper, unguarded, on the six-yard line. She leapt into the air, turned her head toward Pia, and snapped it back to the goal as she connected with the ball and drove it into the lower corner, near post. Goal!

When Catholic kicked off, a charged-up Anglican stole the ball and headed up field for a breakaway. Pia ran the sideline, then darted for center field. Her move froze three defenders and allowed the Anglican girl an angled run to the left. Pia checked the right defense to find open space.

Instead, she saw two dark silhouettes standing in the passageway. The boys. Pia froze. Adisa stole her pass and ran up field. Tania had to have seen them. Pia decided to trust her agent. Her competitive nature kicked in—she sprinted after Adisa and stole the ball back. Flying toward the corner, she sent a cross that her forward tapped in. Goal!

Pia slowed, allowing Adisa the chance for an equalizer goal. Neither of them wanted to tip the balance for their teams. They played on until the pre-arranged time limit, then Pia and Adisa hugged and walked off the field together to cheers from the crowd, the score tied at three.

Pia found Tania on the hillside chatting with a tall man, a fresh beer in her hand. The warnings echoed in her head, 'short attention span' and 'a screw loose'. She approached the pair, stopping a yard away.

Pia said, "Did you catch them?"

Tania's smile waned. "Catch who?"

CHAPTER 29

27-May, 3AM

"PIA! PIA! ARE YOU OK?" Tania shook her.

Pia looked around. An unfamiliar room, a sleepy looking Tania bent over her. A faint gray light leaked in the window. A cross on the wall. The convent.

"Yeah, I'm OK. Sorry, did I wake you up?"

"Damn, girl, you woke the dead. Screaming about getting that sonofabitch and I'll kill you. Talk about dropping f-bombs. You sure you're OK?"

Pia smacked her dry lips and looked around the room. She said, "Yeah, I just … I have these dreams."

"Nightmares about your parents' murders?"

Pia snapped a look up at her. "You know about that?"

"Everybody knows about that. There's a paragraph in the employee manual that says we're not supposed to talk about it. Oh."

"Holy shit." Pia shook her head. "Employee manual? So everyone in the company knows?"

"Just the section for those on guard duty at your estate. I tried out for it once. But. Um. Anyway, I asked the Major about it in a roundabout way and she didn't know anything."

"Maybe she paid attention to the part about discretion. So, what's it say?"

"Your parents were murdered when you were four. Alan Sabel was the first on the scene and adopted you the next day. Then someone tried to kill you when you were ten. So he started the Security division to keep you out of danger. So, is that it? You dream about the murders?"

"That would be too cliché. My mother yells at me about working harder, doing more. Just now, she was screaming at me for letting Ezra die."

Tania dropped on her bed. "Whoa. That would suck big time. My mom can get a little wacko but she'd never haunt me. I hope."

"Don't worry about it. I confused the best psychologists until I gave up on them."

"Yeah, I bet." Tania shook her head. "Wasn't your fault. You know that right? I mean, Ezra had his own reasons for going out there."

Pia asked, "Hey, those boys still across the street?"

"Yeah. I still say we should take them down and—"

"No." The next step required something outside Tania's core strengths. "Go back to sleep."

Tania lay back, pulled a sheet up, closed her eyes, and commenced snoring.

Pia pulled on running shorts and shoes, strapped on her waist pack and gun, slipped out the door, and down the hall. She passed the napping church guard in the convent's lobby, went through the cathedral, made her way to a side door, and crept outside.

Thick clouds that smelled of rain obscured the moon and stars. The lone streetlight on the block hung on the cathedral's far corner, giving her plenty of shadows. Clinging to the darkness, she leaned out—just far enough to see two pairs of shoes in a dark doorway a hundred yards up the street.

Turning in the opposite direction, Pia made her way to the far end of the lane, crossed over a block, and worked her way back toward the boys, approaching from behind.

She studied them. Backlit by the cathedral's light, she could see they were nervous. They squirmed and paced and talked and took an occasional peek at the convent's front door. Either they were waiting for someone or building up the courage to do something dangerous.

She slipped closer, her back to the wall, moving sideways one foot at a time. With each step she felt for loose stones or objects with her toe. Once within range, she took aim and thought through how the Major might handle the situation.

One of them lit a cigarette, which made her want to dart him right then. His inhale turned the burning end white before settling back to red. He sucked it in, then blew out a small cloud. His friend coughed and pushed him away. The smoker walked down the block, around the corner and out of sight. She considered her options. The safest was to dart him and be done.

But that wouldn't answer any questions.

The lone boy waiting in the doorway turned, putting his back to her. She took three quick steps and pressed the gun to his neck.

"Shh…"

The boy trembled. A feeling she understood all too well. She made him turn to the door, put his hands high up, and spread his feet. She patted him down, found a phone and a small revolver she slipped in her waist pack.

"Second time I nailed you," she whispered. "You get in trouble the first time?"

He nodded.

"Then I'll let you walk away if you answer two questions, What were you supposed to do here tonight? And who sent you?"

He didn't speak.

"Option one, your boss finds you asleep on the job with your phone missing," she said. "Option two, you report in and say I was surrounded by people the whole time, then you go home. Which one do you want? If you don't start talking in three seconds, I'm going to dart you and offer the deal to your buddy. First question, who sent you? Three… Two…"

"I don't know," he whispered.

"Last chance. Who pays you?" She pressed her gun harder into his skin.

"Monique Tsogo."

Pia sucked in a quick breath and squeezed her eyes shut for a few seconds. She said, "What were you supposed to do with this gun?"

"Kill you."

Pia pulled her trigger. The boy fell to the ground.

"Changed my mind about the dart," she whispered.

She heard the second boy heading back around the corner at a trot. She backed into the doorway, waited until she sensed him close enough, then spun around the wall and into his path. She fired. He fell.

After taking his cell phone and gun she formed a rough plan in her head. Risky, but she had the advantage of the early hour. She'd wandered many cities around the world at this time of night and knew how empty they were. Security patrols were at their lowest ebb. People were at their weakest. Her plan might work.

After injecting the antidote, she propped the boys up in a doorway and called a cab. The tired, grumpy cabbie declined the midnight drive to Douala until she offered a large bonus. His enthusiasm skyrocketed when she produced three crisp hundred euro notes. As they drove, she looked through the text messages on the captured cellphones. Nothing useful.

Half an hour into her trip, her phone rang. Dad.

"You know, one day you're going to wake me up," she said.

"I just read Jonelle's report. You led a successful mission, you saved those women, you—"

"Dad ... Ezra died."

"And he wouldn't have been the only one if it weren't for your leadership. You've done it, Pia. You proved you can face down killers and win. From here on, let the professionals handle it. I want you packed up and home as soon—"

"No."

"Pia, we all know what you're really trying to prove. If you'd just been a little older, maybe six or seven, you'd have stopped those bastards before—"

"Do you have the information on international banking I asked for?"

"Everyone I spoke to agreed it had to be a high-ranking insider laundering the pirate money," he said. "Either the bank president or the director general, nothing less."

She said, "But those officers are dead."

"Maybe another bank is involved, or someone gained access. Hacking into a bank is nearly impossible but not completely. The fact that it went on for a year has all my banking friends saying it was Marot or Wölfli or both."

"Suicide pact? I don't see that. Maybe they wanted out? Or maybe they cheated the pirates?"

"Jonelle will figure it out. She's been figuring things out for twenty years. Just get on the jet and come home."

Pia paused for a moment. "Why are you so fixated on me coming home? What are you afraid of, Dad?"

He sighed.

"Are you afraid I'll learn something from field work?"

CHAPTER 30

PIA STOOD AT THE END of a block and looked at the walls around Monique Tsogo's home. It was nestled in a tidy neighborhood of Douala's upper middle class and stood out as the finest on the street. The cabbie slumped down to nap while he waited. Pia gathered a few things including a rubber floor mat and approached the house on tiptoe.

She threw the mat over the broken glass embedded on top of the security wall and scaled it. In the middle of a small estate spread out on an acre of land was a two-story house, small by American standards but huge for Cameroon. She crept around it in a wide circle. The thick grass in the front yard smelled freshly mowed. A groomed garden of peonies and King Proteas took up much of the backyard. A footpath down the middle led from the back door to a bench surrounded by more flowers. A light shone through drawn curtains in one downstairs room. Everything else was dark.

A path of white gravel led from the street gate to the front door. A swinging bench hung on the front porch. She looked in the windows to get a feel for the layout. Kitchen, dining, family room, and the lit room downstairs, presumably bedrooms upstairs. Pia tried the back door and found it locked. The door's window, however, slid up easily. She reached in, unlocked the door, and opened it with a delicate pull.

She took one of the confiscated phones, placed it on the bench among the flowers, turned the speaker on high, hit redial, then snuck back into the darkened kitchen through the back door. She flattened herself against the interior wall and waited for the phones to connect.

"Allo?" Monique's voice echoed from both inside and outside the house. Monique walked down the hallway, repeating *Allo?*

Pia slipped behind her, put her in a headlock and pulled back tight.

"Are we alone?" she whispered.

Monique said nothing.

"I asked, are we alone?"

"No. My husband, my children, upstairs. Please don't hurt them."

"I'm not going to hurt anyone. Here's the deal. You answer a couple questions, I let you sleep in your own home tonight. You don't, I dart you, drag you back to Limbe, and let my friend Tania beat the crap out of you. She's been in a foul mood since a bunch of your friends tried to kill her yesterday. So what's it going to be?"

"Not my friends. I swear to you. What do you want to know?"

"Why did you send the boys to kill me?" Pia said.

Monique took a deep breath.

"After you hired me I found Calixthe, just like I told you. Until the shooting started, I thought she was genuine. But the day before you arrived, a different woman called from Austria and hired me to send her information about you and what you were doing. I had no idea—"

"Save it. I asked why you sent them to kill me."

"Please, I have never been in trouble before. I didn't know what to do."

"You've done pretty well for yourself. The house is worth much more than what you charge in fees. You're deep in this piracy thing, aren't you?"

"No, no! My father is the head of surgery at hospital. He gave me this house when he and my mother bought a larger one. My husband is also a doctor—"

"Who are they, then?" Pia squeezed her arm tighter. "Who wants me dead?"

"Someone in Austria. She didn't give me a name, just told me to call her le Directeur."

"That's masculine, isn't it? Shouldn't you call a woman by the feminine version, whatever?"

"La Directrice. I don't know, le Directeur is what she said."

"How did she pay you?"

"She left a bag with cash and phones at the gate."

"Your whole fee in advance?" Pia asked.

"Ten percent. The rest is in Vienna. I am to meet her at Kaffe—"

"Yeah, Kaffehandels. I've heard of it. Who's Elgin Thomas?"

Monique frowned. "I do not know."

"Conor Wigan?"

Monique shook her head.

"When do you meet le Directeur?"

"Tomorrow night. I am to bring proof."

"That I'm dead?" Pia said. "Great."

She relaxed her arm and frisked Monique, turned on a light, pushed her to the dinner table. They sat opposite each other. She said, "OK, Monique. Never been in trouble and all of a sudden you're in the murder for hire business?"

"It was not like that. Yesterday, I was horrified. You saw me. I was a coward in the pilothouse, hiding in the corner. I was ashamed. I am not like you. I am not brave. Then she called me and told me either you or I will die today. What else could I do?"

Pia darted her. Monique slumped onto the table.

"Sure I understand," Pia whispered. "What else could you do?"

Pia tapped her fingernail on the table while she stared at her sleeping traitor. After a good think, she got up and darted the two children and a snoring husband. She administered the antidote injectors and checked that their airways were clear. They would awake in the morning, groggy and motherless but otherwise unharmed. She left a note for them then searched the rest of the house, found a packed suitcase, two cellphones, a notebook, and a passport she carried to the kitchen. In a small office downstairs she found evidence of a normal investigative firm: bail bond records, court services, investigations for legal firms. Nothing to contradict Monique's story. She locked the back door and the window and secured the rest of the house.

Out on the street, a gray mist floated to the ground. She ran to her cabbie and woke him. While he pulled to the curb, Pia carried Monique out of the house on her shoulder.

"Sleeping pills," she told the cabbie.

An hour and another three hundred euros later, the cabbie helped carry Monique past the sleeping church guard and into her room. They put her in Pia's bed and the cabbie left.

Tania looked over her shoulder with bloodshot eyes. She sat up, rubbed her face in her hands, then squinted at the woman in Pia's bed. "Wait, who's that? You picked up a woman last night? Whoa. Didn't know you swung that way."

"It's Monique Tsogo." Pia turned around quickly. "Wait, what do you mean? Did you think I picked up a … You think I'm gay?"

"Are you trying to say you're not? 'Cause you know what they say about female athletes."

"No, I'm not gay. And they say the same thing about female soldiers."

"True that."

They stared at each other in awkward silence for a moment.

"Oh, uh, so, are you gay?" Pia asked.

"Me? Hell no. But, I could learn… y'know, if there's a promotion involved."

"No. No. I'm … not that way."

"OK." Tania looked out the window and sighed with relief.

Pia rolled her eyes. "Look, none of that matters. We're taking her to Vienna—"

Something beeped in a duffle bag at the foot of the bed.

Tania grabbed it, pulled out a sat-phone, checked it. She said, "Looks like the Major left us the tracking unit and some other gear. Stuff they'd never get on an airline. Someone's in trouble, wonder who?"

"Conor Wigan. Why couldn't they take stuff on an airline?"

Tania pulled two M4s out of the bag and held them up. Pia shrugged.

"Have you ever flown on a commercial airline?"

Pia shook her head. Tania sighed.

Pia looked at the beeping phone. She said, "What does this mean, life alert?"

Tania looked over her shoulder. "Means Conor is dying. The tracker in his sock takes vital signs. When the nervous system erupts or his pulse drops off, it sends a warning. Sometimes we get a false positive, like if he's exercising. In Conor's case, I think he's dying. Not dead yet, but critical condition."

"Then let's get going." Pia headed for the door and dialed her favorite cabbie.

"What about sleeping beauty here?"

"She'll sleep another two hours. C'mon, let's try to save Conor."

"The guy who held you at gunpoint?" Tania said. "Why?"

"He needs help."

Pia's favorite cabbie took them to an apartment building across town. They got out, checked the neighborhood, and headed in.

A hazy predawn horizon lit the hem of low clouds moving inland. Dawn would break, but little sunlight would reach them. The fine mist turned to small raindrops.

Pia opened the gate and began checking the apartments. Tania tapped her on the shoulder and pointed across the courtyard. A door stood halfway open.

Tania pulled her Glock. Pia did the same.

They crossed the way, lining up on either side of the door to peer in the narrow opening. A rough outline of furniture was all Pia could make out. They'd go in blind.

Tania nodded to Pia and burst through the door, moving to the right. Pia rushed in behind her to the left. They swept the room: cramped kitchen, dining area filled with boxes, living room with a worn-out couch and two cane chairs. They moved into the hallway, a bathroom on one side and a closed door on the other. They listened. Nothing.

Pia swung into the bathroom. Empty. She turned and stood on one side of the bedroom door. Tania turned the knob, took a breath, and ripped open the door. They jumped in, Tania on the far corner, Pia toward the bed.

Conor Wigan was propped upright with his back against the wall. His head sagged over his shirtless chest, his arms at his sides, the sheets beneath him red with blood. Pia checked the closet then holstered her gun. Tania flipped on a light. Conor lifted his head, recognized Pia, and smiled a gruesome smile. Losing his energy, his head sagged again.

"You're... bloody cooked, girl." He was barely audible. His chin touched his chest.

"Who did this to you, Conor?" Pia asked.

"Those Swiss…bastards. They…"

Pia looked him over from a few feet away, trying to figure out where the bullet holes were. Tania gestured that he'd been shot in the back.

"Sent Mustafa…" he said. "Bloody… traitor. He…"

"Save your breath, Conor. An ambulance is coming—you'll be all right."

Tania shook her head at Pia. She said, "No. Keep him talking."

"Bloody hell … Mustafa thought he would take the…"

"Take what, Conor?" Pia said. "Stay with me now. Don't go to sleep."

Conor listed sideways, leaving a smear of blood on the wall. As Pia moved to help him Tania reached out and pulled her back.

"Touch nothing. We were never here." Tania hissed.

Pia nodded. She choked and wiped her eyes.

"What is Mustafa taking, Conor?"

"God it hurts," Conor said. He groaned loudly, spasmed, then relaxed. Black bile oozed out his mouth.

They stood in silence for a full minute staring at Conor's corpse.

"Let's go," Tania said.

"We can't leave him like this."

"All we're doing is messing up a crime scene. We take the trackers out of his shoe and pocket, wipe down anything we touched. Then we're gone."

"Guess you're right. Seems cold."

"Yes. It is."

They cleaned up and left. From the cab Pia called the police to report gunfire in the apartment building. After that, the ride back to the convent was silent, each woman lost in her own thoughts.

The sun rose and streaked the clouds' underbelly in bright orange before quickly disappearing above them.

They climbed out and gave the cabbie another hundred euros. He folded the money, pledged his silence and pulled away.

Pia tugged Tania's sleeve. "You implied you could trade sex for a promotion—"

Tania laughed loud. "Hey, I wasn't setting you up for a lawsuit. I swear, I was just having a little fun, checking out your ways. I would have said no. Probably."

Pia shook her head, pulled open the convent door.

"Sexual harassment is not something we joke about."

Tania said, "Yeah yeah yeah, whatever." They walked inside. "You are gay though, right?"

CHAPTER 31

50,000 feet over North Africa
27-May, 10AM

PIA COULD HEAR EVERY WORD and she was not pleased. But she kept focused on reading the report on her pad.

"I could get used to flying around in this thing," Tania said. "Just look out that window, Monique—that's Tripoli down there. Tripoli! As in Libya. And we're going to fly right over Rome in another hour." She pointed. "See the map on the wall? That's where we are, and the line shows where we're going. Isn't that cool?

"Now, here's the thing." Tania leaned forward. "If you say *NO* one more fucking time, I'm going to throw you out the window and you're going to face-plant in Tripoli. You got that, bitch?"

"Tania!" Pia shouted down the aisle. "She just woke up. Let her sort out a few things out first. Don't make threats."

"No threats here, Ms. Sabel. I only make promises." Tania turned to Monique, held her index finger up between them. "Ms. Sabel looks the other way for one minute, just one minute, and it's whoosh, out the hatch."

Pia turned to the window as Tania came up the aisle. Tania plopped in the chair facing her.

"OK," Tania said, "so don't invite me to sit down."

Pia shrugged and looked out the window.

"You know," Tania said, "you've got everything. Smarts and skills. Not to mention jets and cars and servants and mansions. And here you are, looking like—"

"Only thing money does is make other people jealous."

"OK, let's trade. Everything I have for everything you have."

Pia leaned across the polished table between them.

Tania pulled back and said, "Hey, I was just kid—"

"Did your mother teach you how to cook?"

"Yeah, as little as she—"

"Mine was teaching me how to chop celery when the killers came in. He wore a red shirt, grabbed her by the throat and held her off the ground while he strangled her. The other guy went into the home office and shot my father in the head."

"I'm sorry, I—"

"I'll give you everything I have if you can give me five more minutes with my mom."

Pia leaned back, turned to the window.

Tania sat still for a long time before wiping her nose. She said, "What the hell triggered that?"

Pia turned back to face her. She said, "Conor, I guess."

"Survivors are always on a rollercoaster. Silly one minute, depressed the next. We were joking when we went back to the convent. That was the high. Guess what this is. Yeah. So talk to me. What else is it?"

"Alphonse." Pia tapped a fingernail on her pad. "Our people in DC sent me his background check. High school in DC, college in Paris, a promising career in the Army. Then a court martial, but the charges were dropped. He joined the gendarmes in Lyon."

"Hey, don't worry about the court martial. They toss those out like party favors. Been there, done that. But Lyon—didn't the gendarmes try to arrest you in Lyon?"

"It can't be him."

"You don't sound so sure."

"The Major thinks it's him. And then the report came in. I was so sure before."

"Call him, talk to him. Use your female senses."

Tania went to the back of the jet. "Hey, Monique, you know how to play poker?"

Pia dialed Alphonse.

"Clément Marot was to meet in Vienna with the man named Elgin Thomas," he said. The appointment was made the same day he called

Sabel Security."

"We keep hearing that name. Major Jackson thought it was made up, then she found a reservation to Brussels."

"We find nothing about him in Geneva. The secretary knew nothing of the name, yet they were to meet tonight at ten."

"I'm … leaving Cameroon," Pia said.

"To Vienna, as we discussed? Capitaine Villeneuve has cleared my travel. I will be there late this evening. Where will we meet?"

What should she say?

"You are the quiet one, oui? What troubles you?"

No way out of it.

She bit her lip and took a deep breath. She said, "Alphonse, every time I tell you where I'm going, someone tries to kill me."

Pia counted ten seconds before he responded.

"I see."

She waited.

"I understand," he said. "We do not need to meet in Vienna. I do not want the, ehm, suspicions."

"I'm sorry, Alphonse. It's just that I have to be sure."

"No, no. I understand. I will be in Vienna anyway. I have the reasons to trace Marot's planned meeting. And then there is the opera."

"The opera?"

"Oui. Mme. Marot is not just the fan, she is also the big supporter of the state opera. She made many financial commitments to funding them, yet many payments are not made. Capitaine Villeneuve thinks there could be the motive there."

"Her husband stopped her philanthropy so she killed him and four others?"

"Sometimes we just do what our capitaine says."

"I'm sure my employees think I have dumb ideas too." Pia glanced down the aisle at Tania. "Say, Alphonse, when you were in the army, where were you stationed?"

"London, Oslo, Berlin, and so on. I was the NATO liaison."

Pia felt her stomach squeeze tighter. "What do you know about Elgin Thomas? Do you have any background on him?"

She could barely speak much less hear his answer. Her voice had betrayed her and she knew it.

"Only that he was on the calendar of Clément Marot," Alphonse said. "Are you all right? You sound tired."

"Fine. Did the other banks have too much money like Banque Marot?"

"Capitaine Villeneuve sent in the *juricomptable*—ehm, the forensic accountants. No report is expected before the next week. Oh, and she is ready for the help of Sabel Security, but she has the minor concern."

"I'll have the Major work it out with her. I have to go."

They clicked off.

Pia didn't like the feeling of that call. She thought about what she'd learned from their conversation. Everything fit Elgin Thomas, yet nothing was definitive. He just didn't feel like a killer to her, but then she had no real experience interrogating killers. Besides, Alphonse backed off when she confronted him. Was that genuine? Or did he have other means of finding her?

Oh, god—the phone.

Pia called the Sabel Security communications team and ordered them to turn off the GPS system on the phone she gave Alphonse, a safety precaution she kicked herself for not taking earlier.

She trusted Alphonse—just not completely. But should she trust him at all? Damn! Pia pounded her fist on the table.

Tania and Monique craned around their seats to look at her. She shrugged.

Tania caught Monique's gaze. She said, "Boyfriend trouble. You know how it is."

Monique nodded and looked back at her cards.

Pia called the Major next and filled her in: her conversation with Alphonse and Villeneuve's willingness to work with them, her abduction of Monique, Conor's death, and Monique's planned meeting with le Directeur, as well as the gender confusion.

"For all we know, Elgin Thomas is le Directeur," the Major said.

"A bank executive isn't going to run a pirate organization from that far away."

"So maybe Conor ran the pirates, and the phantom banker came down from Geneva on paydays."

"The banker would have to have investments in Cameroon that justified business trips," Pia said.

"Possible. I'll check it out on this end."

"What about the female voice who told Monique she was le Directeur?"

"Girlfriend, voice changer, hired help—who knows?"

"We know Monique has a meeting," Pia said. "I'll make sure she's there. We'll see who shows up." She paused. "Did you get more agents out of Berlin?"

The Major cleared her throat. "Well. Uh. We have a problem in our Berlin office. Of the six employees we had, four resigned when your father appointed you. We have one agent who was in a car accident and has a broken leg, and we have the business manager. He was a male nurse before coming to Sabel. No field experience. Never fired a gun."

"Guess Tania and I will figure it out."

"I sent the nurse—I mean business manager. Extra eyes and ears if nothing else. He arrives on a late flight this evening."

Pia said, "And I have more experience with firearms than he?"

CHAPTER 32

Vienna, Austria
27-May, 1PM

THE LIMO DROPPED THEM IN front of the *Wiener Staatsoper*, the Vienna State Opera. Tania and Monique seemed mesmerized by the magnificent stone building.

"Holy… This is the real thing, right?" Tania said. "Those towering arches with little angels up there, they represent stuff—themes from operas. Heroism, tragedy, fantasy, comedy, love."

"Come on," Pia said. "We don't want to be conspicuous out here. We get checked in, then we do the recon, then we catch le Directeur or whoever shows up to pay off Monique."

"Won't Elgin Thomas be here too?" Tania said. "He was supposed to get cash to pay off Mustafa, al-Jabal or whoever. His boys killed Ezra. He's the one I want."

"Either way, one will lead us to the other."

They made their way around the opera house to the Hotel Sacher. While Pia checked in, Monique and Tania stared at the marble cherub in the lobby center. Above it hung a chandelier of crystal and brass. Their eyes swept the ground floor, taking in the white marble walls with red marble trim, the life-sized bas-relief sculptures of ancient Greek goddesses, the glass vases four feet tall. Beyond the lobby was a wood-paneled parlor filled with exquisite antique furniture and more chandeliers.

Pia booked the best penthouse suite and two extra rooms. Snapping her fingers before the eyes of her awestruck companions, she broke their trance and led them to the elevators.

The bellman led them to the top floor and stopped in front of double doors engraved *Zauberflöte*.

"Hey, that's named after a Mozart opera. *The Magic Flute*, right?" Tania said.

Tania and Monique waltzed in first and wandered through the suite. It had a yellow and white living room with antique furniture. The bellman opened glass doors to a balcony that wrapped around two sides of the top floor.

"Whoa, this is incredible," Tania continued gushing. "Look at that, Monique; they got a red marble fireplace in every room. The red kind is the most expensive, comes from Egypt or something. And did you see those bathrooms? Marble tub, marble sinks, marble showers. Hey, Pia, you sure know how to live. What do our rooms look like?"

"You can stay in here if you'd like," Pia said. "I've got the room across the hall next to the elevator."

"You shittin' me?"

Pia dismissed the bellman with a generous tip.

"If the bad guys get ahead of us, they're going to come in here and shoot up the place," she said. "Sleeping in here, nice as it is, could be bad for your health."

"I'm OK with that," Tania said. "If I have to die, may as well be on sheets like this. What about you, Monique? There's two bedrooms in here. Hell, the beds have those four poster curtain things on them. You could rip off a triple before they even stumble across a couch in the dark."

"Let's hope it doesn't come to that," Pia said. "Hey, Monique—you OK? You look a little green."

"I can't do this," Monique said.

Pia stepped in front of her and looked down. She said, "You sent two teenagers to kill me and they failed. That means le Directeur is going to kill you before she comes after me. At least, she's going to try. You're going to pull yourself together and help me win this."

Monique sank into a silk-covered chair, her face in her hands. She looked up, panic-stricken, her voice near hysterical. "I can't do it! I'm scared. I'll ruin it. She'll kill me! I can't—"

"You think these guys were planning to let you live?" Tania said.

"You're what killers call a loose end. If they win, you're dead. It's just a matter of time."

Monique stood up, trembling, terrified—and defiant. "I'll run."

Pia put an arm out and held Tania back.

"They already told you they would kill you if you didn't kill me. They were going to kill you anyway, maybe your family too. You're not going to run, you're going to lead us to le Directeur. I'm going to take them down and turn him or her over to the police. After that, you can go back to Douala and live the rest of your natural life without looking over your shoulder."

"I should have killed you myself—"

Pia grabbed her hand and jerked hard. Monique's body twisted and flew over Pia's right hip, sending the woman crashing to the floor. "You can't. And neither can they." She gave Monique a hand up. "I only play to win."

Monique got to her feet, turned her back and hid her face in her shoulder.

"You're going to make a couple calls, sit in a coffee shop for twenty minutes, and I'll do the rest," Pia said. "I broke up the gang in Limbe. Now they're weak and wounded I'm going to mop them up here in Vienna. I'm your best chance at staying alive. Just do your part and you're on the next flight back home."

Monique stared at her. Tears welled and rolled down her cheeks.

"Go ahead, have a cry," Pia said. "Then pull yourself together—Tania and I have to find Kaffeehandles and figure out some details."

Monique sniffed, wiped her face on her sleeve, and headed for the bathroom.

"See, that's what most people do when they know they're going to die in a couple hours," Tania said. "Fall apart. Monique is normal. She's freaking out. That's what Eric was talking about. But he was wrong about you. You know you're going to die and you're all chill. You got a gift, girl."

"Shut up," Pia said.

★　★　★

HALF AN HOUR LATER SHE strolled up Karntner Strasse in a black T-shirt, black leather jacket, and black jeans. Tania wore a Bundesliga hoodie pulled up over her hair. After asking around, they determined the Kaffeehandel never existed—it was a general term, not a specific shop.

They found a bench in the shopping district. Pia told Monique how the call should go, what she should say. Monique nodded like the condemned and pulled out her phone. Pia and Tania linked into the call, but le Directeur sent her to voicemail. Pia took Monique's phone and sent a text.

```
Am in Vienna. Where do we meet?
```

Several minutes later the reply came back.

```
You failed.
```

Pia texted:

```
No. Delayed. Will finish tonight. You can
verify. Final payment required.
```

They waited twenty minutes for the reply:

```
Instructions coming at 10PM tonight
```

"What took le Directeur so long?" Tania asked.

"Guess they had to confer," Pia said.

They went to the hotel and ordered dinner. Silver service arrived in the suite's dining room with all the pomp and ceremony one would expect from a top hotel. Tania ate with abandon, Monique picked at her food.

"What am I going to tell her?" Monique said.

"We went over this," Pia said. "If they want to kill me you can lead them to me. I'll be looking up and down Karntner Strasse for a place called Kaffeehandel."

"Then le Directeur will kill me?"

CHAPTER 33

Geneva, Switzerland
27-May, 4PM

AQUAMARINE SKYLIGHTS AND WINDOWS MARKED the architecture of the most modern gendarmerie the Major had ever seen. She and agent Miguel were ushered through its long hallways by a short middle-aged man who introduced himself as Lieutenant Berardi. He'd been asked to translate for Capitaine Carla Villeneuve.

He led them to her office. It was an interior space that might have been a utility closet pressed into service for her temporary assignment. Capitaine Villeneuve sat at her desk, typing furiously on a laptop. Berardi took up a position beside her desk. Fluorescents filled the space with both light and a low buzzing noise. Villeneuve nodded at two steel chairs and the Major took a seat. Agent Miguel stood to one side, slightly behind her, mimicking Berardi's posture.

The Major took a quick look around the office where medals and certificates were propped on shelves. The awards were in French with recognizable words like *Sauver* and *Alpinisme*. As Mme. Marot had warned them, Villeneuve was a decorated mountaineer, not a murder investigator.

Villeneuve stopped typing with a flourish and looked up at the Major.

"What can we do for you?" Berardi asked.

The Major spoke slowly, allowing Berardi time to translate.

"We came close to catching Mustafa Ahmadi yesterday, known to you by the name al-Jabal. We followed a slim lead and discovered a good deal about his associates. We're here to offer our services to the canton of Geneva."

Berardi talked with Capitaine Villeneuve at length, more than the

Major's preamble warranted. Once they settled things, Villeneuve smiled at her guests.

"As a matter of formality, we need to confirm the arrangement," Beradi said. "We understand Sabel Security is offering assistance free of charge?"

"Sabel's fees will be paid for by Ms. Sabel directly."

"Why?"

The Major explained Pia's anger at the attempt on her life as well as her desire to remain independent. The two officers conversed. Again the conversation seemed longer than necessary. Then Capitaine Villeneuve smiled and leaned back.

"The canton gratefully accepts your generosity," Berardi said. "We look forward to working with you. Naturally, there are some ground rules. First, you will work independently and not with any officers already investigating the tragedies. Second, you will report directly to the Capitaine at ten in the morning every day to disclose what you have learned. Third, you will not act on behalf of the canton or as officials in any capacity. Is this understood and agreeable?"

The Major looked directly to the Capitaine. "Yes, ma'am."

Capitaine Villeneuve glanced at Berardi, then dropped her eyes to her desk. After gathering her thoughts, she looked up and spoke.

"One last thing," Berardi translated. "She hates to mention this, but it is important to Switzerland that your agents be careful. The last time Sabel Security helped Geneva, a store owner was beaten and shots were fired indiscriminately in an alley and later from the bridge."

"No shots were fired by Sabel Security personnel," the Major said. "Mustafa fired on Ms. Sabel on the bridge. I returned fire using only darts. Sabel Security personnel caused no damage and presented no public danger. And your store owner was aiding the fugitive."

Berardi hesitated, a cloud of confusion crossing his face, before translating.

Villeneuve drummed her pencil on the table and thought for a minute before responding. She sat up, smiled and responded.

"These things are in the past," he translated. "We look forward to your informative and helpful assistance. If you would interview the survivors that would be most helpful. We have already finished those interviews but could have missed something. Thank you and good evening."

The Major rose and turned to leave.

Agent Miguel stopped in the doorway and looked at their translator. He said, "You're good. You moonlight? We might need a native translator, and Sabel is generous."

Berardi handed over a business card.

The Major marched through the gendarmerie's lobby. Miguel caught up, and out they went.

"What do we do now, Agent Miguel? Does the Grand Duchess of Sabel listen to you? 'Cause I don't think she hears me."

Miguel kept silent.

"And we have no official capacity except to tell Villeneuve things? That's nice–we come up with something, hand it over, she gets credit. We cause problems and she'll say she doesn't know us."

"You guys acted like vigilantes last week," Miguel said. "Did you expect a free hand?"

The Major gave him a stern look, then said, "Why did you get that guy's card?"

"He was surprised about something you said. I'll ask him about it later."

"Did I miss anything in there?" she said. "They talked a lot more than he translated."

"Nope. You got it. She was trying to figure out how to get credit for our work."

"OK," she said. "Let's see what the next of kin have to say."

They made a list of the victims' survivors and made calls. Most of them were anxious to discuss the investigation. Anxious to get it moving forward, anxious for an arrest, and unhappy with the police for their lack of results.

THE FIRST PERSON AVAILABLE WAS Marina Bachmann, sister of Sandra

Bachmann, VP of Banque Genève International. Sandra was the second victim, killed upon returning home from the ill-fated dinner party. Marina, a cordial older woman, had come to live with her sister five years earlier after both went through divorces. They had a quiet social life, involving themselves in a charity and attending the Lutheran church once or twice a month. Marina hadn't worked since moving to Geneva from Zurich but had considerable savings. She could think of nothing in Sandra's life that would precipitate murder. But they rarely talked about business.

"Did you know anyone named Mustafa Ahmadi?" the Major said.

"No," Marina said.

"How about Elgin Thomas or Conor Wigan? Calixthe Ebokea?"

Marina shook her head.

"Ever hear the term le Directeur?"

"Yes, every company has them."

"I meant more like a nickname. Someone people refer to as le Directeur?"

Marina shook her head.

When they were ready to leave, she saw them to the door.

Agent Miguel pointed to a crystal sphere with a French inscription. He said, "The award for charity. Which one are you involved in?"

"La Crèche de Tangier," she said. "They aid abandoned babies until they're old enough for an orphanage. A great cause."

RAMONA WÖLFLI, THE YOUNG WIDOW of Eren Wölfli, Banque Genève International's president, answered her penthouse door in yoga pants and stiletto heels. The black tights left nothing to the imagination and her pale blue top clung to every surgically enhanced curve. Her blond hair was cut boyish and short. She led them into a modern white living room and jumped cross-legged onto the couch.

"Why are you interested in this?" she asked in English with a German accent.

"Two reasons," the Major said. "First, the killers tried to kill our company president. Second, they killed one of our agents, Ezra Goldstein."

Ramona shrugged. "What can I tell you? I already told the police that I would have killed him if someone else had not beaten me to it."

Miguel shot the Major a look. She kept her eyes on Ramona and raised her eyebrows.

"They did not tell you this?" Ramona said. "He carried on with his ex-wives as if they were still married. One night with Sylvia, his first, the next night he spends with Eniko, the porn star from Budapest. Then he comes home to me. What do I want with him? He made me sign a contract before we married. I get nothing. Anyway, I made plans to live with my brother in Bern. I will move there next week. Let Sylvia bury him."

"We were interested in a few people your husband might have known," the Major said. She launched into the list, Ramona listened to each name and shook her head.

She said she knew nothing of the banking business—she noticed only that her husband became upset after a call from Sandra Bachmann. He left abruptly and went to his office. She had no idea why.

"For most of the night," Ramona said, "I assumed it was he who did the killing."

"I thought he and Marot were friends," the Major said.

"Best friends. That meant nothing to Eren when it came to money. He cheated anyone he could. The only thing he cared about was Banque Genève International. He would never let anything happen to that ancient institution. He would not put up a dime if I needed medical treatment, but nothing was too good for his bank."

"How did the killer get to him?"

"He hired security guards. They came to our house but he was at his office with Reto. When he went to his car, the killer was waiting."

"I'm sorry."

"No, no. It was perfect."

"Was he involved in any charity?" Miguel asked.

"Ha! His libido was his charity, and he was most generous with it. Sandra handled the real charity."

"Thank you," the Major said. "Those are all the questions we have."

"When you get back to the gendarmerie, be sure to tell the French whore I'm leaving next week. She thinks I'm a gold digger, going after the boy, Marot."

The Major raised her eyebrows again.

"He's not my type—I need maturity." Ramona paused. "But if I wanted him?" She snapped her fingers, "I could have him like that."

JOEY CAMPBELL—MID-FIFTIES, HANDSOME AND ATHLETIC—SMELLED of alcohol, his knees sagged when he stood, and his eyes were bloodshot. He recounted everything he'd already told Lieutenant Lamartine: he was unemployed since arriving in Switzerland, stood to collect two million euros of insurance following his wife's death, and had taken no interest in her work. He pointed out that the insurance money was a quarter of what his wife's income was worth to him had she lived. He was an artist from New York with no following in Europe. None of the pirates' names sounded familiar to him. His wife had never been involved in any charities, thought church was for fools, read crime novels, and would never have an affair because no one would want her. She'd answered the door after getting a call and was shot in the face. All this he told them in the foyer where Sara Campbell died. He held the door open the whole time they talked.

"She had to have known her killer," the Major said on the drive to Madame Marot's estate. "She got a call, expected someone, answered the door, and could see at least a rough shape through the glass. Four bankers were murdered just hours earlier—she'd have been on her guard. Had to be someone from the bank or one of the wives."

"No police detail," Miguel said.

"Right, Lena Marot said they were going to arrange private security. They hadn't done it yet? Or did the killer present himself as the security? Why were there no police standing by? Is that because there are more banks in Geneva than you can shake a stick at?"

"How many?" Miguel asked. "Thirty? Fifty?"

"Seventy-five," she said. "With four or five potential targets at each. Yes, guard detail would overwhelm the police."

"Only two banks involved, though."

"They didn't know that in the first twenty-four hours. And Villeneuve couldn't protect one without protecting all of them. Still, they could have made an effort for Banque Marot's ranking officer, right?"

"I would."

"So why did Sara Campbell open the door?"

MAISON MAROT WAS A SPRAWLING estate with a stone mansion centered on a rise above Lake Léman. A butler opened the massive oak front door and ushered them into the drawing room.

After a long wait, a sallow young man dressed in black came in. At a glance, it was obvious he'd not slept in days, his face pale, his eyes hollow. At first he said nothing, just stood with his hands on the double doors as if summoning the strength to speak.

"Philippe Marot? I'm Major Jonelle Jackson. We met at the Banque—"

"Oui. Parlez-vous Français?"

Miguel answered him in French and they exchanged brief pleasantries. Philippe explained that his mother had already answered all the questions the police asked of her. He asked that they respect her privacy and check with the police for any information needed. Twice he mentioned she was grieving and needed rest. In the end, he recommended they make an appointment to see her some other time. Miguel got up to leave.

"Wait a minute," the Major said. "Tell him we have an update on the investigation. Pia Sabel asked me to deliver the update in person."

Miguel translated. Philippe stood still for a moment, then sighed and went to get his mother. Miguel looked at the Major and waited for an explanation.

"She's a racist," she said and shrugged.

Several minutes later, Mme. Marot took a seat in an overstuffed wingback chair, her son at her side in a matching chair. The Major sat on an ottoman in front of her, Miguel stood to the side. Mme. Marot studied the Sabel Security agents for a moment, then nodded.

"Madame Marot, Pia Sabel gave you her word she would try to find your husband's assassin. I went with her to Cameroon, and we found him. Unfortunately, we were unable to catch him. We believe he was working with others and that some of them may have ties to your husband's bank. Could you tell me if any of these names sound familiar? Elgin Thomas, Conor Wigan, Mustafa Ahmadi, Calixthe Ebokea?"

She shook her head and made it clear that she associated only with Switzerland's finest families—she didn't mix with French or English. She quickly added that she harbored no ill will toward them, simply had never made time to seek them out. She hadn't even associated with Clément's family in Geneva despite owning the family estate. She spent most of her free time with her own family.

"And where does your family live?" The Major asked.

"Wien."

"Ah, the opera," the Major said. "Mozart, *Die Zauberflöte*."

"*Don Giovanni*," Mme. Marot said with a smile. "You are a fan of the opera?"

"My aunt was a singer with big dreams and a great voice. She played Carmen in Santa Fe one summer. That's as far as she got." The Major looked away. "Bad choices in men."

Mme. Marot nodded knowingly. "Men, a necessary evil."

"Do you get back to Vienna often?" the Major asked.

"I am on the board of the state opera. My daughter, Daniela, goes with me to all the opening nights. My son," she nodded at him, "will go if I bribe him. He would rather drive to the mountains. My husband went three times, but that was twenty-five years ago. He hated it."

"Are you involved in any other charities there?"

"Opera fills all my time, especially when I have to live so far away. Philippe has a charity, I think—African children or something."

She turned to him and spoke in French. A crimson hue rose upward from his neck as he replied in short clipped sentences. She turned back to the Major. "I'm afraid he was dragged into that one by his father's friend, Mme. Bachmann."

The Marots were called to dinner after a few more minutes. The butler showed Miguel and the Major out.

DRIVING TO THE NEXT WITNESS, Miguel pulled out the police translator's business card and called him.

Lieutenant Marco Berardi answered. "Unfortunately, I cannot translate for you."

"Shame," Miguel said. "I have a question. Something Major Jackson told Capitaine Villeneuve surprised you. What was it?"

"The incident on the bridge—there is a small discrepancy in the report. No matter."

Miguel said, "I can send you Major Jackson's report. She said three shots ricocheted off the guard rail in front of the hydroelectric plant before she drew her weapon. Her reports are always accurate."

"I am sure it is nothing but I will check it out."

He clicked off.

★   ★   ★

ANTJE AFFOLTER ANSWERED THE DOOR of her lakefront home in a robe—no makeup, over forty, waves of glossy brown hair framed high cheekbones. She apologized in German, then English.

"You have been to see Joey," she said as she led them down the hallway. "It is bad he drinks, ja? I tell him, have a good cry. He says no. Such a man always."

At that, Antje broke down. The Major and Miguel waited. After a minute, she motioned for them to go ahead of her and sit. In a weak voice she offered drinks, cheese, and crackers, all of which they declined.

"Reto was the best thing that ever happened to me," Antje said. "I was just a schoolteacher, no hope for a privileged life. And I was the best thing for him. He was an accountant, overweight and not much to look at but good at math. I trimmed him up, he gave me an allowance. Our children go to the best schools. Now, all that is gone. It is my fault. I am punished, ja?"

"Punished?" Miguel asked.

"For my attentions to Joey." Antje looked around the room, coming back to the Major. "Reto found out. He was so angry—for days he would not speak to me. The night Clément was murdered he worked with Eren all night. Then both killed. I never had the chance to…"

The Major got up, found a box of tissue, handed it to her, and sat again. After Antje blew her nose, the Major asked, "You said they killed him?"

"Ja, the men on the video, two of them. The men who kicked him and shot him."

She described how the police showed her the video in which Reto Affolter was beaten by two men. One fit the description of Mustafa, the other his blond accomplice. Silent and monochrome, the action occurred in a blurred corner of the screen. Despite the distance, it was clear from the body language that they were interrogating him. After they'd learned everything possible, they shot him.

"Same as Eren Wölfli?" Miguel asked.

"Ja. Lieutenant Lamartine thinks thirty minutes apart."

The Major pursed her lips. "Why did he show you this video?"

"Capitaine Villeneuve wanted me to identify Reto. She asked me if I knew what they were asking him."

Surprised, the Major glanced at Miguel. He shrugged.

"Did you?"

"No. We talked always, Reto and me—he told me everything about the bank. Things that make me sleepy, but I listened. Reto was everything to me. But he was so mad, he did not speak to me that week. Only to say he must attend to something at the bank with Eren and would be home late."

The Major ran through the list of pirate names with no luck. When Miguel asked, she explained that Sandra Bachmann had been in charge of charities. Antje helped her with La Crèche de Tangier. They went there several times to inspect the place.

When asked about bank finances and having too much money, Antje said Reto never mentioned it.

"Did you hear about the ship that was hijacked a few months ago?" the Major asked.

"*Objet Trouvé*? Yes, Clément ruined a dinner party telling us all about it. Telling us too much. Reto said Clément should have gotten out when Banque Genève got out. All those ships, all that risk."

"All what ships?"

"*Objet Trouvé* was the fourth or fifth ship of his that was ... what did you call it, hijacked."

"He owned them?"

"Oh no—he invested in voyage charters. A charterer hires a boat to take cargo from one place to another. Clément was the master of timing oil markets. He would buy the oil, hire the ship, and sell the oil when it arrived. His secret was to hire the oldest, slowest ships. They are cheaper and the price of oil rises during the voyage. He made a killing, except for piracy. At first he was insured, but after the third, well, he could get no insurance. So he was most angry. The *Objet Trouvé* was a total loss, fourteen million euros."

"Yeah, that could sting," the Major said.

"Reto always said this would happen." She sniffed. "He thought tankers were a bad investment from the start. He invested in Cameroon's oil services business. Much less volatile."

The Major pressed her on Banque Genève International's ties to Cameroon.

"Reto went once a year to sign papers, make sure everything was in order. I went once. I thought it would be an adventure. But such poverty. It was not fun."

That was all.

DOWN THE ROAD, THE MAJOR called Sabel headquarters to have someone track down Reto Affolter's travels. She wanted to verify Antje's story and to know when any trips to Cameroon might have taken place.

After a few minutes of silence, Miguel said, "Sounds like Reto was involved. How many Swiss bankers would invest in Cameroon?"

"If there's money to be made, all of them. But even if he was le Directeur, why did they kill him? And who took over?"

CHAPTER 34

Vienna, Austria
27-May, 8PM

PIA IMAGINED HOW LE DIRECTEUR would want things to go: One, meet Monique and get all the information possible out of her. Two, kill her. Three, find and kill Pia Sabel. Pretty simple. Le Directeur would probably have Mustafa with him—or her, if le Directeur actually was a woman. The meeting place was top priority. No doubt le Directeur and henchmen would set a trap. Tania and Pia needed to perform flawlessly, and not just to keep Monique alive. One little mistake and they could all end up dead. The complexity of the whole thing made her sick.

She recalled the Major's snide remark back in Washington: *Let me ask you—worried?*

Pia muttered aloud, "Yes, I am."

Tania stared at her with a fork of broccoli halfway to her mouth. She said, "Yes you are what?"

"Worried."

"Good. The only time you're not scared is the second before you get killed."

"You have to work on your pep talks, Tania."

"Hey, where's the hottie from Berlin?"

Pia shook her head. "He's a nurse, not a hottie. Due in on a ten-thirty flight."

"Guy nurses are hot, if you put them in tight shorts and make them dance." She laughed at her joke.

Pia shook her head. "Not going there."

"We women have a lot of payback coming, y'know. The men of the world owe us some ass-wiggling."

Pia gave her the shut-up look. Monique giggled.

"Why bother bringing him in, anyway?" Tania said. "We look like we need a nurse? What's he going to do, help us get dressed in the morning?"

"The Major sent him. He's all we have this side of London."

Three tiered trays of cookies, pastry, and Sacher's famous chocolates arrived after the third course. No one picked at the chocolates. They fought over them.

The Major called. She gave Pia a rundown of everything the next of kin said in the interviews, and Pia reviewed her plan for intercepting le Directeur.

"Make sure you and Tania stay far apart," the Major said. "Keep the earbuds open all the time, maintain visual contact. They'll be doing the same thing. There'll probably be three of them. I doubt they'll bring more because of the public setting, but there could be a fourth, a driver or someone hanging back."

"Got it, thanks."

"What bothers me most is that at least two of the victims knew their attacker. Sara opened the front door for her assassin. Pia, you know anyone would open the door for Alphonse."

"Or for flower deliveries," Pia said. "Or a co-worker, or family."

"Whoever knocked on Sara's door called first. Her phone was missing."

"Just like the others," Pia said.

"I'm telling you, do not trust anyone. Not Alphonse, not a delivery man, not an Austrian official, no one. Especially if they call first."

"I talked to Alphonse and I'm pretty sure he's true."

"Ever have a man lie to you?"

Pia could only say goodbye and clicked off. The sick feeling in her gut kicked up a notch.

"The two of you are scaring me," Tania said. "You need to let go of your fear and start getting pissed at these guys. Nobody cares that they killed a bunch of bankers, but they killed Ezra and they wanna kill us."

Monique's phone beeped.

Café Frauenhuber, 5 minutes

"Let's go." Pia said and pulled up Monique.

She swapped Monique's phone for a Sabel Security phone and sent her to the Radisson Blu Palais on Parkring via cab. Pia and Tania jogged up Karntner Strasse. When they turned onto Himmelpfortgasse, Tania went ahead with her hoodie pulled up. She walked past the coffee shop on the opposite side of the street and reported back on her earbud comlink.

"Four heads visible: the barista, two at a table, and someone reading a paper. Can't see past the paper. No one suspicious on the street. I'm in position, ready when you are."

Pia stood in the foyer of the Danieli Restaurant across the street and texted le Directeur:

```
Have to change plan. Meet me at Raddison Blu
Palais, table in my name.
```

No reply.

A car turned out of the alley a block away, swung onto Himmelpfortgasse, and stopped in front of the coffee shop. The newspaper reader in the café ran out, jumped in the car, and sped down the street.

"That would be the bad guys," Tania said. "You plan on them having a car?"

"Everyone walks in Europe. How was I supposed to know?"

"Hold up. That could have been coincidence or it could be intended to flush us out. Stay where you are. Have Monique take a bathroom break until we get there."

Pia smiled. Tania definitely had her moments. She texted Monique:

```
Go to the restroom, make sure the maître d'
knows where you're going. Stay there until I
text you again.
```

Her hoodie pulled low, Tania stepped out when the car approached and walked up the sidewalk until it passed her.

"Calixthe!" she shouted into her earbud. "It's Calixthe and some old guy."

Pia ran into the cool night air and looked for a cab. No cars in sight. Breaking into a sprint, she quickly closed the gap between her and Tania.

Ahead of her, a man stepped out of the Café Frauenhuber and broke into a trot.

It had been a trap. The man ahead of her would be the third—was there a fourth? She looked around but glimpsed only a middle-aged couple moving down the street. No one else in the café appeared interested in events outside.

Running too fast to pull her gun, she overtook him instead. As she closed in she saw a sun-bleached mop of hair and leathery skin—the pirate who held a knife to Tania's throat in Cameroon. Tania hadn't recognized him in the café because she never saw his face when they fought in the Zodiac. Pia grabbed his collar, planted her feet, pulled him backwards, and threw him to the ground.

He landed on his back, his arm extended.

Only then did she see the gun in his hand.

He fired.

"Pia, you OK?" Tania on the earbud. "I heard a shot."

No time to reply.

Pia jumped on him and smashed her knees into his belly. His gun fired into the air again. She batted his wrist in an unsuccessful attempt to knock the gun away. Three rapid punches to his windpipe choked him. When she reached for her own weapon he brought the barrel of his gun to her face. He was still lucid enough to kill her, or at least try.

She swatted at it again and tried grabbing his wrist. He struggled to breathe as he twisted beneath her, enough to throw off her balance. She leapt to her feet in time to see the gun swing back at her. She ducked sideways, slammed a foot into his head. He rolled away from a second kick accidentally trapping his gun hand underneath his body. She smashed a powerful kick into his kidneys. He writhed in pain. She darted him.

"I'm good," she said. "Subdued your pirate pal. Keep going. Cover

Monique."

The middle-aged couple stopped and stared from across the street.

"Rufen die Polizei!" she called out to them. Which she hoped meant, Call the police.

Their eyes widened. The woman tugged at her escort and the two ran away as fast as their dress shoes would allow.

"No problem," Pia called after them. "I can handle it. Better for my street cred if I do it myself anyway."

She looked down at the pirate. She wasn't about to kill an unconscious unarmed man. Leaving him alive meant she'd better win this thing tonight—otherwise he'd be up and around in a few hours, one more adversary to deal with when she was already outnumbered.

She pulled the Sabel dart out of his body, hit him with an antidote injector, and took off for the Radisson.

While running, she called the polizei herself. The language barrier was too high for the time she had left—best she could tell, they thought she'd killed someone. She gave up.

She caught up to Tania in three city blocks, passed her and found the boutique hotel's street door.

"Hey, do NOT go in there alone!" Tania called on her earbud. "You hear me?"

"Yeah." Pia said. "I'm waiting."

Tania came up behind her a few seconds later. She whispered, "Holster that thing, you'll start a panic. Look, over there—the car that stopped at the café. Empty. There were two people in it when they passed me. We're looking for two hostiles inside, got it?"

Pia nodded, holstered her gun, texted Monique:

Go back to the table now. We're here.

No reply.

Tania whipped out her knife and slashed the car tires, then they walked down the narrow curved steps to the hotel's basement lobby. The small entryway had three openings: elevators, Sapori Restaurant, and the H12 bar. Tania searched for a back door while the maître d' led Pia to a table in back.

Monique looked beyond terrified, drained of all hope. She was seated between a man with his back to Pia and Calixthe Ebokea.

"So you're le Directeur," Pia said.

Calixthe smiled. Without a trace of accent, she said, "We're all here. Pull up a chair and join us. I have a pistol jammed in your friend's ribs, so mind your manners."

Pia stepped up to the table.

"Hardly a friend. She was going to kill me. So go ahead, shoot her."

Calixthe nodded to her companion. "You've never been properly introduced. Pia Sabel, allow me to present Elgin Thomas."

The man in the chair rose and offered a slight bow. Average-sized, dark hair streaked with gray, a thick goatee around a thin-lipped mouth. Pia tensed, her fists clenched, her teeth clamping down hard. His eyes rose to meet hers. He twitched a smile. She caught the glint of the P225 in his hand, half concealed beneath his leather jacket.

"You both have P225s?" Pia said. "What, you guys stole a truck full of them somewhere?"

"Good intel," Tania's whisper came over her earbud. "Keep it coming. I'm slipping through the kitchen."

Calixthe said, "Sit down."

"I'd love to," Pia said. "But there's only three chairs, and there's no way I'm sitting with my back to the door and you two on either side of me."

"We were planning on killing you someplace nice and quiet, but we can do it here if you'd like." Calixthe smiled and nodded to her left. "You'll notice there are no security cameras in this hotel."

"Exactly why I chose it," Pia said. "So far you haven't pulled the trigger, so you must want something. I want something too." She tipped her head at Monique. "Before we negotiate, get that vermin out of here."

Calixthe looked her captive over the way an owner looks at a pet and shook her head. She said, "Sorry, I'll keep her alive for now. I suspect you're one of those bleeding hearts who can't stand to watch another human being die, even if she did try to kill you. So like I said, pull up that chair and sit."

"No. Tell me what you want."

"I want to know where your backup went. You're green, but you're not dumb enough to come in here alone."

"Agent Jacob is waiting for you in the lobby," Pia said. "Agent Marty's on the street outside, covering the service entrance. Nowhere to run, Calixthe."

Elgin Thomas flicked a glance at his companion.

Pia shifted her weight and moved her right foot backward. Elgin's gun followed her. She took a step closer to him. He looked confused and stole another glance at Calixthe.

Pia turned her back on the others and faced him. She said, "You didn't sign up for this, did you, Elgin? You had no idea she wanted you to shoot someone in an overcrowded restaurant with only one door out. You'll never get out of here. You'll be pinned for murder here in Austria. But I'll bet she finds a way out."

His eyes wavered a moment before swinging to Calixthe.

"Did she tell you Elgin Thomas is the code name of their mastermind?" Pia said. "Did she mention all of Interpol is looking for this mythical Elgin Thomas? He's wanted for murder in Cameroon and conspiracy in Geneva. You're the fall guy. Why else would she ask you to be here?"

Pia Sabel was considered the best in women's soccer at the header—smashing the ball with the crown of the head where the skull is thickest. She smashed the crown of her skull into Elgin Thomas's nose.

Blood poured out of him like a faucet. His hands flew up, his gun aimed at the ceiling. Pia smacked the gun from his hand and landed three quick blows into his soft body. He doubled over in pain.

A deafening blast exploded. Sound waves reverberated in the small concrete room as Monique slumped to the table. Pia drew her gun. Elgin staggered toward the front door. She turned to aim at Calixthe, only to find a gun aimed right at her head.

Pia's endless training at ducking kicked in. She pivoted right as she dropped six inches. Calixthe's second shot went over her head and into the wall behind her. The gun barrel lowered before Pia could bring hers up. She launched herself into the space Elgin Thomas vacated. Bringing her gun around with both hands, she took aim only to have horrified diners, racing for the exits, knock her down. From the floor, she saw Calixthe running for the kitchen.

"Tania—she's coming your way!" Pia shouted.

"I see her. Damn! No shot, no shot. Too crowded. Giving chase."

Pia got to her feet, pressed her fingers to Monique's neck and felt a pulse.

Monique lifted her head, her sad eyes looking at Pia. She tried to speak but only gurgled. Two diners moved in next to them.

"Doktor?" she said.

"Nein," one of them said.

"Um, Arzt rufen?" she pleaded. Hoping that meant, *Call a doctor*.

"Krankenwagen—ehm, ambulance," the other man said. He pulled out a cell phone to make the call.

The man and his friend seemed concerned. They also knew she was the good guy here. Pia turned and ran through the lobby. Several patrons cowered in the bar to her left. She looked them over. No Elgin Thomas. She ran up the steps to the street.

Near the top of the short staircase, she saw her shadow on the wall ahead of her. He would have seen her coming. She jumped backwards, pressing her back to the left wall. A bullet shattered the glass door. Screams and footsteps followed. Pia scrambled over the broken glass and through the door to the street. Three people ran down one sidewalk, two more in the opposite direction. Two young Chinese women in fur coats cowered against the building.

"Where'd he go?" Pia asked.

The women pointed into the park across the street just as more shots rang out. Pia dropped to the ground. Concrete chips fell on her. She slid backwards away from the door to a darkened patch of sidewalk. She got to her feet, glanced at the traffic. Cars in both directions had stopped. Terrified drivers stared at her as she ran in front of them.

Where might he have gone?

She darted across an open area to a tree in the deserted park. She caught sight of him running across a wide-open plaza toward a statue. She aimed and fired three shots. All misses. Too far.

She gave chase, only a flower garden between them. He fled behind the statue. He didn't look to be stopping there but going past. Pia approached the statue. A white marble arch decorated with an orgy of naked people framed a golden man with a violin. *Johann Strauss* was carved into the pedestal. Thomas's footsteps receded behind the arch. She ran past the statue to get a look.

A bullet pinged the marble. Her eyes located the source just in time to see the barrel pointed directly at her. A flash. She dove backward.

Another chunk of marble chipped away. She ran around the arch to the right, pressed her back to it, clutched her gun with both hands. She took a deep breath and spun around the marble just in time to see him running toward a long balustrade.

She followed.

He took a set of dimly lit stairs. She ran wide, passing his last position, then leaned over the railing above. Below her stood Elgin Thomas, in an alcove, his gun aimed up the stairway.

Her body stretched awkwardly over the tall balustrade's wide stone top. She tried to aim. Below her was a riverside promenade that ran left and right as far as she could see. Elgin Thomas was alone. She aimed and fired.

Missed. He heard the shot, wheeled and fired at her. She fell backwards unhurt.

On her earbud she heard shots. Tania shouted obscenities and fired three of her own. One more shot rang out. Tania screamed. "Fuck! I'm hit! That bitch!"

In the distance, police sirens filled the streets. Lights flashed against the buildings beyond the trees. Pia considered her options, then stood, planted her hands on top of the balustrade, and launched herself over the top.

She landed, her feet stinging from the impact as she leveled her gun. Elgin ran down the river walk behind her as she staggered a step for balance. Spinning in place, she fired until her gun emptied. She pulled the spare magazine full of lead bullets from her purse and stepped out from the stairwell. Bullets pinged off the ground to her left. She stepped back into the stairwell. Elgin Thomas was gone. Her gut twisted up in knots.

"Tania, you OK?" Pia called out and cupped her hand over her earbud. "Tania? Talk to me. Tania, are you all right?

CHAPTER 35

28-May, Midnight

"PUT HER IN THERE." PIA pointed to one of the suite's bedrooms.

"I can walk!" Tania shouted at Agent Klaus, their newly arrived nurse from Berlin. "Leave me alone, dammit."

A single crutch under one arm, Tania hobbled into the other room and dropped on the bed. She shrieked in pain when her leg bounced. Klaus ran to her side, grabbed Tania's trembling shoulder with one hand, and cradled her leg with the other. He eased her down while moving her leg over the edge of the bed. He stacked pillows next to the injured leg, raised it, then swung it over the pillows and lowered it gently. Tania smiled.

Pia stood in the doorway.

"Ain't this nice?" Tania said. "Y'know what would be cool? Score a room like this, find Tom Cruise in the lobby, bring him up here and leave a bunch of wet spots all over the sheets. But no—when I score this room, I have a nine-millimeter hole clean through my leg and the wet spots are blood. Fuck!"

"At least it didn't hit any bone—"

"You say that one more goddamn time, I'm putting a bullet through your quad so you can speak from experience. I don't have to be friends with you, y'know."

"Sorry," Pia said. "Look, for the last time, this suite is the bait. I'm expecting them to get here between two and four. You aren't mobile. I need you in the other room."

"Hey, Klaus, can you believe this shit?"

Klaus looked from her to Pia, shook his head and put up his hands. Language barrier. Pia waved him off. Not worth trying her hand at

German again. He backed up and sat in one of the antique chairs next to the bed.

"C'mon, I don't get to live like this," Tania said. "Just put some of those extra Kevlar jackets under the covers and hand me the M4. Tell Calixthe I say, 'Bring it, bitch!'"

Pia placed body armor over her chest and left an M4 within easy reach on the edge of the bed. She pulled the comforter over the top.

Tania said, "You know what I really like about hanging out with you? Those lawyers. Last time I ended up in a police station nobody showed up until dawn, just chilled with the drug dealers and hookers all night. Not you. You got it made."

Pia didn't recall her legal team being extraordinary. Two senior partners showed up in the middle of the night to calm an overzealous police detective, exactly what she paid them to do. Detective Janko was offended that Pia brought a shootout to his peaceful little town. Fortunately, his boss knew what a good legal team could do to their careers.

What pissed her off was Detective Janko's suspicious, anti-rich attitude. Janko had bullet holes in walls, victims in the hospital, and witnesses lined up, but no one in jail. He wanted someone to blame and she was handy. The jerk.

Pia asked, "Want the lights out?"

"Nah, I'm ordering a movie. Don't worry, I'll put it on mute and read the captions."

Pia had no way to explain the danger to Klaus. He had no way to weigh the risk of staying in the suite. She put him in the room furthest from the trouble. Bandage check and re-dressing would happen later. Until then, he would wait.

She entered her room, the one facing the suite. She pressed her back to the door and slumped to the floor. Resting her arms on her raised knees, she buried her face. She recalled Calixthe leading her through the jungle to Boa. She should have seen it then—the woman knew how to run. She was an experienced operative of some kind. The only reason Pia was alive today was because Calixthe underestimated her. Unlikely she'd make that mistake again.

She picked up her phone and saw a voicemail message from Dad.

She wanted to listen to it. But she knew what the message would say. He'd ordered her to come home. Alan Sabel hated it when people, especially Pia, didn't do what he wanted. He meant well, he was just overzealous about her safety. Which was nice—sometimes. Nothing said *I love you* like defying the demands of a self-made billionaire with a Type-A personality. She pressed delete, bounced the phone in her hand.

I'm already dead. Every day I live is like an extra day.

Was it her fault Ezra ran out of extra days? Had she been living on extra days since her parents' murders?

Face it, things had gone badly and the whole mess just kept getting worse. She'd expected to have a healthy Tania for her end game. Now she was outnumbered: Calixthe Ebokea and Elgin Thomas versus Pia Sabel. Two experienced criminals against one gold-medal footballer.

She contemplated her plan and the variables. She came up with a second plan and discarded it. Then another, and another. An hour later she was thinking up yet another plan when she heard the elevator doors open.

She rose and peered out the peephole. Two men, familiar-looking but unrecognizable through the distorted lens, approached and faced the suite across the hall. One raised a fist to knock. Pia stepped out of her room and leveled her gun at them.

"Who are you?" she asked.

They turned around in unison and nearly jumped out of their skin.

"Detective Janko." Pia lowered her weapon. "Sorry, I didn't recognize you from the back."

"Ms. Sabel," he said, "you must not wave guns around. This is not Texas. There has been enough damage—"

"Which I didn't cause."

"We understand your viewpoint. Nonetheless, you are obviously anticipating trouble."

"I am." Pia motioned to her room. "Please come in."

They dutifully stepped inside, then looked around the room. Double beds, smallish space, not what they expected for an heiress. She closed the door and pressed her back against it.

"What can I do for you?" she asked.

"We could not find any reason to hold David Benson, the man you tranquilized. During the few seconds we could get him coherent, he wanted to press charges against you for assault."

Janko held up a hand to hold off her objection.

"We found his gun. It was licensed to him. That creates a problem in your story. Officials in Cameroon were not available to confirm any outstanding warrants for extradition. As for you, well…your story is plausible at best. Unfortunately, we found the Belgian tourists you mentioned. They had a very different version of events. They say you jumped the man from behind and beat him mercilessly without provocation."

Pia stared at the detective, then took a long deep breath. She said, "So what do you want?"

"You must come back to the station to answer questions. There may be charges."

Pia felt a laugh welling up inside her. At first she fought it, then she laughed out loud.

"The guy you turned loose, David Bonehead? He's going to come here with a real gun with real bullets to kill me. Would it be all right with you if I shoot him first, then come to the station?"

"This is no joke, Ms. Sabel. I must confiscate your weapon right now. Then you will come with us."

"Tania Cooper has a bullet hole in her leg, Detective Janko. Monique Tsogo is in critical condition in your hospital. Are you going to provide security for them?"

"If you wouldn't mind, hand me your weapon." Detective Janko held out his hand.

Pia pulled out her Glock.

She looked at it, checked the chamber, balanced the weight in her hands, and darted both men.

"Yes, as a matter of fact," she said. "I would mind."

IF SHE HADN'T BEEN IN trouble before, she was now.

At least she could get her money's worth out of those attorneys.

How long before Janko and his pal were due back at his office? Would anyone miss them at this hour? Hopefully the reinforcements were lazy enough to wait for dawn. She dragged both men to the far end of the room and propped them up in the narrow space between the bed and the window.

She thought through her plans one more time. David Benson wouldn't be fully awake for another hour. The polizei might have brought him around with smelling salts but that couldn't last long. Currently, the odds stood at two to one with Benson as a wild card. The detectives would sleep until six or seven in the morning. That should get her past the expected attack. If the attack never came, she'd have to leave Austria in a hurry.

She returned to the door to keep watch.

After half an hour, someone reached the floor via the central stairway. Her peephole didn't give her a view that far down the hall. Holding her breath with her eye pressed to it, she waited.

A tall lanky figure finally sauntered into view.

She ripped the door open, stepped into the hall, and darted Lieutenant Alphonse Lamartine. His body hit the floor hard.

"Welcome to Grand Central Station, Lieutenant," she said. "Hope you find your stay restful."

Tania called her about the noise.

"Everything's OK," Pia said, "but we might need to leave in a hurry."

Tania made it clear she would stay until someone pried her cold dead fingers off the silk bedcovers.

Klaus poked his head out. She waved him over and together they dragged Alphonse into her room and on the bed. In her mind, he deserved a better resting place than Janko. Her gut still told her he was a good man, but she couldn't overlook the facts. Alphonse showed up at her hotel—a hotel she purposely hadn't mentioned to him. Good detective work? Inside information? Must have been the Austrian polizei. Her hotel address was required during the interrogation. But did they tell Alphonse, or did Calixthe?

She checked his pockets. He came unarmed—a small mark in his favor. Paging through his texts she found nothing incriminating. No one named Calixthe or Conor or Elgin was in his contact list. His boss, Villeneuve, texted about ten times an hour for updates on the case. Another set of texts in English involved someone named Susan Duncan, an inquiry about NATO soldiers. Another exchange from Pierre Lamartine and another from Marie Lamartine in French. And one from Duchamps, the hapless street cop.

The most recent text from Capitaine Villeneuve, just two hours ago, piqued her curiosity.

> Nous n'avons plus besoin de vos services. Je
> vous prie de bien vouloir retourner à Chamonix.

She had a feeling she knew what it meant but verified it on a translation site. Villeneuve had sent him home to Chamonix. Before or after he hopped a plane to Vienna?

She took up her position against the door and waited.

SOMETIME AFTER THREE IN THE morning, she heard people coming down the hallway from the central staircase. The swishing of their clothes gave them away. When they came into the peephole's view she recognized Calixthe, the man posing as Elgin Thomas, and David Benson. All three wore trench coats. They were learning. The coats were as good as body armor against her sleeper darts. Leaving her with headshots only. And she wasn't exactly a sharpshooter.

Her stomach clenched. Tania was in there. She had to do this or die trying. Calixthe was opening the suite's door. Benson was holding his gun up, prepared to follow. Elgin was guarding the hall and stairs, looking away from Pia.

She pulled the door open as quietly as possible.

She stepped into the hall at the same moment Calixthe stepped into the suite. Pia fired three times at Benson. All three misses.

Her hand was shaking. She'd been warned about the body's response under pressure.

Thomas and Benson turned around, shocked.

She took a breath and fired again, hitting Benson square in the nose. He dropped.

Calixthe was inside, out of sight.

Pia hugged the wall, looking down her Glock's sight directly at Elgin Thomas. His gun was aimed the wrong way, into the suite, to cover Calixthe. His face looked directly into Pia's barrel and turned white. Her hand was rock-steady. She held her fire on instinct, motioned instead for him to lie down and toss the gun aside. He complied, lying flat on the far side of the suite's doorway from Pia. She guessed Calixthe was standing in the doorway ready to shoot anyone who came around the corner—and Pia was doing the same. A classic standoff.

Pia's mind spun through options and ideas. She could dart Elgin Thomas and go after Calixthe. But her adversary was crafty and tenacious. Pia stood a good chance of losing. She could try to draw the older woman out. Or she could hope Tania would help from inside.

"Hey, Calixthe!" Pia called out. "There's only one door in that room. Only one way out. Sooner or later you'll have to face Detective Janko."

Calixthe stayed silent.

Pia knew what that meant: come and get me.

She patted down David Benson fast while keeping her eyes and her gun trained on Elgin. One P225, one money clip, one stiletto, one phone. She tossed them into the hallway behind her.

Elgin Thomas's eyes kept darting back and forth from Pia to inside the suite. That could only mean one thing: he was guiding an attack from Calixthe. Those back-and-forth eye movements provided Calixthe intelligence about Pia's position.

She picked up Benson's gun, aimed it at Elgin, and rose off her knees to a squat. With her fingers, she indicated he should raise his eyes as if he were watching her stand up. At first he pretended not to understand. She sighted down the barrel of Benson's gun.

He raised his eyes.

Calixthe's footfalls were silent, but her creaking ankle gave away her position. If Pia's calculations were correct, she'd burst around the corner and fire at head level. She might even do it without looking. Pia remained in a crouch, aiming her Glock up and her confiscated P225 at Elgin. Another ankle creak. Another footstep closer. If Elgin gave her away, or if she were wrong, Pia's life would end in the next ten seconds. It was all she could do not to force the issue by rolling out and firing wildly. Her breathing stopped. Her heart raced.

She caught a shift in Elgin's pupils. Calixthe's reflection.

Pia pushed her Glock around the corner and fired three darts.

"Dammit, Pia!" Tania's voice rang out before Calixthe hit the floor. "You forgot she was mine?"

CHAPTER 36

28-May, 3AM

"SORRY," PIA SAID.

She heard a body hit the floor. Tania screamed in pain.

Pia looked at Elgin Thomas. She said, "Get up. Unbuckle your belt, drop your pants to your ankles, keep your hands as high as you can get them. Stand in the corner. You move and I'm going to empty Benson's magazine in you. Got it?"

Elgin nodded and complied.

Behind her, Pia heard a loud gasp.

Down the hall, Klaus stood in the doorway.

Pia rolled her eyes. "It's OK. Um … Sie sind Räubers, Schurkens. Bad guys. Look, just get Tania, she needs your help. Helfen Tania."

Klaus flew into the suite, stepping over the bodies in the doorway. He scooped up Tania in one hand, grabbed her crutch with the other, and carried her back to bed.

Pia picked up all the loose items in the hallway and made Elgin drag the bodies into the suite. After a quick look around the hall to make sure everything looked normal, she went inside. Klaus joined her after settling Tania. She held Elgin at gunpoint and called the front desk.

"I need four rolls of duct tape," she said. "Duct tape. Gray, thick, wide. You know?"

"Klebeband," Elgin said. "Filament Klebeband."

"Filament Klebeband," Pia said. "Right away, bitte."

Three minutes later she tipped the bellboy ten euros and closed the door.

"Elgin Thomas." She tossed him a roll of tape. "What's your real name?"

"Walter Walcott."

"One thing I've learned about your gang is that you guys love using fake names. Not hard to guess you're not Elgin. But then, Elgin is the boss's name. And let's face it, you're no boss."

"I could be."

"You kept looking at Calixthe for answers."

He blinked his swollen, tired eyes.

"You ready to switch sides, Walter?"

He looked ready.

"Right, I wouldn't trust you if you said yes. So here's what you're going to do. You help Klaus prop these guys up in the dining room chairs and bind them up with Filament Klebeband. Then I've got three more stashed across the hall."

With Walter/Elgin's help translating, she communicated the work to Klaus and began securing Calixthe Ebokea, David Benson, then Alphonse. When it came time for the detectives, they had a little fun. They propped them in compromising positions and took pictures. Finally, they taped up the polizei with the others. Each prisoner's wrists were secured to the arm of a chair, each ankle bound to a chair leg. Their heads were held upright with a ligature attached to the chair's back. When she finished, the dining room looked like a horror-comedy with awkward zombies taped into antique chairs at an elegant table.

"Your turn, Elgin, Walter, whatever your name is. Sit in the chair, Klaus will tape you up. I'm not going to dart you if you talk. As you can see, Calixthe is going to jail. Her operation is done. If you work with me, I'll help you out as best I can. Calixthe can't hear you, so you can talk all you want. They'll all wake up within an hour of each other. Won't that be fun?"

He looked sick.

"First question, who runs the Cameroon operation?"

"Elgin Thomas."

"C'mon, tell me the truth."

"I am."

"Did you know your buddy Conor Wigan is dead?"

Walter looked up, his eyes searching hers for the truth. She stared back, cold and honest. His face paled as the truth sank in.

"Just before he died, he told me the Swiss ordered Mustafa Ahmadi to kill him. Guess who's next? Especially since you failed tonight." Pia leaned toward him while Klaus finished binding his hands to the chair's armrests.

"Who's going to take the blame? Calixthe? Oh no. She's going to nail you, my friend. How does the real Elgin Thomas reward abject failure? The death penalty?"

He glared at the sleeping woman next to him.

"One more time, who runs the Cameroon operation?"

He nodded at Calixthe. "Susan Duncan."

Pia's heart stopped. She turned to the pile of phones and guns on the side table and plowed through them until she found Alphonse's phone. She flipped through the texts.

Alphonse Lamartine:

```
I am looking for the friend of yours named
Elgin Thomas. Berlin four years ago. You have
kept in touch?
```

Susan Duncan:

```
No. Thought I'd never hear from you again. How
have you been?
```

Alphonse Lamartine:

```
Fine. Thomas is serious trouble. Murder. Geneva
Police, Sabel Security, Interpol.
```

Susan Duncan:

```
If I see him, I'll let him know.
```

Pia reeled. A coded warning? An innocent inquiry? Official police investigation? How did he know her?

"Who is Susan Duncan?" she asked. "Where is she from? Why was she in Berlin four years ago?"

"How do you know Conor's dead?"

"I was there." Pia filled him in. "He never mentioned Calixthe, or Susan Duncan. He said Mustafa killed him. I'm guessing Mustafa never did anything unless Calixthe told him to."

"Well. That's partly right," he said. "Bloody little bastard followed her around like a puppy dog until last week. Now he's full of himself."

She squinted at Walter. "She was Elgin Thomas? She ran everything?"

His eyes flickered for a second.

"Right now," Pia said, "the only thing I have on you is guilt by association and pointing a gun at me. With a good attorney, you could probably distance yourself from these guys and slink back to whatever hole in the ground weasels like you live in. All I need from you is enough information to turn the tables on these guys."

He stared at the wall.

"OK, here's the deal." Pia paced the dining room. "You want something. I want something. You help me, I'll think about helping you. Now tell me what you want."

"I want to walk out of here."

"You know, I might actually let you do that." Pia smirked. "But I'd have to verify your story first. So start talking."

Walter sighed. "Yeah, she had us call her Elgin Thomas. Even to her face. Calixthe Ebokea was her Cameroon name. Elgin was her business name. Susan Duncan was her real name. Used to be the American liaison to NATO." He paused. "Hey, you OK love? You're looking a bit sick. Anyway, Conor was stationed in Stockholm with her when they were young. Had a baby. She was a piss-poor mother. Conor raised that boy alone, best he could. I met them both when I was stationed in Rome. So the deal was, someone asked for a guy named Elgin, it was a sign they were not to be trusted."

"Wow, you guys are clever. OK, she ran the Cameroon operation. Conor already told me that much. Who was she working with?"

"I don't know. She and Conor kept the whole thing secret."

"Le Directeur?" Pia asked.

"Don't know what you mean. Who's that?"

"Are you that stupid? Or do you think I am."

"I swear I don't know what you're talking about."

"Le Directeur, the money laundering in Geneva. How'd you get paid?"

"We'd come up here to Vienna. Me, Conor, and Davey Benson escorting Susan. We'd put up in a little shack across the Danube, then she'd head out to meet someone. Come home with a bag of cash, every time."

"And as insurance, you followed her a couple times. Just in case she tried to cut you out. Right?"

Walter Walcott's head spun around to face her, angry and straining against the duct tape.

"Is that what Conor told you?"

"No, you just did. Conor wasn't bright enough for insurance. Besides, he figured he and Calixthe, or Susan, were married for life. You didn't have that kind of guarantee. You needed something else. What was it?"

"Married? Calixthe would never marry him. She just let him think that." He looked down at the table. "Yeah, I followed her. Never figured out much. She met a young man one time. A good-looking woman another. I followed her five times. Three times it was the young man, once the woman. Two weeks ago it was both. Cafe Tirolerhof on Führichgasse every time. The young man was one of those soft types. The woman was either madly in love with him or the best gold digger you ever saw."

"What language did they speak?"

"Bloody hell, you think I'm that stupid? I never got close enough to hear them. Calixthe would have shot me on the spot."

Pia pushed between two zombies, leaned across the table, planting her palms in the middle. She asked, "Where is Mustafa Ahmadi?"

He smiled at her. "In the lobby."

"Nice try," Pia said. "If he was, you'd never have talked."

"I have no idea where he is. He came to Brussels with us. Split up at the airport. Never saw him again. But you should be scared. Conor was crazy, but only when he went off his meds. Mustafa's a real nutcase. He finds you, you're one dead footballer."

"Guess he never told you," Pia said.

Walter looked confused.

"I tackled him after he murdered Clément Marot and turned him over to the police," she said. "I scared him off on the Rhone. I ran him out of ammunition in Cameroon. He's actually afraid of me."

"You bested him? Three times?" Walter Walcott laughed deep enough to make himself cough. Then he cleared his throat. "Well then, you're just the lass who can help me out. See, I need to get that young man out of my life for good. He plans the same for me as he did for Conor. I could tell something was wrong with him on the flight up here. Knowing he killed Conor, it all makes sense now. So, here's the deal. You cut me loose, walk me to the door with no guns in your hands, and just before I make a run for it, I tell you where you can find him."

"That's funny, Walter. You're a riot."

"I'm serious, love. You can have the bugger. You get the killer, I get a chance. What do you Yanks call it? A win-win?"

"OK, you almost got a deal. Almost. First, you tell me how to find le Directeur. That was a code name for the young couple, right? The same way Calixthe was Elgin Thomas?"

"Guess so," Walter said.

"You followed them but never got close enough to hear them talking. That would be only halfway smart. I think you're all the way smart. I think you found some way of getting in touch with them just in case something happened to Calixthe, or whatever her name is. Now, you tell me how to find them and I'll think about helping you out with Mustafa."

Walter Walcott stared at the table for a long time. Finally, he looked up.

"You'll think about helping me? You want Mustafa, don't you?"

"I used to. But now that I know he's planning to kill you, I'm thinking, what a great opportunity to get rid of you both. I just tell the polizei about him after he kills you and my work in Vienna is done. If you want me to take care of him for you—that'll cost you."

Walter shook his head slowly before looking back at her with pathetic, pleading eyes. He said, "How do I know I can trust you?"

CHAPTER 37

Geneva, Switzerland
28-May, 6AM

"…BECAUSE WHERE SHE GOES IS important," the Major said.

Agent Miguel took the keys and the bagged breakfast and headed out into the morning mist without a word.

The Major nodded at the hotel's doorman, who stepped to the street and hailed her a cab. A block from Joey Campbell's house, she got out and hiked up the hillside. Walking was a necessary meditation for her. Alone with no distractions, she could untangle webs of deceit.

If Antje Affolter was telling the truth about her affair with Joey Campbell, sometime in the next thirty minutes, she'd scurry from the Campbell's house and head home. Once the affair was confirmed, the Major would proceed to Bachmann's house. No matter how she looked at it, the Major couldn't see Marina Bachmann as capable of hiring assassins. She most likely stood to inherit something of her sister's but she had no other ties to the banking community. Ramona Wölfli, who would most likely get up some time after ten, was a much better suspect. Not because she hated her husband—which was convenient, believable, and probably honest—but because of her mercenary attitude. Ramona had dismissed Philippe Marot as too young—clearly she saw herself capable of winning another older, wealthier man. Maybe she'd already found one in the money laundering business.

Dawn lightened the eastern sky and the streetlights clicked off. In the dim gray light, she found the view of Lake Léman breathtaking. Early morning bird calls lent music to the scenery. The Major stopped between houses to admire the view. A dome of baby blue sky covered dark blue water surrounded by dark blue mountains. She took a mental picture and kept walking.

Reaching the end of the lane from which she could still observe the Campbell's residence, she turned around. On cue, Antje tiptoed out of the house, a small bag in her hand, then got into a car and drove off.

The Major put a checkmark on her mental list: affair confirmed, but still a suspect. The woman knew banking, exhibited bad judgment with Joey, had plenty of financial motive. And her husband had ties to Cameroon. If she were ranking suspects by capability, Antje would take first place. If she ranked them by cold-bloodededness, Antje tied for last with Marina Bachmann. Could Antje be a good actress? The Major had seen plenty of great acting jobs in her time. It was possible.

Turning up the next lane, the Major made the short hike toward the Bachmann residence. Two blocks away, she heard her name called. Marina Bachmann, a dog's leash in one hand, waved from a side street.

"Major Jackson, out for a morning walk?" Marina said.

"My body's in a different time zone, so I thought I'd stroll around the lake. Beautiful view."

"Yes, we love it." Marina held a knuckle to her lips and winced. "We used to walk the dog together, you know. It was one of our chores as children. She was older and would tell me what to do, so I hated it. Now, I miss the innocent little fights."

"What did you talk about as adults?" the Major said.

"Gossip. What she heard about this banker, what I heard about that wife." Marina Bachmann laughed at herself. "Sounds so silly, doesn't it?"

The Major smiled and winked. "Did she have anything good?"

Marina turned down the sidewalk and motioned for the Major to join her.

"Did you know Antje Affolter was having an affair with that artist, Campbell?"

"No! Really?"

"And Eren Wölfli lived like a Muslim sheik with three wives in his harem."

"I met Mme. Wölfli," the Major said in her best conspiratorial voice. "Did he choose the others for the same reason?"

"Eren divorced women for the sin of turning twenty-nine."

"Where did he find them?"

"Where do you think?"

They both laughed.

"But then," Marina said, "is it so much worse than older women running around with younger men? They say only young gigolos ski Chamonix now."

The Major laughed again. "Am I too old to take up skiing?"

They walked another block in silence, the Major working over the bits and pieces in her mind. Marina started to say something, then stopped and touched her shoulder.

"Do you know who did it? Who killed my sister?"

"I have a few ideas. I know there were two people in Geneva. I know one had to have banking experience. A rival, a junior executive, a disgruntled employee? We're working on it."

"Thank you, Major Jackson. I'm glad to have run into you. You've told me more than the police. I'm not sure they know what to do."

She watched Marina start up the entryway toward her house, a standard Victorian with a front porch and high-pitched roof. The garage was tucked on the side in the back of the property. The Major stared at the garage.

"Excuse me, Ms. Bachmann," she called out, "did your sister use the garage the night she was murdered?"

"She did."

"Do you have a side door she normally went through?"

"Yes. But the gunman called to her—I heard the voice just before the gunshot."

"She knew him?"

"The police thought so, but she would have answered to anyone who called her name. This is a friendly city full of friendly people."

The Major said goodbye and left.

Around the corner she called a cab to carry her to the hill overlooking Ramona Wölfli's penthouse. Once there, she crossed a small park and found a bench with a perfect view. The binoculars were the right size and power to see directly into Ramona's kitchen. She propped a laser detector on the bench next to her and aimed it at the windows. It would sound a warning when anyone moved through the visible end of the apartment.

For a few moments she watched the sun rise over the Alps. Mists swirled at the eastern end of the lake, still shrouded in the mountains' shadows. She wondered if Sabel Security would open an office in Geneva. She sighed, gave up her delusions, and started pacing.

What about Wölfli's first wife? Or second? What about Mme. Lena Marot? Was it her superior attitude that made her the Major's prime suspect? Or her racism? She stopped herself. No supporting evidence pointed to Marot.

She ran through the mental list of survivors who had connections that could run a pirate ring three thousand miles away. She eliminated the alcoholic Campbell and the domestic Bachmann as incapable. Antje Affolter and Ramona Wölfli had that skill set. Ramona because gold diggers are capable of amazing things when their allowance is threatened.

Back to Marot. Dammit, no matter how much she wanted it to work, she had nothing that connected the woman to any part of this conspiracy.

Someone knew the banking business and had access to criminals. Who was the missing link between a bank executive and Calixthe?

She slowed her pacing. *Think.*

Bankers play golf, vacation in Greece, aspire to country clubs. They don't hang out in dive bars on the waterfront. Could someone have moved the other way? Could a criminal move up the ladder inside the banking business? Unlikely. It would take too long, and criminals aren't known for patience. Still, there must have been cross-pollination. A banker and a criminal got together somehow, somewhere, some place. Ramona made a good candidate for supplying the criminal connections. What banker, other than Eren, would fall into her web?

Any of them. None of them.

Pia Sabel called and reported on her evening's excitement. After darting Walter Walcott for failing to give up le Directeur, she'd darted them all again and taken her normal three-hour nap while Klaus kept watch. Then she'd gone through the captive's possessions. Calixthe carried a packet of matches identical to the one found on Mustafa the night of the murder. Possibly the exact same one, since Geneva lost the evidence bag. Pia had called the number, no answer. She chalked that up to the early hour and would try again later.

"Sabel's intelligence group," Pia said, "dug up interesting background on Susan Duncan, aka Calixthe Ebokea. Two years ago she retired from the CIA. She spent twenty years as a field operative in all the places you might expect: the Hague, Stockholm, Berlin, Lyon, Hamburg, London. Her last two stops were Geneva and Vienna."

"Then she definitely masterminded the pirate operation," the Major said. "That leaves open the question about who the banking connection is. And how did they meet?"

"There were two people, a woman and a man, who called themselves le Directeur. Calixthe met with them, Monique spoke to them, Walter saw them. How do we find them?"

"You have everyone tied up. Wake them up with smelling salts and have them start talking. I'm not sure what you're going to do about the polizei. That could be tricky. Might want to wake up your lawyers and have them on standby. What about Alphonse?"

"My mood shifts by the hour about him. He's dirty. He's clean. Dirty. Clean. How can I figure it out?"

The Major took a deep breath.

"Well, it doesn't matter much," Pia said. "When he wakes up, he's going to hate me for suspecting him. If he's in with her, he's going to make me feel guilty. If he's clean, I'm going to feel guilty. Maybe I should give him a gun and let him shoot me."

"Please figure out a better way," the Major said. "I'm thinking Ramona is the femme fatale and she seduced some junior executive. Oh, hey, my alarm went off, which means she's up and moving around. Three hours earlier than I expected. Got to go."

They clicked off. The Major pulled her binoculars up and steadied her elbows on her knees. Wölfli's penthouse rose above the skyline with picture windows facing the lake and a balcony running the length of two sides. Facing her were a series of expansive windows. She could see some of the kitchen, most of dining room, and half the living room.

As she adjusted the focus, Ramona came in looking like she stepped out of lingerie catalog. She strode through the living room, strutted in front of the picture windows, and disappeared into another room. In that flash of legs and skin, the Major understood Ramona's confidence in attracting a wealthy mate. She had a body men would die for: long lean legs, perfectly round butt, flat tummy, modest implants, and lace around all the curves.

"And I work out for hours just to keep my gut from hanging over my belt," The Major muttered to herself.

Agent Miguel called.

"No movement at Maison Marot, but there are three driveways," he said. "I can only see two. Place has three guest houses, a main house with ten bedrooms, a boathouse on the lake. Only three family members live there."

"You did some recon before sunrise?"

"Sort of," he said. "Property valuations, with detailed estate descriptions, are on the canton's tax assessment website."

"Clever boy. Any of our suspects staying there as guests?"

"No, and stakeouts bore me," Miguel said. "But the boredom is over. The Marot limo's pulling out. Should I follow them?"

"Can you tell who's inside?"

"No."

"Hang on a sec. I lost Ramona." The Major scanned the Wölfli's windows for signs of Ramona. Nothing. She cursed herself for the momentary lapse and pulled down the binoculars. Then she saw them. Two people leaning over the balcony's railing. Possibly the missing le Directeur. One wore a thick robe and held a coffee mug. True to The Major's opinion of her, Ramona put nothing over her lingerie outside. The Major lifted her binoculars to get a better view of the mystery guest—and howled with laughter until she caught her breath.

"What's so funny?" Miguel asked.

"Miguel, you're not going to believe this." The Major laughed again. "That gold-digging little tramp. Her sugar daddy's dead only a week and she's out prowling already. Were my eyes playing tricks on me, or did I just see Ramona Wölfli tying tongues with Madame Lena Marot?"

CHAPTER 38

Vienna, Austria
28-May, 7AM

PIA STOOD BEHIND LIEUTENANT ALPHONSE Lamartine and wafted smelling salts under his nose one more time. His eyes blinked, his head snapped back, and he sank into sleep again. She crushed another dose between her thumb and forefinger and placed it even closer to his nose. At last his eyes were fully open. She peeled off the tape that held his head upright. It stayed up. He shook his head and snorted. While he took a deep breath and got his bearings, Pia slipped around the table and into his line of sight.

Pushing apart the chairs of Calixthe and Detective Janko, she placed her hands on the table and leaned toward Alphonse with an apologetic look.

"Pia?" he mumbled. "What happened?"

"Ah, well. What can I say? You came at a bad time."

He looked around. "Susan Duncan?"

"Yes."

"And the man—Detective Janko, oui?"

"Yes."

"Not the good thing. Not good to capture police officers." He took a deep breath and let it out slowly. He looked down at his arms. "And we are all tied up?"

"Yes."

He took another deep breath and shook his curly locks.

"I have done something wrong?"

"Well, I'm not sure."

He looked up at her. "You suspected me. Then I showed up

unannounced."

"Yes."

"I checked in with the police. They were discussing you. They questioned me. I was worried. I … should have called."

"There was nothing you could do, Alphonse." She looked away. "Before I turn you loose, I have to ask you some questions."

"No, no. Do not turn me loose."

"If you're innocent, and I think you are, then I need your help."

"No, no, no. I am in trouble now with my Capitaine because I came here—"

"I saw the text."

"And when I arrived, I reported my intentions to the local police—"

"Janko?"

"Oui. They detained me an hour. And now—"

"I get it," she said. "If I untie you now, you're in more trouble than if I keep you tied up."

"That is half the problem."

Pia waited.

"If I were you," Alphonse said, "and found so much evidence against Lamartine, I would not trust the man. I do not want to live under the suspicions of Pia Sabel. I ask you—keep me here until you trust me. The decision you make on your own, not because of my persuasions."

Pia stared at him. Not the reaction she expected. It would have been better if he were angry.

"OK then, you stay tied up. Now for the questions. First, who is Susan Duncan?"

"Mata Hari," he said with contempt. "The CIA temptress of the worst kind. She made havoc of NATO soldiers stationed in Berlin."

Pia raised her eyebrows. "She's not exactly a looker."

"Women have the mistaken impression of what appeals to the man. Yes, beauty is an appeal. It is easy to see and easy to identify. But mostly men fall for availability and the willingness."

"What?"

"Most men can only obey Mother Nature. If he finds the woman both willing and available, he will oblige Mother Nature's directives to, ehm, reproduce. Some men have the higher moral code. Soldiers, far from home, listen more to Mother Nature more than moral codes."

"And you—you oblige Mother Nature's directives whenever you find a woman willing and available?"

"I must admit, before I met you, moral codes seemed most inconvenient. Now, my thinking is different. I think the moral code most desirable and worthwhile."

"Yeah, sure." She huffed and paced. She wanted it to be true, but in her experience with men, truth was a moving target. "Why were you dismissed from the army?"

"Heh, heh. Ah, the Mother Nature problem is mine also. The general's daughter, just back from university in America, was willing—"

"Yeah. OK. I get it." She paused. "So Susan Duncan seduced NATO soldiers. Why?"

"She was the recruiter, one who persuades men to share the secrets."

"By sleeping with them?" Pia asked.

"I did not know the details. Only the problem."

"But Walter and Conor were English. The CIA wants spies in the UK?"

Alphonse shrugged. "They were long before my time. But she was still active five years ago. Besides, the CIA is the CIA. They do what they do. They cannot help themselves. Do they spy on the ally to ensure he is still the ally? Or do they spy on the ally because they can?"

"Did you give up France's secrets?"

"I was the cure. Seducing her was my duty, for France." He coughed. "Only for France."

Pia smiled. "So I'm looking at the stud muffin of the French army. Impressive. When I wake her up, will she verify this?"

Alphonse shrugged with a smirk. "After I filed my report, the CIA sent her away within the hour."

"When was the last time you contacted her?"

"Yesterday. I asked her about Elgin Thomas—I thought she might know how to find him. Later I discover he died of cancer two years ago."

"And until yesterday you never contacted her."

"No reason. Her idea of love was full of enthusiasm but without soul.

She called on me many times. I did not encourage her. I even considered getting the … what do you call them in America? The restraining order?"

Pia stopped pacing and stared at him for a moment. Laughter erupted from deep inside her. She looked at Susan Duncan-Calixthe Ebokea-Elgin Thomas. A seductress to Conor and probably Walter. But she meant nothing to France's official NATO stud. At first Alphonse seemed a little embarrassed. Then he laughed with her.

"You think I am full of myself, oui? Ah, I think you are right."

Pia composed herself, handed the smelling salts to Klaus, and pointed to Detective Janko. While the salts tickled his nose, she positioned herself across from him. She pulled up the compromising pictures of the detectives on her phone and held them up. They were the first things he saw.

"Sorry, Detective," she said. "You came at a bad time last night. Sitting next to you is Susan Duncan, a former CIA operative wanted for murder and piracy in Cameroon. With her are two of her associates. I missed the fourth in their party, a man named Mustafa Ahmadi. Either I let these killers go free or I turn them over to you. I'll ask you about that in a minute.

"In front of you is Lieutenant Alphonse Lamartine, recently on assignment with the Geneva Police. He can confirm my story. If he's not enough, the weapon used to shoot both Agent Tania Cooper and Monique Tsogo are here on the sideboard, complete with fingerprints." She let it sink in for a beat. "What would you like to do, detective?"

Janko's eyes seared into her. His wrists strained, his entire body shook with anger. Pia pointed a gun at him.

"Or I can put you back to sleep, email these pictures to your coworkers, and leave you two handcuffed to the bedpost naked. So take a minute to think things through."

Alphonse looked at Janko and shook his head. He said, "Look around you, Detective. She's a twenty-five-year-old footballer who captured everyone at this table, including you and me. She offers you the credit for these arrests. You are the smart man to take this offer."

Detective Janko looked away, his face screwed up tight. He took a few deep breaths and came back to look at Alphonse. He said, "You work with this woman?"

"I am bound as are you, monsieur. Working together is not the good description."

Janko bit his lip.

"Let him think," Alphonse said. "Perhaps his assistant will be the more agreeable one."

Pia smiled. "I don't need either of them. I was just trying to be nice. Next one to wake up is Calixthe."

After several repeated applications by Klaus, Calixthe's eyes opened and snapped around the room. She winced at the sight of her goons tied up and drugged. When she recognized Alphonse, her face flushed red.

"Sucks, huh, Susan?" Pia said. "All those years as a CIA agent and you get zapped by a spoiled rich kid—not just once but twice. Don't make me do it a third time." She pointed. "I'm getting tired of dragging your carcass around. The guy sitting next to you is Detective Janko of the Vienna Polizei. He's looking for the woman who tried to kill Monique Tsogo and Tania Cooper. I've got your gun over there, with your fingerprints all over it, ready to hand over for evidence. Now, I want you to pay close attention Susan-Duncan-Elgin-Thomas-Calixthe-Ebokea, whatever your name is. Here's the deal. You give me a clue, just a little clue, that will lead me to le Directeur, and I turn you loose right now. You get a head start on Detective Janko. Not much of a chance, but a lot better than you have at the moment. All you have to do is tell me something I can believe. Ready? Go."

Calixthe glared at her.

"Oooh, you remind me of the Ukranian captain just before she got a red card for taking a swing at me," Pia said. "But she wasn't tied to a chair. C'mon, think about it, Calixthe. What? I'm not hearing anything. Want the deal? Calixthe? Susan? Hello? No? OK."

"You could have planted fingerprints," Janko said. "While she was tied up. You have no chain of custody documentation."

Something about that phrase struck a chord in Pia's mind. *Chain of custody.* She knew it was important. Everyone stared at her while she thought. Where did it fit in? She concentrated for a moment but the meaning eluded her. It would come to her when she stopped thinking about it.

She turned her gaze back to Janko.

"Are you really a policeman?" Pia leaned into his face. "Monique is in critical condition, but they say she's going to live. You think she can identify the person who dragged her out of the women's room at the Radisson and shot her in the ribs? How about Tania? She's on pain meds in the next room. Want me to wake her up and ask her? We can make a little line-up right here in this room. We have three women to choose from: Calixthe, me, and you—the pussy of Vienna."

Alphonse laughed until Janko glared at him.

Pia caught Klaus's eye and pointed to Walter Walcott. While he administered smelling salts, she leaned across the table into Calixthe's face. She said, "Walter here was less than pleased when I told him you killed his pal Conor. I'm thinking I can skip the whole Austrian criminal justice system and just give Walter a gun. I think he'd blow your brains out, Susan. What do you think?"

"Conor is dead?" Calixthe paled.

"Yes."

"How?"

"Mustafa."

Calixthe looked down at the table.

Pia said, "You want me to believe you didn't order the hit?"

Calixthe twisted in her chair. Her silence told Pia everything.

Pia leaned in close. "Feeling alone, Calixthe?"

The woman glared at her again but couldn't keep it up. She looked away.

"So it's true," Pia said. "Mustafa's taking over. That's why le Directeur didn't come in person tonight. He didn't even send his assassin—he sent you. And we both know why, don't we?"

Calixthe stared at the table.

"He knew it was a trap, Calixthe. He knew I'd win because I always win. So he sent you and you fell for it. You figured this was your chance to get back on his good side. You even brought your best boys for the job."

She walked around behind Calixthe. Leaned down, her face next to

Calixthe's ear. "You lost."

Calixthe tried to move her head. Her teeth flashed as if she were trying to bite someone. Too bad her head was still taped to the chair.

Pia said, "Give me le Directeur and I'll let you make a break for it."

"Why would you let me run?"

"Three reasons. One, I want le Directeur. Two, you're Cameroon's problem. Three, you're ineffective and therefore no longer a threat."

"How can I trust you?"

"If anyone thinks I'm dishonest—raise your hand." Pia looked around the table at her trussed up captives. "There you have it. Unanimous."

She smiled. Calixthe scowled. Pia said, "OK. You have my word in front of these witnesses. I won't stop you. Unless you do something stupid like make for my little gun collection over there."

"OK, untie me and I'll tell you a little."

"You cannot be serious!" Janko said. "You will not turn her loose."

"What is with you?" Pia said. "You try to arrest me for assaulting a killer, you don't take me up on the offer to let you be the hero, and now you want to tell me what to do? Shut up or I'll turn your lights out again."

Janko fumed and squirmed in his chair.

"I have changed my mind, detective," Alphonse said. "I think you are not the smart man. Not at all."

Pia nodded to Klaus and he cut Calixthe loose. Pia kept her gun trained on Calixthe and said, "Quickly now—a good clue or I dart you and you're back where you started."

"I never learned their names," Calixthe said. "I know that he works at one of the banks. He lives well but never has cash. I know nothing about her except that they are lovers."

"That's it? Riddles? You expect me to turn you loose with that?"

Calixthe looked hurt.

"C'mon, tell me what they look like. What language do they speak? Haircuts? Race? Height?"

"They speak French and German. They're both average height. He wore a fake mustache. She wore a shoulder-length blonde wig. They're both white."

Pia rolled her eyes. "You're a waste of time."

She tossed her head toward the door. Calixthe took two steps. A dart popped in from the other room. Calixthe fell to the floor only two steps from her chair.

Detective Janko said, "You lied to her."

"Did I lift a finger to stop her?"

CHAPTER 39

28-May, 8AM

FROM THE LIVING ROOM, TANIA said, "I'm going back to bed now."

"OK, I've heard enough," Janko said. "Cut me loose, please."

"Hang on." Pia recorded him with her phone. "Tell me what you've learned."

Janko recited the evidence as presented and pledged to let Pia leave Austria on her own terms. They agreed that neither of them would benefit from bringing the darting of Janko to light. Klaus cut him loose and woke his partner. And, at Janko's insistence, she reluctantly deleted the staged pictures of him.

Turning to Walter, Pia said, "Listen, this is your last chance. You just watched Calixthe sell out le Directeur. What do you think she's going to tell the Austrian polizei about you? She'll be a witness against you, claiming you're Elgin Thomas. A former CIA agent makes a believable witness. Tell me where I can find Mustafa—I'll take care of him and you'll have one less problem."

Walter's head nodded in tiny bobs. "He went to Geneva. We split up in Brussels."

"Why would he go there? They're looking for him."

"The three of them, both les Directeurs and Susan, hatched the plan together. But she pushed them around too much. Wanted more of the money. Then they met Mustafa. He was like their mad dog. When they send him to kill somebody, it got done. Besides, he was the one who knew the Filipinos. Their kind work cheap and keep their mouths shut."

"Simple economics then," Pia said. "The cheapest killer gets the job. He's in, you're out."

Walter shrugged. Pia wished him luck with the Austrians. Klaus cut everyone loose and Detective Janko took their statements.

When he was done, she packed up and called the bellman. She went downstairs with Alphonse while Klaus and Tania waited for the next elevator. In the lobby, they stopped and looked at each other.

"You want a ride back to Geneva?" she asked.

"I'm not wanted in Geneva."

"Neither am I." Pia tried to smile.

"I am not certain you trust me," he said.

She started to speak. He put his index finger across her lips.

"You are not certain," he said.

She nodded. Her stomach twisted another notch. She clamped her lips and said, "Where are you going then?"

"Back to Chamonix," he said. "She sent me home."

"You can ride with me to Geneva, drive home from there."

He put a knuckle under her chin, raised her face to his. "I would like that very much."

"I could send Klaus and Tania back on a commercial flight. You and I can get some privacy in the jet."

He smiled. "No. This would not be right."

"Wait, wha—"

"I want you most desperately. But, I could not live with your doubts about me. No. I will not take advantage of you until I have proven myself to you." He paused. "And then, I will take every advantage."

Pia's mouth opened and closed several times but no words came out. She backed up a step. Something whacked her thigh.

"If you're not going to kiss him," Tania said, "can I give it a shot?"

FIFTEEN MINUTES LATER, WHEN HER entourage boarded the jet, Pia was still pissed at Tania.

In the air, she called the Major and exchanged updates.

They decided they had to move fast. With Calixthe in custody, the couple playing le Directeur would feel the noose tightening. The Major feared the conspirators would either flee or kill more people.

"Ramona?" Pia said for the third time. "She provides a connection to criminals, but with Lena? Walter said the male was slightly built and the woman was pretty. Ramona could play either role but not both. And even at a distance, Lena Marot wouldn't have been Walter's idea of pretty."

"Why not?" the Major said. "Conor said Elgin Thomas liked opera. Lena is a big supporter of the opera. Calixthe knew her way around Vienna. She didn't hesitate when you moved the meeting to the Radisson."

"We know Lena is a racist. She'd never get into a criminal enterprise with Calixthe."

"Can't argue that one," the Major said. "As much as I'd like it to be Lena, she has no motive and no capability. But Ramona fits."

"Sideways. From your description, I don't think she's smart enough."

"There's that."

"What are we missing?" Pia asked.

"Lieutenant Berardi researched the police reports. There were some discrepancies that didn't match the evidence. Like the shooting at the bridge was reported as we fired bullets at the assassins. A simple mistake that might be setting us up. I still think we need to consider your boyfriend. Conor said the real Elgin Thomas met morally impaired soldiers through NATO."

"It's not him." Pia sat up, looked two rows away where Alphonse stood in the aisle, talking to Tania. "Calixthe intended to kill me tonight. Alphonse passed up several opportunities. He refused a gun. He refused his freedom. He's not interested in killing me."

"Pia, if you think someone's framing him, tell me who and why?"

"When the press asked us questions before a big game, we'd have a plan for handling them, a scripted set of responses. Same for the other side. When I wanted to learn about game plans, I'd listen to the odd things my opponents said in the hallways or cafeterias. Things that didn't fit the rehearsed version. What did people say that was off topic?"

"What do you mean?" the Major said. "Give me an example."

"Something Janko said struck me as odd," Pia said. "Chain of custody. At the time, it was out of place, a stupid thing to say. Everyone says stupid things now and then. But overall, the police aren't stupid.

Chain of custody. Stuck out in my mind, I don't know why yet."

"Bachmann's charity was odd. Long way to go for charity. And Ramona admitted targeting mature wealth for her next conquest." The Major repeated the interview. "Antje knows banking, shipping, and Cameroon. But she doesn't feel like a murderer. She doesn't have that cold edge. Then there's Joey Campbell. I had the feeling he would kill to get back to New York, but that'd be a stretch."

The jet came in for the landing, bounced on the runway twice, and taxied to the executive terminal.

"Let's look at this from a different angle," Pia said. "Where would Calixthe have met someone in the banking industry? Hey, wait a minute. Alphonse said she stalked him."

The jet rolled to a stop. A lone Volkswagen Passat waited outside. Pia squinted at it. She lowered her phone to her chest and yelled at her pilot. He reported the limo drivers were unavailable since word got out that someone was trying to kill her. She'd have to do her own driving.

Alphonse said, "I can drive you around before I go back to Chamonix."

"That's OK, I like to drive now and then. But you could keep me company."

Pia stared at him. Her eyes narrowed as she thought. He raised his brows. She pulled her phone to her ear slowly before speaking rapidly. She said, "I figured it out—well, half of it anyway. I'll join you when you report to Villeneuve on progress. I have to make a stop first."

She clicked off as she heard the Major ask, "Wait, figured out what?"

CHAPTER 40

Geneva, Switzerland
28-May, 9:30AM

KLAUS OPENED THE BACK DOOR to the rental car and lifted Tania in.

"Sorry, Tania, you and Klaus are going to the hotel," Pia said. "I'm in a hurry here."

"No way. I'm your bodyguard and I'm on duty."

Alphonse and Pia craned around the headrests to stare at her. Pink elastic circled her leg, holding in several pounds of gauze.

Her quad flexed as she climbed in the backseat. She howled in pain.

"Damn," she said. "Klaus gave me Novocaine. Guess it hasn't kicked in yet."

"Forget it," Pia said. "You're going to the hotel. You need some rest."

"GTFO, Pia."

"I'll get you another big fluffy hotel suite."

"No way, Pia. You get killed, how am I going to pay for the suite?"

Alphonse said, "You are the sugar mama, nothing more."

Pia slugged him lightly. "Yeah, like Lena Marot. Let's go find the bad guys."

"Now you're talking," Tania said. "I'm going to make them answer for Ezra."

"You're waiting in the car," Pia said. "Crutches make for a slow getaway."

Alphonse said, "Do not worry. I will be the bodyguard today."

"You're supposed to be back in Chamonix," Pia said.

"I would choose to be with you."

Pia stared at him a beat.

Alphonse said, "That is, if you trust me."

Pia leaned over the console and kissed him on the cheek. He smiled. She sent Klaus to the hotel with the pilots and drove off.

Pia said, "Tania, get the Major on the phone."

She drove out of the airport and headed into downtown Geneva. They drove through the residential district to Avenue de France, across the railroad yard, and onto the waterfront boulevards. Pia slowed as they passed the Genève-Pâquis landing, the small park where Clément Marot died a week earlier. She pulled over, parked along the road, and stared at the park. It looked different in the daylight with tourists milling about, but her mind replayed the scene. Mustafa was in cuffs and yet looked calm, as if he knew he would escape.

"They don't answer," Tania said. "Can't get the Major or Miguel."

"Where are they?"

"The Major's on the edge of town near the river. Miguel is at Maison Marot. I texted them both, called and left messages. They must be sneaking up on someone or something."

Pia looked at the park again. The Lake Léman's famous fountain shot high in the sky leaving rainbows in its mists. Serene and peaceful in the sun, the park looked like the postcards. She said, "I know who it is."

In unison, Tania and Alphonse said, "Who?"

Pia looked at Alphonse. "Call Capitaine Villeneuve."

"And tell her?"

"She's not going to answer."

Alphonse looked confused but dialed. It rang for a long time. He said, "You are right. She does not answer."

"She's the one, Alphonse. Le Capitaine is le Directeur."

"This is not possible. She is the professional—"

"*Chain of custody,* I finally figured out why that's been sticking in my head. The first night, when it all began, she had her purse on her shoulder when she put Mustafa, al-Jabal, in the police car. Duchamps should have belted him in. But she did it because she had nail clippers, Alphonse. Remember the curved slice in the plasticuffs? She freed his hands with nail clippers. The kind lots of women carry in their purses. She clipped the cuffs and Mustafa knocked out Duchamps as soon as he went around the corner."

"Anyone could have—"

"No. I tackled him, I searched him, and Marty cuffed him. Villeneuve led him to the car and put him in it. *Chain of custody*. He didn't have nail clippers when I searched him. Marty held him until Villeneuve led him to the car. She had Duchamps start the car while she put Mustafa in the back. No one thought anything of it because she was in charge. You thought she was taking the case personally."

"Oui." His head nodded rhythmically. "But this is not proof."

"You left me standing on the bridge and a couple minutes later Mustafa showed up. The only people who knew I was there: you, and my bodyguards. You're a good officer, you report everything up your chain of command. You told Villeneuve and she sent Mustafa. I told you I was going to Cameroon and Mustafa set a trap for me the next day."

Alphonse stared at her.

"All the victims opened their doors," she said. "Eren and Reto were in their bank but they came outside. Someone called them first and said, *I'm out front, meet me*. Why else would they walk out after two friends were killed? And Sara Campbell, murdered in her doorway. Who would she open it for?"

He shrugged. "Lena Marot, Antje, Ramona."

"Or?"

"Or Capitaine Villeneuve." A snort of disgust escaped him as he turned to the window. "Oui. We knew it was someone close, but…. Le Capitaine?"

"And the Major and Miguel are giving her their report about now. I never told them she was dangerous. I screwed up. Now she has at least one of them."

"God. Dammit!" Tania pounded the door. "Get me there. I'll kill that bitch!"

Pia clenched her hands around the steering wheel and breathed through her nose. Alphonse and Tania watched her. With one deep breath, she pulled herself together, set her eyes on the road, and put the car in gear.

She said, "Which one is closest, the Major or Miguel?"

CHAPTER 41

28-May, 10AM

TANIA LEANED BETWEEN THE SEATS, held her phone's map out for Pia. Maison Marot was only six blocks away. As much as Pia wanted to get the Major, Miguel was closer and could be a valuable asset in locating Villeneuve.

Alphonse tried calling police officers at the gendarmerie and got voicemail every time. Everyone knew he'd been sent home, making his calls low priority. After leaving four messages, he gave up. He suggested they try calling le Directeur on the phone Pia confiscated from Calixthe.

Gravel crunched under the tires as they rolled down the estate driveway five minutes later. Marot's staff would be more difficult to push around than Ramona's doorman. Nothing clever came to mind, so Pia decided to elbow her way through. She trotted up to the door, Alphonse by her side, Tania in the car, and rang the bell. While she waited, she took Alphonse's advice and called from Calixthe's phone. The only number in the contact list was for le Directeur.

The butler opened the front door and they stepped into the foyer. On the right, a staircase swept upwards. In front of them was a small sitting room, to the left a dark hallway disappeared into the mansion's depths. The butler asked them to wait in the foyer while he checked on Mme. Marot's availability.

Seconds after he left, Philippe Marot, his short, slim frame trying hard to look threatening, rushed down the hall. He wore a yellow knit shirt with a red cross. Noticeable for the bad color combination.

Pia's panic level spiked and she nearly jumped. Philippe swore at her and waved them outside. Alphonse protested. Over their raised voices Pia heard a phone ring.

"Quiet!" She held her hand in the air.

Le Directeur's phone was ringing somewhere in the hall beyond Philippe.

For a moment, Philippe and Alphonse stopped and stared at her. She listened to the ringing on her phone. A voice down the hall said, *"Allo? Calixthe?"* A second later, she heard the same words in her phone.

Her eyes locked on Philippe. The shirt, the bad color combination. The ANPSP logo. Philippe wanted to be a professional skier and the local ski patrol leader was Carla Villeneuve. Calixthe said he lived well but never had cash. Walcott called him soft.

Philippe's eyes darted back and forth from Pia to Alphonse. He ran at Pia, his arms and legs flailing.

She turned, stepped into his rush, and jabbed her left fist twice into his Adam's apple. He staggered backward and clutched his throat. She followed with a right cross that spun him around, then swept his foot out from under him and left him on the floor.

"He's the other half." Pia drew her gun. "Mustafa is down the hall."

On cue, Mustafa Ahmadi ducked his head out of the drawing room. Pia and Alphonse dove into the foyer as he fired three shots. Bullets splintered the front door. Pia stuck her gun around the corner and heard Mustafa's footsteps retreat. She stepped into the hall and aimed. No one there. She ran into the dimly lit main house, Alphonse close behind.

Double doors opened into a darkened drawing room. On the far side, a shadow slipped through a door to another room. Pia's first dart hit the oak paneling. She slid laterally to her left, looking into the room before giving chase. Nothing. She pushed the door open with her foot. Behind her, Philippe Marot screamed something unintelligible. She stepped deeper into the drawing room and felt two ineffective fists hit her in the back.

She turned, saw Alphonse restraining the young man, thought about fairness and decided Philippe didn't deserve any. She popped two more fast jabs. The first landed on Philippe's cheek, turning his head to the right. The second connected the heel of her hand to his temple. Alphonse tossed him aside. She fired a dart without aiming, then chased into the library after Mustafa.

Several pieces of large furniture in the dim space offered a hundred hiding places. On a coffee table she saw Miguel's phone, the back removed, an electronic connector sticking out of it. Mustafa was trying to jail-break it to locate Pia. Where was Miguel? Dead? With the Major, held somewhere by the river? She refocused and crept forward. Alphonse stepped in behind her. He picked up a lamp, stripped the shade, and wielded it like a bat.

"Gun?" Pia asked.

He shrugged and smiled. "Do you have an extra?"

She pursed her lips and stepped around a wingback chair, leading her eyes with her gun on outstretched arms, cleared the couch and relaxed her stance. Her problem would be in the next room.

"I will go first," Alphonse said.

Pia shook her head and moved forward to the door. She consulted all her senses, hoping to feel Mustafa's presence. Nothing.

Behind her, Philippe took flight. She saw the dart meant for him stuck in the floor. She'd missed. She fired as he ran and missed again. He disappeared around a corner.

Priority? The greater danger: Mustafa.

Pia threw herself into a roll that landed in the next room. Stopping on her knees, she leapt to her feet and looked around. A billiard room with a bar and stools at one end. A few blades of sunlight streamed through horizontal blinds beyond the bar. High contrast lighting that benefitted the killer. She approached the door, trying to sense anyone hidden in the room beyond. She moved to the billiard table, using it for cover. Alphonse joined her. She whispered to him, he nodded: the slate table would stop bullets. They put their backs under the table and rose up, pushing it over with a crash. Pia duck-walked to the left side to sneak a peek. Sweat rolled off her forehead and pooled in her palms. She wiped her hands on her pants and moved a little farther forward.

The sound of feet shuffled behind her. She dropped to the floor. Three gun blasts shattered the stillness of the room. Something thudded on the floor. She rolled back behind the billiard table. Nothing hurt. She rose to peer over the table leg. Philippe came to the doorway with an AK-47. Pia slid laterally to the side of the table and fired three times. He ducked back. Hearing no thud, she assumed they were all misses.

Then she saw Alphonse lying face up in the doorway. Blood poured from a hole in his head and two more in his chest.

"NO!" She lunged into the library and fired.

The wall beside her exploded in shards of wood chips. Mustafa was trying to shoot her through the wall, and there was nothing in the construction to stop a high-velocity round, making his tactic just as dangerous for Philippe. She dropped, landing an arm's length from Alphonse's body. His eyes stared upward.

Only Philippe could have fired the shots that killed him.

Her body turned cold. She felt no fear. Only anger.

She screamed and stood.

Careful with her few remaining darts, her aim moved from one door to the other. A shadow blocked the light behind her for a split second. She turned and aimed. Nothing there. Wheeling back around, she caught a glimpse of Philippe before he ducked into the drawing room.

Trapped.

Stumbling forward, she charged. Philippe stepped into the doorway, in her sights. She heard Mustafa moving somewhere behind her. She ducked. The wood frame over her head turned to sawdust in a hail of bullets.

He still fired like a movie-star.

"Put the gun down, bitch!" Mustafa Ahmadi called from the billiard room's opposite doorway.

Pia didn't move. "You're not going to kill me?"

"We have a question."

She couldn't see Mustafa, which meant he had to be slightly off to one side, obstructed by the overturned billiard table. If he had a shot at all, it would be a very narrow angle. That's why he hadn't shot her yet—he wasn't sure where she was in the dim light. She put her hands up, surrendering. Her Glock dangled from her thumb. Philippe took it.

"What's your question?" Pia asked.

Her left foot slipped forward, toward Philippe and out of the doorway. Out of any possible line of fire from Mustafa. When he didn't tell her to stop, she knew he couldn't see her.

"Who did you talk to this morning?"

Pia felt the question like a punch in her gut. It was the same question the sick murderous bastard had asked the bankers. Each of them answered, and doing so signed the death warrant for the next banker. She wouldn't have that on her conscience. Besides, the only person who knew the situation lay dead on the floor.

Tania, safe and sound outside, had no idea what was going on inside the thick stone walls of Maison Marot.

Mustafa was making his way around the billiard table and Philippe was holding a gun in her face. Pia resolved to keep her mouth shut no matter what they did to her.

Then Philippe gave her an opportunity. He said something to her in French, some kind of insult if the sneer on his face was any indicator.

Pia cocked her head.

"Speak English, Philippe." She slid an inch closer. "Or do you trust your garçon to ask the questions?"

A real man would have maintained eye contact. Philippe's eyes darted toward Mustafa's last known position in the other room. They could hear Mustafa's footsteps as he strode around the billiard table. They both knew he'd come through the doorway in ten steps and shoot Pia Sabel in the head. They also knew Philippe was in the line of fire and could potentially be a victim of his own assassin. Philippe blinked.

All the invitation she needed.

She exploded off her right leg, her left shoulder shoved the barrel of the gun up and out of the way. At the same time the heel of her hand snapped his head backward with tremendous force. Her left hook smashed his head into the wall. Stunned for a second time, he pulled his trigger, his magazine emptied into the ceiling. As he collapsed on the floor she grabbed the gun barrel, smashed the gunstock into his face, and threw it across the room. Just to be sure, she kicked him in the head.

When the machine gun fired, she'd heard the thud of Mustafa dropping to the floor in the next room.

"Calixthe is in police custody in Vienna," Pia called out. "I caught her and turned her over to police. I watched them question her. She knew you were here to cut her out and go straight to Philippe. That's why she was blaming everything on you—Mustafa Ahmadi."

Bullets streamed through the wooden wall next to her. She dropped to the floor and rolled under the piano. Philippe got to his knees, shaking his head. Pia saw her gun on the floor, scrambled for it, and darted him.

From Mustafa's room she heard metallic clicks. Changing magazines. She had seconds before he reloaded.

Pia scrambled out and ran for the front door. She flew outside, leapt the steps, jumped in the car, and sped down the driveway, swerving as she drove.

Mustafa came to the door spraying bullets. She heard the trunk take several shots before the back window exploded. He forgot the muzzle climb of the machine gun. Most of his bullets went high.

Tania sat up in the back seat and looked around. She said, "What the hell? What happened? Where's Alphonse? Hey! Pia, are you crying?"

CHAPTER 42

BARELY ABLE TO SEE THE road in front of her, Pia followed Tania's navigational instructions. The Major and Miguel still hadn't answered their phones. Pia kept her foot on the gas. The tires squealed around corner after corner. They left Geneva's nicer neighborhoods and found the road toward Chamonix.

Pia closed her eyes for a second only to see Alphonse's eyes staring back.

In the back seat, Tania reloaded her pistol with hollow points. Less likely to penetrate body armor than a parabellum, but more stopping power per bullet. Tania refilled Pia's Glock with darts and tossed it on the passenger seat.

"Alphonse had a hole right through his head," Pia said. "The blood. And his eyes…"

"Eric was wrong about you—you handled the adrenaline just fine. Now you have to learn the other thing, dealing with death while you're still at war. We finish the job first. Then we grieve. Just like we did with Ezra." Tania paused. "Listen. We're driving into a trap. We both know it. But we're going to win here. We're going to take her down. So, pull it together, Pia. I need you sharp and ready."

"Oh god. All that shooting. It was…"

"You thought it was going to be easy. You thought you were going to run onto the field, kick the winning goal, and take a bow. Welcome to real life, Pia. The bad guys have the Major and Miguel. Somebody has to do something about that. Right now, it's down to you and me."

"You're wounded. I don't want anyone else dying. This—"

"You can't stop me. And when we get this done, when we have

Villeneuve and her little boy-toy in the morgue, don't bother inviting me to the next mission briefing. I'm signing up right now. Anywhere you go, I go with you."

Pia glanced into the backseat just long enough for their eyes to meet. She said, "Thanks, Tania."

"Hey, keep your eyes on the road. We have to get there first."

Pia's phone rang. Lieutenant Marco Berardi of the Geneva gendarmerie identified himself. He said, "You were seen fleeing a crime scene. You shot officer Alphonse Lamartine and severely injured Philippe Marot. I urge you to stop this madness and turn yourself in. You cannot fight the entire police department."

"Where's your Capitaine Villeneuve, Berardi?"

"She is not my Capitaine. I work in a different group. Besides, she is off duty today. We are investigating the murders at Maison Marot. You will be better off if you turn yourself—"

"Philippe and his pal Mustafa aren't there, are they? They called it in, right? Mustafa dragged him out. He's cleaning the gunpowder residue off their hands."

"Don't worry about forensics, Ms. Sabel. Think about what you need to do. You need to turn yourself in. You can't run forever. You can't get far."

"You're right. Tell you what, meet me just past Le Bout-du-Monde, where the bridge crosses the River Arve. Off the left side."

Berardi said nothing for a moment. Then, "Why there?"

Pia clicked off.

Tania racked her M4.

Pia turned onto a narrow street and the city's quality declined around them. They passed a ragged amateur sports complex and apartments, crossed the bridge, and took a small side street into the river's flood plain. Low-rent housing lined one side, trees and mud the other. One house had a broken window, the next was unpainted, the one after that abandoned. No more picturesque Geneva. She slowed to a crawl to examine every driveway and parking space. A rusty Citroën in one, the next two empty, a Fiat after that.

Pia's phone rang again. She checked the caller ID: Villeneuve. She picked up, put it on speaker. "Carla, I know it was you. I have Philippe."

A stream of French insults came through the line.

Pia looked at Tania, who shrugged.

"Capitaine, give the phone to Miguel. Um. Donnez le telephone to Miguel."

Noises on the other end: Tromping on boards? She imagined pushes and tugs and tape peeling, heard grunts, a one-way conversation in French.

Miguel's voice. "She surprised us. We're bound in a base—"

A smack. Yelling.

Miguel said, "She wants you to turn yourself in for the murder of Alphonse Lamartine."

"Tell her Berardi figured it out. He's on his way to her location now." She waited for the translation. "Tell her I'm coming to trade Philippe for you and the Major."

After some background discussion, Miguel said, "She says Mustafa has Philippe. You'll turn yourself over to her."

"Mustafa lied, that's why he didn't let her speak to Philippe on the phone. I have him. If she trades right now, she can make a run for it. Tell her to send you out to the street and I'll swap for Philippe. Berardi will be here in ten minutes. Not much time. She has to think fast."

"She agrees," Miguel said after another brief discussion. "Last house on the row."

The line clicked off.

Pia looked at Tania. "Too easy?"

"Yeah too easy. GPS shows second house from the end, not the last."

They squished their earbuds in place and set up their comlink. Pia rolled the car forward, inch by inch, toward the third house from the end, letting the engine idle them onward. Her eyes scanned everything in front of her. As she rolled into view of the second house, something caught her eye—a shadow in an upper story window. She slammed the selector into reverse and smashed the gas pedal to the floor. Her windshield exploded. A bullet passed four inches above the steering wheel, right where her head had been a split second earlier.

The car raced backwards past two houses and stopped. Pia leapt out and shook off tiny shards of peanut-sized safety glass. Tania struggled to keep up, a crutch shoved into one armpit, an M4 in her free hand.

A house with peeling gray paint that looked abandoned stood between Pia and Villeneuve. A broken window gave her a view of an empty room. The fewer innocent civilians between them, the better.

The road followed the river, bending to the left. The houses canted forward enough that the third house from the end, the empty one, provided cover. Pia ran to its front edge. From there she could see the side of Villeneuve's hideout. It had faded and peeling yellow paint with red trim. A red shingle roof with many shingles still in place. Villeneuve's personal car was parked on the near side.

The house featured one large dirty window along the facing wall, a smaller dirty window near it, a basement, a small concrete stoop. A broken children's swing stood rusting between buildings. Pia ran down the side of the empty house. At the back, she slowed and inched along until she could see the backside of Villeneuve's hiding place. An unpainted wooden deck with three steps leading up. A single door with a wide window next to it.

Tania caught up, her limp under control only by her grim determination.

"Miguel started to say *base*, which must mean basement," Pia said. "Upstairs should be clear of hostages. You go around the front and fire at the second level. You might get lucky and wing her. You'll definitely get her attention. I'll use the distraction to go in the back door."

"I'll lay down bursts of three," Tania said. "Four of them ought to do it. They'll be three seconds apart. Make your run right after the first burst. She'll duck, then she'll look for the source. That's your chance. If she's dumb, she'll walk right into the next burst. I'll give you a cue."

"She's not dumb."

"Best chance we have anyway."

Tania limped toward the front. When she was in position, her voice came through the earbud. She said, "Hey, Pia, know what I like about you? You know you're going to die and you're all chill."

Tania fired into the blank wall where the upper floor should start, then counted aloud.

Pia took off running. As she neared the back deck, she looked through the dirty window on the side. A silhouetted figure ran through, headed to the back. Villeneuve wasn't falling for it. Pia reached the steps and raced up them. Through the dim back door glass, she could see the figure coming. She dove for the deck, her hands picking up splinters.

Three shots. The first blew a hole in the door's bottom half. The second and third blew out the glass.

Pia rolled onto her back and aimed at the door. Her shoulders and arms shook with strain and fear. Her breath came fast and hard through her nose. The barrel of a Sig Sauer poked out the window.

She rolled off the deck a second before two more bullets fired into the planks she'd left behind. The Glock skittered across the dirt. Pia froze.

Villeneuve's face came to the broken glass. Her gun and eyes scanned from the left, away from Pia. Faces speak louder than words, and Carla Villeneuve's face screamed hate. Pia's opponent intended to win in a game where winning meant living.

Pia rolled again. She grabbed the gun and aimed with trembling hands. Before she could fire, Villeneuve saw her and slipped into the interior shadows. Villeneuve had fired five bullets. Her Sig Sauer had three left before reloading, four if she started with one in the chamber. Pia rose to a knee and fired one dart with more hope than aim.

Villeneuve's footsteps in full retreat told her she'd missed. Pia retook the back door and bolted through it, confident her enemy had vacated the room. Her eyes adjusted to the dim light. A simple kitchen with bare places where the appliances should have been. It had two entrances, one straight ahead of her, the other an immediate left.

Pia leaned into the left opening. Just enough to get a look around the corner. A bare room opened to a small hallway with one door, probably a bathroom. Beyond it, another bare room. She leaned back into the kitchen in time to see Villeneuve's gun reach around the corner and fire another bullet.

Two left.

Villeneuve's aim was off because she wasn't looking. She punctured the back door again, but her method was effective. Minimal risk for a small chance at success. Pia copied the move, firing three of her own.

She had five darts left. She stepped to the left, into the first bare room. With luck, she could sneak up behind Villeneuve. Without luck, Villeneuve would sneak up behind her. That could still work if she played it right.

She moved down the hall, pushed the small door open and took a glance without breaking stride. A bathroom: tile to shoulder height, small sink, shower and toilet. No wasted space. She continued into the next room and looked through the window that faced Tania's position. Outside, she saw Tania crossing between houses, limping on her crutch, heading for the basement hatch. A dangerous move that made some sense. If Tania lived long enough and managed to free the Major or Miguel, the balance of power in this dangerous game would tip their way. If Villeneuve saw her or fired through the floorboards—

Villeneuve's steps were coming through the kitchen. Trying to sneak up behind her.

Villeneuve fired a shot through the window. Tania dove for the ground, her M4 returning an un-aimed three-round burst. Tania was a sitting duck with an injured leg, rolling on the ground in pain. Villeneuve might have ducked to avoid Tania's burst, but she wouldn't stay down as long as Tania. And Tania was in the middle of an empty lot.

Pia kicked the wall to give herself away, then squatted in the front room. She was near the bathroom wall, about where the sink would be. Two walls of tile and a sink wasn't exactly a bulletproof shield, but it might deflect enough energy from the bullet to help. She tensed her legs, ready to propel her body in any direction necessary. She listened. A board creaked somewhere to her right. Villeneuve was coming for her. That was a good thing, it would buy Tania time. Pia repositioned her grip on her gun and aimed at head height.

Her eye darted to the unexplored room across the hallway that connected to the kitchen. Villeneuve might be coming from that direction. She listened. Her enemy was on the far side of the bathroom. Her ears stretched for more sound, her skin sensed vibrations in the air, her nose sniffed for any scent. Another creak.

She could barely hear over the pounding in her eardrums. She smelled nothing but the dust stirred by her movements. She tasted only the metallic adrenaline seeping through the cellular tissues into her mouth. Saw nothing for the strain as she watched the hall for a moving shadow.

Her skin picked it up first, the tiny hairs on her arms sensed the difference in electricity. A static build up to a lightning strike. Villeneuve was near. Very near. In the room opposite the kitchen.

There was a good chance she was going to die in ten seconds.

Sweat formed on her forehead. Her body trembled with fear. Her limbs felt light, the blood that should be in her hands rushed to her head.

Pia shifted her weight to be sure she could jump when Villeneuve came around the corner and fired her last two bullets. She felt the board beneath her foot give half an inch. A creak echoed through the room like a cannon shot.

Villeneuve fired two shots through the bathroom. The tile did what she'd hoped—the first bullet exited the wall far above her and the second came through fragmented into small pieces. One piece sliced across her back, another slammed straight into her shoulder. Two more came out of the wall in front of her. Painful but not life threatening.

That was Villeneuve's last bullet.

Now was the time for offense.

Pia leapt toward the hallway, reached around the edge, and fired three blind shots. She heard a magazine hit the floor. Villeneuve reloading. She stepped into the hallway and saw her darts stuck in the wall. Wasted ammunition. She stepped around the corner and fired her last two darts.

The first sailed through Villeneuve's auburn hair. The second stuck in the lapel of her wool coat, a thousandth of an inch short of the target.

Villeneuve fumbled to turn the fresh magazine right side up with one hand. Her other gripped the empty gun. She looked up, her face full of shock and fear and anger and hate.

Pia threw her gun at the woman. It glanced off her collarbone, causing a flinch that delayed the reloading process. First steps are the most critical steps in a fight. They define the offensive and defensive positions. Pia spent years working with her trainers to perfect those steps. Her left foot landed inside Villeneuve's gun hand. Her shoulder positioned to fully prevent reloading. Her first two jabs landed on Villeneuve's right eye. Just as Eric told her, Villeneuve's brain was soaking up all the available oxygen to think, leaving her hands to fumble through a clumsy attempt to strike back using the gun as a blunt instrument. Pia's knees lowered her six inches below Villeneuve's outstretched punch. She powered back up, smashed her shoulder into Villeneuve's elbow, and threw left and right shovel punches as she rose.

Villeneuve teetered backward a step. Pia followed with a left hook to the chin, then a vicious right cross. Villeneuve's eyes rolled backward. Pia slammed fist after fist into the criminal's torso. Left and right, over and over. For Alphonse and Ezra and Marty and Jacob. For Clément, Sandra, Reto, Sara. Even for Eren Wölfli. She added a couple more when she remembered Tania's wound. She felt Villeneuve's core muscles slacken and give up the defense. She stopped the body blows and landed one last right cross.

Villeneuve's knees buckled. Her body dropped to the floor and twitched.

"Is she dead?" the Major asked from the kitchen entryway.

"Serious concussion, internal injuries. How long were you standing there?"

"Just got her in my sight when you stepped into the line of fire and started slugging away like T-Rex Shields."

Pia smiled a mirthless smile. Miguel and Tania stepped into the room. Hurried hugs of relief went around the group.

"Tania says the cops are coming," the Major said. "We don't have much time. How do you want to play the next act?"

Pia pulled out Calixthe's phone and called Mustafa.

"Hey, Mustafa, feeling lonely? Don't worry, I'm coming for you. Count on it. But first I have a question for you. See, I figured out a lot of this, but there's one part I just don't get. How did it all start? I mean, we know Carla Villeneuve worked at ANPSP to seduce young rich skiers. She hit the jackpot with little neglected Philippe. She couldn't wait for him to inherit everything because her biological clock was ticking, something like that, right? So they worked out an international piracy ring with her pal Calixthe, the CIA agent who came sniffing around the slopes of Chamonix pining for Alphonse. The operation made money— lots of money. Then Clément discovered the money laundering scheme.

He was pissed, confronted his son, gave him a day or a week or whatever to fix it. That's when he called us. Right so far?"

Mustafa said, "What do you want?"

"So instead of coming clean, Philippe moved the money to Eren Wölfli's bank and called you in to kill his own father. Right?"

"What do you want?"

"I'll take that as a yes. Here's what I don't get—the whole Villeneuve thing. I mean, I'm rich and I can see gold diggers coming from a mile away. Was he that stupid?"

Mustafa huffed.

"OK, maybe you don't know the gossip behind these guys. You just dove for the blood money and a chance to run Calixthe out of Cameroon. A kid wanting to kill his own father didn't bother you at all. You must be one hell of a nice guy, Mustafa."

"What do you want?"

"I have two deals. The first is for Philippe. I've got his girlfriend in the trunk of my car. If he wants her back, meet me at the Pont de la Machine. Midnight."

A long pause. "And the second deal?"

"The second deal is for you, Mustafa. To hear it, make sure Philippe makes the midnight appointment."

Mustafa huffed.

Pia asked, "You're not afraid of me, are you?"

CHAPTER 43

28-May, 11PM

"YES, MUSTAFA," PIA SAID INTO the phone, "I can see you. I knew you and Philippe would come early to set a trap, but I never imagined you'd wear black trench coats. That is just so tacky."

The two killers stood on the Rue du Rhone, a nice street on the southern river bank. Five-story office buildings with restaurants and nightclubs on their ground floors backlit the men. They twisted one way then another, searching the riverside, the sidewalk, the buildings. Their heads swiveled—they had to be frustrated, furious, and scared, all at the same time. They knew she could see them. They had no idea where she was.

A little more than two hundred feet away, Pia Sabel stood behind a cabinet in a darkened café at the Pont de la Machine. An unobstructed view of the moonlit footbridge gave her an excellent advantage. Her night vision binoculars worked so well she could see their lips moving.

"Listen up, Mustafa. You and I have some talking to do. I noticed you're holding the phone to your ear. I assume that means you aren't letting Philippe listen in. If you are, cut him off now, because his girlfriend is selling you out big time."

Mustafa turned to look at Philippe's backside. After a few seconds, he resumed his scan of the office buildings. He checked the roofline, hoping to see a figure outlined against the sky. He would find nothing.

Dressed head to toe in black, recessed in the dark building, Pia was invisible.

"I've got a problem," she said. "You told the police I ran amok at Philippe's house. That I killed Alphonse, Lena Marot, and the butler. One of those all-American rampage shootings. Thanks, Mustafa. Thanks a lot."

Mustafa said, "What's the second deal?"

"We're getting there, buddy. You need to understand how much trouble I'm in here. I'm wanted for murder. But then so are you."

Mustafa said, "Don't worry about me."

"Halfway up the footbridge toward the old power plant, you'll find an audio player. Listen to it. You'll recognize Carla Villeneuve's voice. In her version of events, Mustafa Ahmadi acted alone in killing all the bankers. All the insurance I could get out of her. You and I know that won't help get me out of trouble, but it sure will make your life a living hell."

Pia watched Mustafa looking around. He pointed Philippe one way, then headed up the footbridge.

"Not yet," Pia said. "I have more bad news for you."

He got close enough to see the audio player and stopped. Philippe called out to him.

"Think about this. They set you up. Calixthe never pulled a trigger in Switzerland. Carla Villeneuve never pulled a trigger anywhere. Philippe Marot never pulled a trigger either until this morning, when he pulled the trigger that killed Alphonse Lamartine. Three bullets in the back. The police don't like people who kill one of their own. When Philippe blamed my lack of experience with firearms, they believed him. Now I'm in a world of hurt. You help me out with a couple things and I'll help you out. Deal?"

"Philippe did not shoot him in the back. He aimed at you." She could almost hear the smirk. "Your flic, the cop, saw him and stepped into the line of fire to save you."

Pia's gut flipped over.

Her eyes clamped shut, teeth clenched, insides churned. She struggled to get a grip on herself. She took a deep breath. Alphonse had saved her life by losing his.

If she had let him go first, would she have done the same to save him?

Mustafa said, "How can you help me?"

"I have a jet fueled and ready to go. It's on the executive apron, near a wall easily scaled. In all the years I've flown, they never once looked in the aft hold. I'm not sure the customs agents know there is one. Not luxurious but pressurized and accessible from the main cabin. You tell me what I need to know and you get a ride to Brussels in the hold. Deal?"

"What do you need to know?"

"AK47s all over the place. I counted ten in Cameroon. You probably had twice that many. There were more at Maison Marot. And enough Sig Sauers to re-arm the Geneva police. Where'd she get them?"

"Two years ago, she broke up an arms deal between Libyans and some Swiss in Chamonix. The guns were held in the evidence locker here in Geneva. The dealers pled guilty, the case was forgotten. Last year she checked them out and never checked them back in."

On the shore, Philippe's agitation level was rising fast. He shouted at Mustafa. Mustafa shouted back.

"Wave him over," Pia said. "Show him the recording. Ask him to listen to it. She was his girlfriend, I'm sure he'd like to hear her voice. Especially the part where she sells him out. She said he hired you."

Mustafa shouted to Philippe, who came running. Philippe picked up the player, put the earbuds in his ears. Hit play.

"Did you know they still have the death penalty in Cameroon?" Pia said. "And I hear Vienna is ready to send Calixthe back there. She already told the Austrians you were the mastermind. Backs up Villeneuve's story. When she gets back to Cameroon and faces the death penalty, what do you think she'll tell them?"

Mustafa huffed.

"Tell me this, just curious. Why kill Conor Wigan? Seemed a little unnecessary."

"Who is Conor Wigan?"

"He was dying when I found him. I don't think people lie about that kind of thing when they know they're dying. So why kill him?"

"That useless old man? Did he talk to you? Did he tell you my name?"

"That's it, then? He talked, so you had to kill him. What else could you do?" Pia paused for a minute. "Hey, you fixed for cash if we can get off the ground? I mean, I'll give you a lift, nothing more. Have they already paid you for doing Clément and the others?"

Mustafa's head spun around, searching the buildings high and low. Philippe threw the player on the ground and jumped on it. He shouted into the night and shoved Mustafa away from him.

"He is tired of this," Mustafa said. "He wants Carla. You promised Carla would be here."

"Oh, she's nearby, don't worry about that. But it's not midnight. You're early. Now listen, Mustafa. Philippe's clean, and Carla might get away with it, but you and me? Mustafa, we're screwed. And they screwed us. I need your help. I need a way out of Geneva. I'm desperate. I'll give you a ride if you can give me something that will clear my name."

Mustafa held the phone to his chest and spoke to Philippe. Pia's heart cranked up, she felt the deal slipping away. Was Mustafa telling Philippe what she was asking? No, he was smart enough to keep his options open.

Mustafa put the phone back to his ear.

"We want Carla now."

"So he's giving you a ride out of Geneva, then? You know he's heading for Kiribati or someplace like that. He has a lot of money stashed away somewhere. Has to. If he hasn't paid you yet, has he at least shown you the money?"

Mustafa said nothing. He tensed and breathed deeply. His eyes wandered across Lake Léman. He clenched and unclenched his free hand several times.

"Think about it," Pia whispered. "I have the kind of money Philippe and Carla dreamed about. If your price isn't too steep, I'll pay you to toss your friend in the river right now. Then I can blame Philippe for killing Alphonse. That gives me a shot at getting away. I get away, you get a ride. So just tell me. How much would you charge to kill Philippe right now?"

"Twenty thousand euros."

"That's what they promised you for Clément and the others? Whoa, that's cheap. So how come they never paid you?"

Mustafa huffed.

"Conor told me his cut was a hundred thousand per ship. Did Philippe treat you that badly too? I mean, you know they made seven million off the *Objet Trouvé* alone, right?"

"They what?"

"The last ship, the *Objet Trouvé*, seven million euros went to Philippe. Fifteen guys worked that ship. Should've been more like three or four hundred thousand euros each, right? That means they were skimming more than expenses. They skimmed five million. And you took all the risk for the murders for just twenty thousand?"

"Each."

"Oh. Yeah. Now that makes sense. Five bankers, a hundred thousand euros, you doubled your cut. Nice. Still half of what you deserved for that last ship alone. You should get a manager to negotiate your deals for you."

Mustafa laughed. "You perhaps? How much is your offer?"

"Well, I can get you out of town. Villeneuve got you out of town once. But she's not going to do that this time, is she? Hey, wait a minute. She wasn't the one who got you out of town. She was with the cops the night I found you at the Marrakesh shop. And you were waiting for a ride. Holy crap—it was Philippe, wasn't it? No one would have looked in his car. Not even the best police would be so rude as to search the bereaved."

Mustafa laughed. "You just figured that out? You're so stupid."

He turned to Philippe and said something in French.

Pia turned and shrugged at Marco Berardi and whispered, "Good enough? Or should I keep going?"

Beradi looked at Capitaine Serge Bavaud for approval. Bavaud nodded. Marco barked French into a public address system. He said, "This is the Geneva Police. You are under arrest. Drop your weapons. Put your hands in the air."

From both sides of the river, police in body armor swarmed onto the footbridge, machine guns aimed at Philippe and Mustafa.

Mustafa put his hands into the air, facing the searchlight of the approaching helicopter.

Philippe Marot ran toward the building seeking refuge, unaware Pia was inside. Marco and Capitaine Bavaud stepped out, guns leveled at him.

Pia stepped in front of them and, betting Philippe did whatever a woman told him, shouted, "Sauter!"

She thought that was French for *jump*.

As he ran, he glanced at the landing just beyond the railing and made the same mistake Pia had a few days earlier. If you were desperate, it looked closer. In his panic, her instruction made sense. He swerved and vaulted over the railing.

He made his decision. The cold water sucked him into the penstock.

His body would surface in the morning.

The world was a safer place.

Tania's crutches plonked on the walkway behind Pia. She said, "That was mean."

"Depends on whether or not you believe in free will." She turned and patted Tania's shoulder. "Besides, I spend every waking hour of my life wishing I had five more minutes with my mother and father. He killed his."

The Major joined them.

"When he figured out what his son was doing, Clément called Sabel Security," Pia said. "He didn't call the Swiss police because he wanted us to save Philippe from the pirates."

"He also had an appointment to meet with Elgin Thomas," the Major said. "Maybe to pay off the pirates? He was doing everything he could to help his son—and this is how the son repaid him."

Pia walked over to Mustafa. "Did you guys really think the police were too stupid to check the trigger for fingerprints? Or the shell casings? Or the gunstocks?"

Mustafa hung his head but the hatred remained in his eyes.

The Major tugged her arm and pointed to the waiting limo. They walked away.

Pia's phone rang. Dad.

"Jonelle texted me," he said. "It's all over and you won. Congratulations. I was scared."

"You were scared? Holy crap, Dad."

She gushed the details of her last three days, kept talking as she stepped into the limo and the driver closed the door. She recounted every shot fired and punch thrown. The Major, Tania, and Miguel smiled when she gave them credit for their parts. She choked up when she told him about Ezra and Alphonse. She loved how he listened to her even though he'd already read the reports. He listened without interrupting, without judgment, offering only kind consolations and heartfelt admiration. By the time she wrapped up, they were at the airport.

"I'm glad it worked out," he said when she'd settled in the jet's seat. "But I have to speak as a father, not just as your largest equity partner. I care about you very much. I don't want you running missions. I want you behind a desk or taking clients to dinner. Not dodging bullets."

"Most of what Sabel Security does stays secret, Dad. Our clients don't want anyone to know how long their engineers were held by revolutionaries in Venezuela. But I can do something different here. I can do something good. I can help small countries throw off oppressive generals. I can root out child pornography rings. I can stop drug dealers. I can help people, Dad. Really help people. I've made my decision, I'm going to use Sabel Security to make the world a better place."

"No. Stick to what works. Stick to the government contracts and the kidnapped executives. Don't open any—"

"What's the matter, Dad? Afraid I'll find out who ordered my parents' assassination?"

The End

TO YOU FROM SEELEY JAMES

I hope you enjoyed the story and will join my VIP Readers by signing up at SeeleyJames.com/VIP. I hold a drawing every month for things like gift certificates or naming characters in upcoming books. I also give VIPs the inside scoop on things like how certain characters were named; which Shakespeare soliloquies I ~~plagiarized~~ drew from; what I'm working on next, etc.

Please remember to leave a review! Indie authors live and die by reviews. If you didn't enjoy it, that's OK, sometimes the magic works and sometimes it doesn't.

If you want to chat, please email me at seeley@seeleyjames.com or join me on Facebook: SeeleyJamesAuth. I love hearing from readers.

EXCERPTS FROM SABEL SECURITY SERIES:

Element 42, Sabel Security #1

 The voice in my head returned when I stopped taking my meds. My caseworker said the voice was part of my condition—PTSD-induced schizophrenia—but I call him Mercury, the winged messenger of the gods, and a damn good friend. For years, he was my biggest ally in combat and helped me predict the future. I'm not talking about very far into the future. Sometimes minutes, sometimes seconds, and sometimes just enough to see it coming.

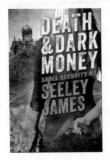

Death and Dark Money, Sabel Security #2

Sixteen minutes before David Gottleib died, I was alarmed that a nearly-naked black man leaned against my refrigerator with a casual grin. It wasn't because he was tall with supernaturally chiseled muscles. Nor was it the lone fig leaf he sported over his substantial manhood. It wasn't the leather sandals or the bronze helmet with small bronze wings either. What alarmed me was that I could see him at all.

No one can see a god.

At least, no one with a shred of sanity left.

Death and the Damned, Sabel Security #3

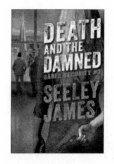

Who to trust is the scariest decision we make in life. I grabbed him by the hair, pulled his head back, and, cheek-to-cheek, we contemplated the sparkling stars dotting the moonless Syrian sky. I sensed his eyeballs strain all the way to the right to look at me. His fingernails dug into my forearm. Anxiety caused him to miss the grandeur of the moment. Too bad. It was stunningly beautiful. You don't see that many stars from over-lit American cities. But I tired of our two-second relationship and drew my blade across his throat, severing his carotid artery and larynx before he could scream a warning to the others. I dropped his carcass on the other jihadi at my feet. He trusted me because I speak Arabic. Bad idea.

Death and Treason, Sabel Security #4

The president, a billionaire, and a disgraced FBI agent were talking about disrupting democracy with the casual air you and I might use to pick a movie. It made my blood boil. Back when I was an overconfident, pimply-faced teenager, I joined the Rangers and swore to protect the Constitution from all enemies, foreign and domestic. That commitment still anchors my soul. My outrage nearly caused me to miss the conspirators' after-thought scheme to kill my boss, Pia Sabel.

Death and Secrets, Sabel Security #5

A voice in a dream said, "Do you remember who shot you?"

Someone tugged me through a murky world. When the gray globs in my vision thinned, I recognized my sister. She kneaded my right hand and said something underwater. I blinked. Tubes hung down around me, metal rails on either side. A rack of machines with flashing lights towered over my shoulder. On my left stood a man in a white lab coat with the educated gaze of a doctor.

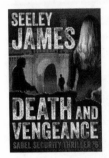

Death and Vengeance, Sabel Security #6

Annie Wilkes had been expecting to spend the rest of the day in emergency calls about the bombing. That changed when she stepped out of the ladies' room. A pistol peeked from under an overcoat draped over a stranger's arm. She scanned the Mumbai Hilton's lobby for her security detail. Five yards away, her lieutenant lay face down on the floor. Farther away, her chief of staff struggled against restraints and a gag, his arms held in check by two men in business suits.

ABOUT THE AUTHOR

His near-death experiences range from talking a jealous husband into putting the gun down to spinning out on an icy freeway in heavy traffic without touching anything. His resume ranges from washing dishes to global technology management. His personal life stretches from homeless at 17, adopting a 3-year-old at 19, getting married at 37, fathering his last child at 43, hiking the Grand Canyon Rim-to-Rim several times a year, and taking the occasional nap.

His writing career ranges from humble beginnings with short stories in The Battered Suitcase, to being awarded a Medallion from the Book Readers Appreciation Group. Seeley is best known for his Sabel Security series of thrillers featuring athlete and heiress Pia Sabel and her bodyguard, unhinged veteran Jacob Stearne. One of them kicks ass and the other talks to the wrong god.

His love of creativity began at an early age, growing up at Frank Lloyd Wright's School of Architecture in Arizona and Wisconsin. He carried his imagination first into a successful career in sales and marketing, and then to his real love: fiction.

For more books featuring Pia Sabel and Jacob Stearne, visit SeeleyJames. com

Contact Seeley James:

mailto:Seeley@seeleyjames.com
Website: SeeleyJames.com
Facebook: SeeleyJamesAuth
BookBub: Seeley James